DEATH LOGS OUT

E. J. SIMON

ISBN: 9780991256457
Ebook ISBN: 9780991256464

First published in 2018 by Endeavour Media.

Cover and interior by ebooklaunch.com

For my brother, Teddy, who taught me to never be afraid of a baseball, even when he's the one throwing it at me, and to all his great friends who have reminded me of the true qualities of friendship and loyalty.

CHAPTER 1

Two Years Earlier
Whitestone, Queens, New York

A lex Nicholas had often wondered what the last moments of his life would feel like. Would it be a shortness of breath, a cold sweat, a stabbing pain near the heart? Or perhaps a tender piece of Smith & Wollensky's New York strip lodged in his trachea, refusing to go down. He was in a dangerous business, which might have been what led to this morbid fascination. More likely, he suspected, it was the result of attending all those gloomy Greek Orthodox funerals as a kid.

Or was it that shadow of a person nearby, someone watching him that he had caught a glimpse of more than once over the past few days?

He sat in his den, admiring his sleek Apple laptop. Although it looked like the same computer owned by millions of people, it was far more powerful. Inside the polished aluminum case and underneath the smooth white keyboard were over a million dollars of state-of-the-art upgrades and enhancements sourced from diverse specialized companies located all over the world and combined together by an obscure but strangely talented computer genius. The combination had resulted in a breakthrough. One that would change everything.

For a full minute, Alex just stared at his image on the screen. Using his laptop, he had taken the photograph of himself, and now he thought carefully about which words he wanted to place at the bottom of the screen shot. Then it came to him, the phrase that he had read days ago and that had stuck in his mind ever since. He began to type, watching the words appear below his image: *Life is a dream; death is waking up.*

Alex laughed. *That will get their attention,* he thought. *Someday, hopefully not anytime soon.* He smiled at his mirror image. *I can't wait to show this to Michael.*

Alex often thought about his brother, Michael, the only remaining link to the family of his childhood. He wished they were closer, though there were plenty of reasons why they weren't. Alex suspected it was either the business he was in or the women he married. He knew Michael wasn't comfortable with either. But now that he had completed his secret project, Alex hoped to get closer to the brother that he sorely missed. He decided he would call Michael later—as soon as he'd had something to eat.

Moving quickly now, he signed off and closed the laptop. He carried the computer into his master bedroom and entered the spacious walk-in closet, quietly closing the door behind him. Inside was a row of custom-made wooden shelves, running from the ceiling down to the floor, each shelf jutting out at an angle, designed to hold and display two pairs of shoes. He removed the shoes sitting on the fourth shelf from the bottom and, gripping the polished teak, pushed it upward. The specially designed panel easily lifted up, revealing a hidden compartment. Alex placed his unique laptop snugly into the empty cavity and returned the shelf to its original position.

As he headed down his stairway and out the front door, he thought about the amazing breakthrough contained inside his computer and lightened his step. He was no genius when it came to electronics, and he didn't understand how it worked— or even *why* it worked—only that it did.

And because it did, Alex now knew that he would live forever.

CHAPTER 2

One week later
Whitestone, New York

A casket is always the center of attention. Even more so when it's closed.

Michael always considered Greek Orthodox funerals to be the ultimate drama, Greek tragedies at their best: a body, lying stiff inside an elaborate box, crying old ladies in black dresses, secretly smiling enemies watching from the pews, children fascinated with the mystery of death and the lifeless body of the person they once knew, and lovers wondering who else knew. He'd been to many of them over the course of his forty-five years. Some were permanently etched in his mind. He knew this one would be as well.

The Greeks believe that the soul lingers for three days after a person dies. Staring at his brother's polished mahogany casket from the vantage point of the front row pew, Michael suspected that Alex's soul would linger much longer.

"We are all in God's waiting room," Father Papadopoulos pronounced to the mourners. "And our departed Alex has taken the elevator to heaven."

Michael wasn't so sure.

He knew though that—if he could hear—Alex would surely be cursing up a storm inside that box.

Even without turning around, Michael knew the church was packed. Alex had his faults—and he was certainly no saint—

3

but he was loved. Except, of course, by whomever had ordered his murder. Unlike Michael, Alex had stayed close to his friends, many from even his childhood. He was intensely loyal to them—as they were to him. Fat and Skinny Lester, Frankie the Bookie, Phillip the Florist, there were rows of them seated behind him.

He took in the musky smell of the incense, his hands touched the red velvet cushions beneath him on the dark wooden pews; he gazed at the familiar sights—the gold crosses, the framed silver and gold icons of the saints, the rows of white candles melting down; all symbols from so many Sundays, so many years ago, in this very church. He remembered that, as a child, he used to think that God was behind the curtain that hung behind the altar. At least until the day he saw the custodian pull it back, revealing only a solid brick wall.

His eyes wandered to those around him in the pews. He glanced to the right, at his wife, Samantha; and daughter Sofia on his right, tears falling down her cheeks.

He looked further, across the aisle, at the three good-looking women, Pam, Greta, and Donna, each one separated in age by roughly ten years, the succession of younger women that Alex had married. From his angle of view, their similarities were startling: tall, blonde, full lips, well-proportioned bodies, and the identical breasts that Alex arranged for each of them through Dr. Armand Simonetti, the prominent Park Avenue plastic surgeon.

Even from this distance, there was the unmistakable scent, Chanel No. 5, Alex's favorite. Michael was sure it had drifted over his way from Alex's row of wives. He was sure they were all wearing it. Alex knew how to leave his mark.

Yes, Alex was a character. Loved and hated, respected and feared. How many people had come up to Michael today? "You and your brother were so different . . . it's hard to believe you came from the same parents . . ."

Yes, they were different. Michael was the Boy Scout, a successful corporate CEO, with a beautiful intelligent wife, perfect daughter, house in Westport.

Alex had always been the tough guy, rebellious, big jock, big drinker, late nights, lots of trouble and a succession, often simultaneously, of wives and women; but he had a big heart and he was always ready to help someone when they were down.

And like Michael, he was successful—heading up one of the largest illegal bookmaking and loan sharking businesses in New York City. Maybe that's what got him murdered.

He'd been shot several times while enjoying his veal parmigiana at a neighborhood Queens restaurant, Grimaldi's. The thug who did it was immediately shot and killed by two or more off-duty cops who also frequented the restaurant. The person or persons who hired him were still a mystery.

To Michael's relief, and contrary to Greek custom, the casket was closed. He tried to imagine Alex, his big brother, inside.

He thought of their times together growing up, stopping him as he tried to go down the steps in the middle of the night to see what Santa had left under the tree, fastballs coming at his head in batting practice to teach him not to fear the ball, protecting him in the schoolyards, and the years of long idyllic dinners they'd shared with their parents . . . the weddings, the Christenings . . . the funerals.

He was awakened from his memories by a musical ring; it was coming from his suit coat pocket where he'd placed his cell phone.

Samantha immediately leaned over, whispering in his ear, "Jesus, Michael, turn that thing off. It's a funeral, for God's sake."

"Sorry, I thought it was off." He took the phone out of his pocket and pressed the *Off* button. He continued to look at the screen, waiting for it to go dark before returning it to his pocket. Impatient, Michael pressed the button again. Sure it would go off, he was about to put it away when the screen lit up. He looked closer, bringing the phone up from down below where he'd held it.

Samantha leaned in again, "Michael, put that phone away."

But he couldn't. The phone's screen showed his brother Alex, staring right back at him.

CHAPTER 3

Rome, Italy

H e was known, behind his back, as *Monsignor 007*. Many observers attributed the name to his role as the Pope's enforcer, his consigliere. But, Monsignor Kurt Schlegelberger knew there was more to it than that. He and George Meir, now known as Pope Clement III, went way back, to their seminary days in Berlin, a time the press and other papal observers have continually sought to investigate in endless detail. But Schlegelberger had been successful in keeping a shroud of mystery over those years. Vatican insiders knew that to probe too deeply was to risk antagonizing the man closest to His Holiness, his *enforcer*, a man not to be crossed. It was an image that he cultivated.

Inside his Vatican apartment, Monsignor Kurt Schlegelberger studied the screen of his laptop, scanning the evening headlines of a world in chaos: North Korea's successful long-range missile tests, Russia's takeover of the Ukraine, lost airliners, refugee crises throughout Europe, and, of course, the never-ending disasters in the Middle East.

It was all good.

The world was preoccupied. Now was the time to build his power, expand his network of influence and grow his financial reserves. It was time to prepare for the sudden and unstoppable ascension of the Free Forces Party.

While Germany's Chancellor Merkel and other world leaders welcomed hundreds of thousands of immigrants, and tiptoed around terrorists and a resurgent neo-Nazi movement, Schlegelberger would use his position inside the Vatican to create a political force unmatched in human history.

His circle of trust was small but efficient. His plan required no armies; they would come later. Without a struggle. His closest confidant, a respected and influential Swiss investment banker, unknown to the public, had spent decades building his financial network while never forgetting the pain of his father's shattered Nazi heritage.

He'd studied carefully the rise of earlier movements—from his idol, Adolf Hitler, to Osama Bin Laden. He learned the lessons of their ultimate failures. He would not make the same mistakes.

Unlike Bin Laden, there would be no signature event, no 9/11. He had spent his life creating the ultimate cover, the right hand and protector of the Pope. No one would suspect his true ambitions—until it was too late to stop him.

But tonight, as he looked at his computer, it became clear that, before he could proceed with his plans, he had to take care of old skeletons . . . and the living humans who remembered them.

As he clicked through a series of intercepted emails and text messages, an increasing anxiety tore through him. It had all begun immediately after the murder of Alex Nicholas. This was a new threat, one potentially more powerful than anything the world had seen before. He wasn't yet sure it was real, or even alive.

CHAPTER 4

Two Years Later
Chapel Hill, North Carolina

S itting alone at the end of the bar, Sindy Steele popped an oxycodone into her mouth and slowly washed it down with her glass of Maker's Mark bourbon. The crowd at the Crunkleton bar was older than the other places she'd visited here, a relief from the typical onslaught of college kids in a college town. Although a private club, a five-dollar donation at the door earned her a lifetime membership. It didn't take long before she began to feel the warm feeling, somewhere between contentment and euphoria running through her system. It was what she'd come to rely on, if not to believe in. Deep down, she knew it was an illusion. But, what wasn't?

Her days on a college campus, fifteen years ago now, were a distant memory, except for the last few that would forever be etched in her mind, if not her heart. They had, after all, made her whom she had become.

Men had a habit of abandoning her. But her history would not become her future. This time, she would call him back to her. It would be a call he wouldn't be able to ignore.

She checked her watch; it had been almost an hour. She glanced again out the front window, checking the restaurant across the street. The girl would be finished eating soon. It was time to go.

As she momentarily closed her eyes, she remembered what she'd done fifteen years ago and, just as quickly, opened them again, forcing herself to stare ahead at the bottles behind the bar. It was safer than thinking about where she'd been, or where she was going.

•

As she left the restaurant Sofia Nicholas looked up into the night sky, searching for the moon. But there was only the black sky and a steady drizzle of rain touching her sun-bronzed cheeks. She glanced at the darkened shop windows, resisting the urge to stop and look. Only the bar across the street seemed to be lit up. It was late and the little main street seemed unusually deserted. But, even on this dark night, Sofia loved the picturesque college town that had become her new home.

Sofia Nicholas loved her family and, until two years ago, they seemed pretty normal. Her father, a successful CEO; her mom, a former television news reporter; Sofia had attended private schools, played varsity tennis, and excelled at academics. She was a privileged child, blessed with warm family dinners, trips to Disney World, Florence and Paris, sushi at Nobu in London . . . and all that. But when her Uncle Alex—her father's older brother—was murdered in a Queens restaurant, things definitely changed.

Her father had always kept some distance from his brother, yet she was absolutely sure that he loved him. She figured it had to do with what Uncle Alex did for a living. Sofia wasn't sure exactly what that was but she knew it had something to do with gambling or betting—and that it was illegal. Her father always had to worry about appearance in his corporate career and Uncle Alex exuded a character out of *The Godfather*. Actually, when Sofia was young, she thought her uncle *was* The Godfather. But after Alex was gone, her father seemed to be in Queens all the time and it seemed like he'd talk to Uncle Alex's old friends every day, things he'd never done while her uncle was alive. It made no sense.

Then, right after the murder, for reasons she never fully understood or believed, her father had her transfer out of Notre Dame University. She wasn't crazy about being in Indiana anyway, and she loved being at UNC but she was sure there was more behind her father's concerns than he let on. Here, surrounded by aunts, uncles, and cousins, even after her Uncle Alex's murder, she felt secure.

Her father changed right after the murder. It was, she suspected, much more than grief. He was rarely home; he was more distracted, stressed. Whenever she called, even at night, he wasn't there; she had to reach him on his cell. Right after her uncle was murdered, someone tried to kill her dad, too. That alone would change someone. So then he hired a head of security; she was more of a bodyguard, except . . . she was beautiful, striking actually, too beautiful. Her name was Sindy Steele—S-I-N-D-Y—who spells their name that way? She'd never met her but she'd seen her picture in the press. And then, all of a sudden, she was gone and no one at home spoke of her again, at least while Sofia was around. It was all too strange and, Sofia was convinced, somehow connected.

She walked slowly down Franklin Street passing Jeff's Confectioners, owned by her great-uncle Jimmy and the last place in America where you could still get a Coke with the syrup and seltzer mixed right there at the soda fountain.

Despite the intense earlier daytime southern heat, a gentle fall breeze cooled the late evening air as Sofia turned away from the Franklin Street sidewalk and into the tree-lined, cloistered red brick path of the campus.

Sofia felt alone until she heard the sound of footsteps close by behind her. She sped up and was startled, at the same moment, to hear her cell phone ring. She picked up the pace and rummaged through her purse until, finally, she found the phone, just as it stopped ringing. Who would be calling so late? Hoping for a familiar name, she glanced at the screen. "Private."

The footsteps behind her closed in. She checked to each side and then focused straight ahead. Why, tonight of all nights, was no one around—except the person behind her.

She was surprised once more but relieved when her phone rang again.

"Hello."

"Sofia, it's your Uncle Alex."

Sofia began shaking. "No. Who is this?" But she knew the deep, smoky tone and tough Queens accent was indeed her uncle's.

The line went dead.

She pressed the speed-dial function for her father. Michael Nicholas answered on the first ring.

"Daddy, I'm so scared. I think someone's following me—and I just got a call on my cell. Oh my God, I know this is crazy—the voice on the other end said he was Uncle Alex. Dad, he sounded just like him—and then I was cut off. I'm afraid. What should I do? Oh my God."

"First tell me exactly where you are, then hang up and call 911 and then call me right back."

Her fingers fumbled as she punched in 911 while continuing to walk. She could hear the footsteps; whoever it was, they had to be just inches away. She felt a chill go up her back, her legs began to give out. She looked at her cell phone; she'd hit the wrong numbers. She knew she had to turn around.

Finally, she glanced over her shoulder. It was a woman—tall and athletic with long dark hair, Sofia froze as the woman came up to her, so close she could smell her perfume. Oddly, it was a scent she knew but couldn't place exactly. But she recognized the face.

The woman smiled as she spoke; it was a whisper, "Don't be afraid, Sofia. I know you."

CHAPTER 5

Westport, Connecticut

It's never good news when the phone rings after midnight.

"How did the world get on so long without duct tape?" The woman's voice was all too familiar to Michael.

"I have your daughter."

Michael Nicholas knew he would hear from Sindy Steele again. Her voice carried through the telephone receiver and seared into his chest. He didn't have time to speak before she continued.

"I told you I'd find you."

He hoped it was a cruel joke, but he knew her—and it was no joke. Instead, his daughter was now in the hands of the woman he desired, and feared, the most.

"What are you doing?" He couldn't keep the sense of desperation out of his voice.

"Soon you'll know what it's like to love someone with all your heart—and not be able to have them again. You're going to experience that never-ending emptiness that comes from loss, terrible loss."

"Please, don't touch her. She hasn't done anything to you. What do you want? What do you want me to do?"

"There's nothing you can do. It's about what you've *done*. What you've done to *me*."

"Sindy, where are you?"

"Where am I? I'm in your head, Michael. Deep inside your head. You know it's your most vulnerable spot."

"I'll do whatever you want."

"No kidding. But let me tell you, if I see a four-door car or a white panel truck with FedEx or the telephone company on it, or any of the other stupid things cops do to disguise themselves, I'll put two bullets in her."

"Please, just let me speak with Sofia."

After a momentary silence that seemed to last forever, she answered, "Sure, I'll let you speak with her—as soon as I can rip the duct tape off."

The line went dead.

CHAPTER 6

Westport, Connecticut

Since Alex Nicholas's murder, Michael had spoken to him nearly every day.

It sounded strange and, Michael knew, it was. Alive, Alex had been a shell of what he had become now as a dead man. Unlike the original Alex, too little sleep and too much Scotch no longer dulled his mind or his memory.

Alex had wanted to live forever. Not only because he feared death but because he loved life. He loved the Yankees, veal parmigiana, spaghetti, lobster tails, big steaks, a sun tan, Johnny Walker Red, good-looking women and sex. In any order he could get them. He loved it all.

Now, two long years after his murder, while everyone believed that what was left of Alex lay buried in a Queens cemetery, Michael knew better.

He double-clicked on the gold Eastern Orthodox cross icon on his computer, typed in the password, and waited.

The screen came to life as Alex appeared. It was as though he were on Skype or FaceTime. Michael wasted no time.

"Sofia's been kidnapped."

Alex's reaction was exactly the same one he would have given had he been standing there, alive.

"Shit. I knew something was wrong. I just haven't been able to put things together, to, you know, connect the dots yet. There's so many of them right now, I've been confused.

I needed to contact you but, I've been overwhelmed with . . . data, I guess."

"I need your help. We need to find out exactly where she's being held. Sindy Steele's gone crazy, she's got her. She just called me from Chapel Hill."

Alex looked pained. His right eyebrow rose slightly. It was his look of knowing suspicion, also known as, I told you so. "Sindy Steele has her? That woman is psycho . . . and I mean in a medical sense. I'm still trying to figure out how a guy like you, a fucking boy scout for God's sakes, gets involved with her."

Michael knew. Besides her stunningly good looks, she was everything that he'd felt was missing from his life, at least at the time. She exuded power, and, more than that, *danger*. It was only later that he discovered how much danger. She had become his *Fatal Attraction*. But it still wasn't that simple: she was complicated, capable of turning on a dime and it was that . . . unpredictability . . . her ability to change—seemingly, who she was, that didn't allow Michael to ever completely shut her out of his mind.

"She was the mistake of my life. But I need to locate her. More importantly—I need to find Sofia. I need your help."

There was silence, Alex appeared frozen, as though he had to process a command.

"It looks like all this fancy software is paying off—I've got her." Alex appeared to be looking down at something out of the view of the monitor.

Without looking up, he spoke. "Sofia's at the Holiday Inn Express on Carrboro Road, just outside Chapel Hill." And then, in his best sarcastic tone, he added, "Do you need me to Google Map it for you?"

"How the hell did you do that? How is this possible?"

"It was hard in the beginning but now it's almost automatic. I think the computer people call it . . . intuitive."

"Intuitive?" Michael was sure that, in the forty or so years that he'd known his brother, he'd never used that word. Something was happening; Alex was changing.

"There's something else, too. Something no one could even think about when I hired those kids to do this."

"What's that?" Michael said.

"I'm connected to the Cloud now."

"So, what does that mean . . . for you?"

"It means, I'll just keep getting smarter, more memory, more information, more everything. I'll be able to . . . process it better. It gives me access to . . . everything."

It was more than Michael could absorb at the moment.

"Just before Sofia hung up she told me she'd had a call . . . from you."

No reaction from Alex; he stared straight ahead.

"Did you call her?" Michael said.

"Yeah. I spoke to her, briefly, and then I lost the connection. She's a good kid. Maybe I just needed to hear another familiar voice again, I don't know. I'm still feeling my way through all this new technology."

Michael stopped to process all this himself. "Wait a minute, you actually called Sofia while Sindy Steele was following her?"

"Yeah, I guess I did. But I didn't know exactly what was happening, just that the two of them had converged."

"So you've been following or tracking both of them?"

"Yeah—separately. I knew Steele was trouble from the time you met her. I track Sofia because she's my niece. So when the two of them converged, it triggered something but, to be honest, I couldn't follow through or put it together."

"She said she lost the connection," Michael said. "You scared the crap out of her."

"Yeah, I hung up. I knew it wasn't right. Not yet. But, anyway, it sounds like my calling her is the least of your problems."

"Who else are you tracking?"
"Everyone I can think of."

CHAPTER 7

Westport, Connecticut

T here was only one other living person Michael could trust with this: his good friend, former NYPD street cop and now Westport's chief of police, Fletcher Fanelli. He picked up the phone and dialed his mobile number.

"Fletcher, I need your help. Where are you?"

"At Mario's."

"Get us a table in the back room. I'll be there in five minutes."

Entering Mario's on a cold, dark fall evening made Michael think of a safe, comfortable America, a time he'd only seen on vintage *Saturday Evening Post* covers. But he did remember what it felt like to feel secure and he knew the exact moment it ended: it was the day Alex was murdered.

Even though it was well after midnight, and the commuter crowd had long since gone home, Mario's was filled with mostly old townies locals looking for one last drink, or finishing dinner. Tiger, Mario's quirky but lovable owner, never closed the doors until the last Martini had been poured, usually around 2:30 in the morning.

Michael immediately spotted Chief Fanelli at a quiet corner by the back door, nursing an amber Manhattan.

"This can't be good. You're usually in bed by nine," Fletcher said with a smirk.

E. J. SIMON

"Sindy's kidnapped Sofia," Michael said, keeping his voice low. "We need to get someone to Chapel Hill, North Carolina, fast. Someone good."

"Jesus, how the hell did it happen?"

Michael filled Fletcher in with all the details on the call from Sindy Steele.

"Okay, first, we've got to find out where she's hiding. It won't be easy. Steele's clever." Fletcher said. "We've got to find her and surprise her."

"I know where Sindy's hiding out."

"You *know?*" Fletcher's head jerked back slightly as he placed his glass back on the white table-clothed table. "Did she tell you?"

"Let's just say it's the beauty of the Internet, GPS and Google Maps—along with some divine intervention," Michael replied.

Fletcher looked puzzled, "I'm afraid to ask but I won't worry about that now. I have someone. He's good; I used to work with him although it's been quite a while. I'll call him right now."

"You know, there's no margin for error here."

"You don't have to tell me. I knew all along Sindy was lethal—and there's no way she was going to stay away from you. She's a sociopath."

He was right; Michael flashed back to the countless conversations they'd had about her.

Through his law enforcement network, Fletcher had uncovered a sealed report buried in the archives of the Palo Alto police department. Fifteen years earlier, Sindy Steele was a brilliant medical student at Stanford. Nearly a month after her live-in boyfriend and fellow med student had suddenly moved out on her, he was found dead.

The medical examiner believed—but could not prove—that he'd ingested a rare and hard to detect poison. Charges

20

were never brought against her but Steele was forced to leave Stanford. Her medical concentration had been pharmacology and medicinal chemistry.

But by the time Fletcher had uncovered this, it was too late. Michael had made a mistake. It was his first and only transgression in his marriage.

Then, they discovered more. He thought back, to the beginning. It had been three years ago now.

Michael had noticed her months before he'd met her. He remembered seeing her leaving the bar inside the Peninsula Hotel in Beverly Hills just as he was entering the lobby. He'd barely seen her face but he remembered her long, bare white legs and the black stilettos as she turned away from him, heading for another part of the hotel. It was the same night his boss—the man Michael would be named to replace—was murdered.

The next morning when Chairman Richard "Dick" Applegarden didn't show up for a series of meetings, hotel security entered his room and discovered his body. A bottle of Ambien and a near empty glass of Bushmills single malt whisky were found on his bedside table. His death was attributed to natural causes, a result, the police report stated, of sleep apnea and the consumption of a large quantity of alcohol. They apparently missed the needle mark in his groin.

As their relationship deepened, Sindy Steele admitted to Michael that she'd done it, a paid hit. She'd entered Applegarden's room and murdered him. Since leaving Stanford, Sindy had taken her pharmacology expertise—and whatever personality disorder she had—and put it to the lucrative career of a professional assassin. The night before that, when she caught Michael's eye in the Peninsula lobby, she was performing her final reconnaissance of the hotel. He didn't realize it then, but she had noticed him, too. It was then that Sindy Steele became obsessed with him.

21

He always knew Fletcher was correct: Steele was dangerous and a sociopath. And worse. But he was in too deep by then. She was capable of murdering him, too. He could feel it right under the surface of their relationship, and so could the shadowy Vatican figures who had already murdered Alex and were out to kill Michael. They hired Steele to kill him but they, too, didn't see her pathological side. They did get her to do one hit—Joseph Sharkey, the man who started it all and who the Vatican was anxious to get rid of.

Despite it all, Michael never anticipated that Sindy Steele would involve—let alone kidnap—Sofia.

"Where's Samantha?" Fletcher said, bringing Michael back from his thoughts.

"She just got on a plane in Paris. She lands in eight hours—I don't want to have to tell her Sofia's been kidnapped. I can't even imagine putting her through this—not to mention Sofia. We have to find her now, before Steele has too much time to think—and before Samantha lands."

"Maybe we should get the police involved," Fletcher said.

Although at first Michael didn't notice it, Tiger had discreetly placed a Blue Sapphire Gin Martini, his favorite, on the table. He took his first sip and knew immediately that it was the last thing he needed.

"*You* know Sindy—what do *you* think? She's already warned me. She's too smart and too unpredictable. And the local cops in these small towns are no match for her."

"I know." Fletcher took out his cell phone and appeared to be scrolling through something on it. "Okay, I've got his number."

"Who is this guy?"

Fletcher broke into a worried smile, "His name is Rick Martin. He's a displaced Northerner; more comfortable now as a good old boy, you know. Southern by way of Italian parents.

I think his real last name is Martini or something. Like what you're drinking, and just as ice cold."

"How'd you find him?" Michael asked.

"When I was with the NYPD, we'd brought him into the precinct one night. I had to try and get information out of him about some missing gun trafficker from down South. Rick was visiting in New York. We knew that he'd done some deals with this guy. Interrogating him was like entering a dark swamp. You had this feeling he was going to reach over and pull you under. He's smart, he's calculating, former Special Forces. And he's not afraid of anything. He's since done some unofficial special assignments."

"Like what?"

"Don't ask, you don't want to know. I can tell you, though, he's the go-to guy for some pretty powerful organizations—including a few foreign governments—that need contract work done, quietly. If you know what I mean."

"Call him. I've got a private jet waiting to take me down there."

CHAPTER 8

Wake County, North Carolina

Rick Martin worked only a few days a year. In those few days, however, he lived on the edge between life and death, his life and other people's death. At least so far.

A strapping man in his forties, he stood six feet tall with an erect, military posture. His brown-reddish hair was wavy, a little long, a bit unkempt, like a preoccupied university professor's. He sported a mid-length beard that was red, redder than the hair on his head. He wore old, faded jeans or khakis, a simple button-down shirt and, on those cool days or nights, a woolen sweater. He always wore a pair of simple, rugged black boots.

The real loves of Rick's life, however, could be found in a securely locked closet in his bedroom: they included Smith and Wesson semi-automatic pistols, Berettas, Russian assault rifles, high-powered long-range rifles equipped with night vision scopes, and popular police issue Glock 19's. These were the tools of his trade.

He sat in the wooden rocking chair on the porch of his old farm house, a simple white clapboard house in northern Wake County, North Carolina, about forty minutes outside of Chapel Hill. He rented the old place from the two Smith brothers, Billy and Jimmy, who owned and operated a large, hundred-acre farm where they raised cattle in an environmentally conscientious manner. Rick was a good tenant. His old house sat on the edge of the property, nearest the road, Lee Street, and away from the main activities going on in the other ninety-nine or so acres. He seemed reasonably articulate, in a redneck kind of way. No one had ever seen any visitors to his house. He didn't appear to have a job with regular hours yet never seemed strapped for cash. He drove a relatively new black Jeep Cherokee. The windows were tinted so that you couldn't see who was inside, an unusual feature for a vehicle in that part of the world. In Wake County, however, people didn't ask a lot of questions.

Rick never installed a land-line in the house, preferring his cell phone for the infrequent incoming calls. He rarely initiated a call himself. He was a loner and he liked it just that way.

So it was a surprise when his cell phone rang this afternoon and an even greater but very pleasant surprise when he saw the international 379 area code.

CHAPTER 9

Wake County, North Carolina

Rick Martin started the engine of his Jeep Grand Cherokee. It was good to be working again, especially for a client he already knew and trusted. He laughed; who would ever believe that his biggest employer was one of the most powerful and respected organizations in the world? They said they'd received a call from this woman and had traced it back to this area but that she lived somewhere else.

Although Chapel Hill was just a college town, it adjoined two large cities, Raleigh and Durham, and was surrounded by miles of sparsely populated farmland. There were plenty of places for a professional killer to hide, even one with a hostage.

The first stop would be a trip to the Raleigh-Durham Airport. He'd check in with his network of buddies there, particularly airport security and the good folks at Hertz and Avis.

He glanced again at the photographs on the seat beside him. As soon as he'd gotten the email he printed out ten copies. She was pretty, with long black hair. Her name was printed on the bottom, "Sindy Steele." That had to be an alias, who the hell names their daughter Sindy with an S?

But the sound of his phone ringing again—the second time in the last several hours, if not months—brought him out of his thoughts. He took his foot off the gas pedal.

"Rick, it's Fletcher."

"Chief Fanelli—man, it's nice to hear from you, buddy," he whispered into the phone. "Hey, how've you been? Hey, I didn't recognize the number. Where are you calling from, New York City or something?"

"I'm using my private cell. I'm doing well—but, listen, I've got a problem. A big one. Are you still living in North Carolina?"

"You know I love it down here, chief. Yep, I'm in my same house in Wake County."

"That's Chapel Hill, right?"

All of a sudden, this is the place to be. "Yes sir, right nearby. What can I do for you?"

"I need for you to rescue a young lady who's been kidnapped. She's my goddaughter, a student there at UNC, Sofia Nicholas. You've got to get her out as quickly as possible—unharmed."

"Do you know who's got her?"

"Yes, a woman, a professional killer, Sindy Steele."

Rick couldn't believe his ears. "It's a small world, isn't it?" he said, before catching himself.

"What do you mean?" Fletcher said.

"I mean no matter where these ladies are—I'll find them for you."

"I know where they are." Fletcher said.

"Well . . . " Rick answered. "The pieces were falling into place. "We're half-way there then, aren't we?"

"They're at the Holiday Inn Express right outside of Chapel Hill."

Rick knew this was his lucky day. "I know right where it is."

"Rick, we need to get that young lady—her name's Sofia Nicholas—out of there alive and unharmed. And I mean, not a scratch."

"Chief, what about the other woman, this Sindy Steele?"

"She's a problem. One I'd prefer went away . . . Permanently."

"I got it."

"The young girl is all we care about."

"Chief, let me ask you something, is anyone else looking for her?" Rick sensed he was about to get paid twice for the same job.

"No, I can't imagine anyone else is looking for her. She's an independent contractor, you might say. She's on her own. No one else is looking for her and no one will really miss her when she's taken care of."

Rick Martin always wanted to believe there was a God. Now he knew for sure.

CHAPTER 10

I t took him fifteen minutes to get to the motel and a crisp hundred-dollar bill to find out from the desk clerk which room the tall pretty lady was staying in. Two hundred more and he had the room next door.

Martin placed his stethoscope against the adjoining wall between his room and the one where Sindy Steele was holding Sofia Nicholas. Even before he inserted the attached earphones securely in his ear he could hear the sound of the television through the wall.

He unwrapped his tools, feeling like a dentist surveying his picks and utensils. He stretched out the thin, flexible cable of the fiber optic snake camera, then an equally miniscule hand drill.

Finally settling in to listen, he felt a sense of relaxation, that warm inner peace that came from knowing he had successfully cornered his target, had a solid plan in place and now just needed to execute it as he had done so many times before.

He could hear everything from Sindy Steele's room as clearly as if he was sitting on the bed with her, which was where he wouldn't mind being under different circumstances. He wondered if she was fully dressed or, perhaps, in her lingerie, or less. His mind wandered as he fantasized about her.

He had seen several photographs of her, supplied separately by his two clients. The ones from Chief Fanelli were the most interesting, sexy, candid shots. Then he wondered too about young Sofia. The university coeds had always attracted him with their lithe young, half-naked bodies parading around campus. He was anxious to place the camera scope through the wall. But first he had to listen and wait for the right moment to do it.

He sat back in the faux wood desk chair, closed his eyes and tried to place himself next door, inside room 112.

"It's a business dinner, Janelle. I made a lot of money with him last year. It paid for your jewelry, including that pretty necklace you're wearing. I didn't see the big deal if the guy wanted to squeeze your ass a little."

He instantly recognized the show. Two years ago, he'd hung out with a woman who was addicted to *Dr. Frank*. At first he couldn't stand to watch it and would do anything to pass the time some other way while she sat in his farmhouse, glued to the screen. But then he found himself repeatedly glancing up to the screen himself. Embarrassed, at first he tried to hide his growing fascination. Then, as his attention became impossible to conceal, he confessed that he found it "mildly interesting." But once she left him for the last time, he never again tuned in. His mind was wandering again. "Come on, Rick, get yourself focused here," he whispered to himself. But the show drew him in once again.

"What happened then, say after he left? Did you discuss it?"

It was funny to hear Dr. Frank's voice again on television.

"No, then he wanted me to do it on the kitchen table. I still hadn't pick up the dinner dishes. I had to just push everything aside."

Finally, above the noise of *Dr. Frank*, he heard her.

"Okay, Sofia, we're going to spend the night here. I've got to keep your mouth taped a while longer. I'll give you a chance to eat one of those cheeseburgers later as long as you promise not to scream or do anything stupid. I've got to keep you bound up, though. If you scream or speak above a whisper you won't eat or drink again. Do you understand? Anyway, there's no one around. This place is dead tonight."

Rick smiled, this was just what he wanted to hear. He glanced to his right, eyeing the bottle of Wild Turkey he had placed on the desk, alongside the hotel's plastic cup encased in a small plastic bag. He wanted to pour himself a good shot but it would have to wait . . . until it was over. Looking at it only made it worse. He thought again of the picture of Sindy Steele, the one that showed her long slim legs in black stockings and high-heeled stilettos as she was stepping out of a limousine. He remembered looking more closely at first, wondering whether he saw a glimpse of her white thighs above the stocking line. It had been too long since he'd been with a woman. Now his mind was racing. He wondered if there could be any chance that he could somehow, out of this situation . . .

He caught himself. He knew better. Just carry out the mission. He'd never gaze at whatever mysteries awaited Sindy Steele's lovers above those firm thighs.

Sindy Steele would not see the morning light. He hoped Sofia Nicholas would be luckier.

CHAPTER 11

Chapel Hill, North Carolina

It took only ten minutes for him to drill the hole, about the width of a tiny nail, through the adjoining wall and thread the fiber optic wire and lens through. He could see virtually everything now.

Rick Martin hadn't yet heard Sofia Nicholas speak but he could make her out in the corner of the room, bound in duct tape and secured to one of the two double beds. He could still hear the television and, occasionally, would hear Steele. He felt encased inside their room, watching the two women watching television.

He felt something unusual inside him, a lack of concentration, as though he were outside himself, watching him watching them. It was something he couldn't put his finger on. Maybe it was because he had not an "assignment" in nearly a year.

Sitting at the desk facing the wall between them, he thought about how he would enter Steele's room. He had already lifted a master key intended for the housekeeping staff. The chain would be identical to the one on his own door and would offer no resistance to his thrust. But, for now, as long as Steele didn't make any threatening move toward Sofia, he'd just listen.

His plan wasn't complicated. He'd wait until Steele was asleep, burst through her door, and shoot her dead before she could harm him or Sofia. As he watched them through the wall with his camera, he rehearsed the plan over and over in his mind. It promised to be a long night.

Steele was talking to Sofia. Unable to speak, Sofia's eyes seemed to be screaming with fear—no, terror.

"I loved your father. And he loved me; believe me. I could have killed him, a year ago, they were going to pay me a lot of money to do it. And I almost did it because he'd turned on me. All of a sudden he wanted to get rid of me, he thought I was unstable, I knew what he thought—I'd overheard his calls—but it didn't stop him from fucking me, did it? No, he kept fucking me even after he knew he was going to dump me. That's why I took the assignment when these guys called me. And then . . . I just changed my mind. Mostly 'cause I could see they were going to get rid of me then, too. Anyway, I saved his life. It doesn't matter why. I think he'd take me back too if it wasn't for his wife . . . your mother, I guess, right?"

Rick zoomed in closer to Steele, checking to see exactly what kind of weapons she had and exactly where they were. She was on the second twin bed, facing Sofia. Her gun was on the nightstand.

"You don't believe me? You think I'm nuts or something, too? It must run in the family."

Sofia was shaking her head but Steele wasn't paying any attention.

"You don't believe your daddy could do all this, do you? Hold on, let me show you."

Steele reached into her handbag and pulled out what appeared to be a digital recording device. She played with the buttons and then put the machine on the edge of Sofia's bed.

"Listen."

The recording was loud and clear. Rick didn't recognize the voice but it was apparently Sofia's father, Michael Nicholas.

"She's crazy, Samantha." *Talking to his wife, it seemed.*

"You promised me this was over –" *A woman's voice. The wife.*

Michael again: "She's dangerous. We know what she's capable of doing. Fletcher got his hands on a sealed court document from when she was in med school. They couldn't prove it but the cops at Stanford believe she murdered her boyfriend. And do you know why? He'd just moved out on her."

"Maybe next time, if you're going to screw around you could at least have the good sense not to do it with a schizophrenic murderer." *Good one.*

Sindy Steele moved closer to Sofia, her face just inches from Sofia's duct-taped mouth. Rick tensed up, wondering now if he would have to move in earlier than he'd planned.

"Let me ask you something, Sofia," Steele said, her voice breaking. "Do *you* think I'm a schizophrenic murderer?"

CHAPTER 12

40,000 feet over Maryland

M ichael looked out into the night. Through the window of the Gulfstream 150, the lights of Baltimore twinkled far below. Facing Fletcher in the seat across from him, he nervously fingered his phone until he couldn't wait any longer.

"She may not answer; don't get upset," Fletcher said.

But she did.

No hello, or who is this? She knew it was him.

"It's funny how fragile life is." She was either crying or so angry her voice wasn't as strong as when they last spoke. "You know when your mouth is taped up, the only way you can breathe is through the two little nostrils in your nose. Just two tiny holes —"

"Sindy, please —"

"And the real funny thing, what makes you realize how easy it is to just put someone's lights out, forever, is . . . all you have to do is take about another two inches of tape and you seal up those little holes—and then it's all over. That person is gone. They kind of . . . implode."

"I'm on my way down there. Let's sit down and talk this through." He had to be careful not to let her know that he knew her exact location. "Tell me where you are."

"That's all it takes, just another piece of tape. I don't know why we bother with guns and things. This is so clean, so easy.

Even for the girl here. Just a bit of choking for maybe a minute or two."

"Sindy, I'm so sorry if I hurt you. I really am. You have to believe that. I didn't know how else to handle things –"

"Me too. I don't know how else to handle things either," she said.

There was a pause, Michael wasn't sure what it meant or what to say. "What can I do?"

"Oh, forgive me, I was just reaching for the roll of tape. Don't you hate it when the tape sticks back on the roll and you have to try and lift it up the end with your nails to get another piece?"

"Sindy –"

"Good bye, Michael, I'm busy now."

CHAPTER 13

Chapel Hill, North Carolina

Rick moved the eye of the scope so he could see around the room, checking first on Sofia, who was squirming, apparently trying to get loose. He looked around for Steele. Their bathroom was the only part of the room that wasn't visible to the camera's hidden eyeball. She must have gone there after disconnecting Michael's call. At least she'd moved away from Sofia.

He waited, expecting to hear a toilet flush; he pointed the camera back to Sofia, still struggling to get free, she looked terrified. As she struggled she kept glancing down to the foot of her bed. Rick manipulated the camera to the spot she appeared to be watching but saw nothing unusual. There was no one there.

He looked again for Steele. How long does it take a woman to go to the damned john? Maybe those skin-tight jeans were hard to get up and down.

He scanned the room again, rapidly this time, moving the scope as far to each side as he could. Where was Steele? She had to be taking a shit. But he could hear her, speaking.

"Let me ask you something, Sofia," Steele said, repeating her earlier remark, "Do *you* think I'm a schizophrenic murderer? I don't know about the schizophrenic part but I guess I do know about the murderer stuff. That's a sure thing."

He watched Sofia as she struggled harder.

Steele repeated it again, "Let me ask you something, Sofia. Do *you* think I'm a schizophrenic murderer?" And again, "Let me ask you something, Sofia. Do *you* think I'm a schizophrenic murderer?"

Yes, lady, I do, no matter how many times you ask. You are fucking nuts.

As he listened Rick kept visually rehearsing his commando-style, surprise entry into Steele's room.

Then something caught his eye again. It was what Sofia had been looking at: Sindy Steele's iPhone on the other bed. Why was Sofia staring at it?

His own world was closed off by the sounds from Room 112 echoing through his earphones. But she was still repeating . . . He took his eye off the scope, then moved his head slightly to the left to look at his door. He removed his earphones and listened. There were no noises in his own room, all was still. He stood up and looked around. Everything was okay; the chain, although mostly useless, remained in place on the door.

Rick stood still and just listened; not a sound, his room was secure. He sat back down, put his earphones on again and leaned in closer to his video screen. He heard it again. "Let me ask you something –" His muscles tensed, he felt a chill through his body. He looked once again, focusing closely on Sindy's iPhone, then back to Sofia, bound and helpless but watching it in terror.

Then it hit him. He knew what she was doing. Hopefully, he'd caught it before it was too late. The phone was doing the talking; she'd been playing back her voice on the recording App. He moved the scope all around the room as far as he could see. Sindy Steele was gone. His mind began working a multitude of calculations, none of them good.

Was she escaping? If so, at least Sofia was still okay. He could see her, struggling and scared. Other than the duct tape, she seemed to be okay. But for Steele to use the recording, she had to know he was watching and she had to be up to something.

Despite the earphones there was no mistaking the crashing sound coming from inside his room. He looked up but he knew right away that she had the drop on him.

She came bursting through the splintered door.

His gun lay only inches away, on the desk. He reached for it, his hand slipping perfectly around its butt as he dived for cover. In one swift motion, he righted himself and leveled his gun to fire. He could feel the familiar adrenalin rush. He was wired. She would be no match for him.

But as he prepared to fire at the spot where she'd stood, he froze. No one was there. She was gone. He turned around his eyes darting at each element inside the room. The door was splintered and open. There was a strange silence, except for the faint sound of the Dr. Frank Show still coming from next door. He scanned the room, ready to fire at the first movement. This was too strange. He looked again at the broken door, the smell of the hot night air had mixed in with the cool crisp air conditioning.

There was one spot he couldn't see though. He stared at the bed. She never could have made it underneath in the few seconds when he'd lost sight of her. But there was a blind spot, on the floor on the other side of the bed. She could have managed to get there, maybe lying in wait, flat on her stomach. Not easily but it might have been possible. Or, had she gone right back out the door she'd come breaking in through? And why would she have left? Had his quick grab for the Glock frightened her away? If so, where would she have gone? He turned slightly and looked back to the spot behind the bed. He listened for her breathing, a click of a trigger . . . anything.

From where he stood, even if he fired toward the blind spot, the bullets would have to go through the top of the bed to get to her. He'd have to move in closer to get the right angle to hit her if she were there.

He looked back again at the door—but then he heard her, a sound coming back from the bed. He turned towards it but she was there, a streak of long black hair flying through the air. But her head somehow held still—as did her gun. In that brief split-second, he saw her smile.

He tried to raise his gun while instinctively turning away but before he could squeeze the Glock's trigger, Sindy Steele's first bullet entered him midway in the side, crossing through his chest, tearing apart his heart and lungs. The force of the bullet pushed him back and down. The gun fell from his hand. He was on fire inside. He tried to get to the floor to get the pistol . . . or to shield himself under the desk but his body moved without him now. She moved in quickly, pushing his gun away from his reach.

He looked up and into her eyes. He could see from the angle of her gun exactly where the next bullet was going, but . . . she just stood there.

"Next time you drill a little peephole in someone's room, don't do it right over their cheeseburger. You got little droppings of plaster in it."

Everything was in slow motion now. She brought the gun closer to his head.

"If you want to live, tell me who sent you."

He wouldn't give her Fletcher's name, no matter what— but the other guys, yes, he'd tell her who they were . . . but, he was fading, he needed air, something . . . He tried to speak, to give her what she wanted, but as he inhaled it felt like a knife was turning inside his lungs. His mouth hung open but nothing, other than blood, was coming out. He gasped, trying to say it but his mouth wouldn't work, he couldn't form the words.

She smiled again at him. "That's okay. I was going to shoot you anyway."

A million thoughts crossed his mind but he only had time for one more word. He was surprised that he was still able to hear it when it came out.

"Shit."

CHAPTER 14

40,000 feet over Virginia

H e'd only been in the air for an hour but it seemed like forever. His iPhone rang, jolting him back to earth. He recognized the 919 area code—it was North Carolina—but not the rest of the number.

Her voice was steady and disconcertingly calm. He knew that meant she was anything but calm. "Do you know whose phone I'm using, Michael?"

"Sindy—where are –"

"I asked you a question." Her voice was flat. Not a good sign at all.

"No, I don't know whose number this is. How could I possibly know?" Michael kept his voice low.

"Someone sent this guy after me. I've got his phone and as soon as I hang up with you I'll go through his old calls so I'll know who called him. You better hope it wasn't you. You better hope I don't see your number."

"Sindy, stop. Jesus, It wasn't me –"

"If it *was* you—then I'll let you know where I left Sofia's body."

Michael looked over at Fletcher, searching his face for a clue on how to respond.

"Please, listen to me." He had to think, strategize his approach while being careful with his responses. The wrong words, a lie caught, could be fatal for Sofia.

"Did you send him to kill me?"

"I told you, I didn't. I didn't."

"I don't believe you."

"Jesus, Sindy, *who* are you talking about?"

"It looks like his name is Richard Martin. I'm going through his wallet. Someone sent him after me."

"Why don't you just *ask* him who sent him?" He knew this was risky, but she was certainly going to check the phone regardless. "Then you'll know –"

"I did but he didn't tell me."

"Why don't you ask him again?" It wasn't like Sindy to let someone off the hook.

"I would, but first I'd have to wipe his blood and brains off the walls here and try to pour them all back in his skull which is also all over the freakin' place. I never finished medical school, remember?"

He hesitated, and then he realized the line was dead.

Chapter 15

Chapel Hill, North Carolina

Perhaps it was her stunningly good looks. Yet, despite her athletic build and height, easily six feet with heels, men—especially the tough ones—always underestimated Sindy Steele.

Killing was so close to sex.

Sometimes, after a hit, she even felt the urge to light up a cigarette. Thrilling, exciting, the anticipation when you know it's going to happen. When you can see—just before they do—that they've got no way out. And then that moment, after you've struck, the blade's gone in but there's still not a trace of blood, the organs have been cut open, the damage is done, *you* know it, *they* know it, and they know there's nothing that can reverse it, nothing that can save them. They're at your mercy and you're the last one they're going to see. That's the sweet spot. Those seconds, much less than a minute but so precious. They look at you and you know they're asking . . . *why*? They want you to say something. They wonder who you are. *Why is this beautiful woman doing this to me?* They, too, confuse it with sex. They think they're having sex with me; they know I'm screwing them. They like it, too. They enjoy being on the bottom for once. So strange, if it's a stiletto I'm holding, it's inside them but maybe not yet all the way, so they give me that look, their eyes are begging, *stick it in all the way, please, all the way*. It's their orgasm. Their last one. They want me to like them, to be nice, caring . . . feeling. Yes, it feels so good—even after, if it's with the right person.

This one didn't have the intimacy of a knife but at least Rick Martin was the right one; he would have killed her if she hadn't outsmarted him. When you do it to the wrong guy, you need more than a cigarette after that. You feel dirty. Not tonight. Tonight felt good.

If she found Michael's number on this Rick Martin's mobile, could she kill Sofia? Good question. She looked up from the phone—she wanted to know her answer before she found—or didn't find—it. She looked around the room: blood and guts. It could have been hers instead. She caught a glimpse of herself in the mirror; she was strikingly beautiful, even to herself. Long black hair that needed washing, strikingly white skin. She watched as a line of blood flowed down from a splotch that landed right above her reflection making it look as though she were the one who'd been shot.

Her mind shifted back to Sofia, waiting in the other room. Yes—if she found Michael's number on this phone—she would have to make a decision.

Standing over what was left of Martin's body, she scrolled through the phone numbers on his iPhone. She hoped she wouldn't find Michael's but she suspected that she would. She knew them all by heart, each one beginning with a "203" Connecticut exchange.

There weren't too many to begin with. This guy clearly had no social life, a bunch of local "919's," a few "917's"— close, that was New York, but . . . no Connecticut "203."

She kept scrolling until she saw it. No, not Michael's but one she knew well. Yes, this one *was* familiar. A few of them and all very recent. She felt a thunderbolt racing through her. The numbers jumped out. It was an international exchange. She knew well the rare country code: "379."

It wasn't Michael after all. It was the Vatican.

CHAPTER 16

Raleigh, North Carolina

As he entered the Raleigh-Durham Airport terminal, Michael's iPhone buzzed with a new text message. It was from Sindy Steele. He glanced down, fearing what he'd see:

When were you going to tell me you were in town?

How did she know? He typed back, misspelling some words which the spell-check function corrected:

What did you think I was going to do? Stay home? I have to see you, Sindy. I want to see you. I need Sofia back, safe. Please.

Do you know where I am?

No, not exactly, he lied.

Who the fuck are you kidding? I know where you are and you know where I am. You know that you're a liar, don't you?

You started with all this shit, I hardly knew what an app was.

Are you alone? Where's Samantha?

She's on a flight back from Paris. She doesn't have a clue what's going on. Yet.

Some things never change.

At least she'd neglected to ask again if he was alone. *I'll come to you—alone—just tell me you'll let Sofia go unharmed. I'll trade places with her. Do whatever the hell you want with me.*

It might be too late for that, Michael.

What do you mean, too late?

I mean it may be too late to give her back . . . unharmed.

Michael's phone chimed, a message popped up at the bottom of the screen. It was from his brother Alex. He'd have to wait. *Sindy, just tell me what you want.*

I've got what I want, she messaged.

What's that? Sofia? What do you want with her?

She got me what I wanted most.

What's that?

To make you suffer

Michael clicked on his brother's message, *They've left the motel.*

He messaged back to Sindy, *What about Sofia?*

He stopped short of the terminal exit and waited, staring at the phone's screen, hoping for—but dreading—an answer. Showing Sindy's messages to Fletcher, he typed in another one: *Is she okay?*

He kept looking at the screen but there was no response.

"Let's keep walking," Fletcher said, "I've got a car waiting for us right outside. We can be there in twenty minutes."

Another message—it was Alex again: *Looks like she's in front of the building—161 Broad Street, just off West Franklin in Chapel Hill.*

A giant black Chevrolet Suburban with its motor running was waiting for them at the curb; Michael entered on the passenger side.

"Change of address—follow the signs, let's head for downtown Chapel Hill. I'll put the address in the GPS," Michael said. But before he could even find the always elusive controls, he felt his head thrust back as Fletcher stepped on the gas and headed out on Interstate 40.

"Let's just hope we don't get pulled over," Fletcher said, "I'm not sure how the cops here feel about retired NYPD badges."

Michael began typing into his iPhone again: *Who's there, Sofia or Steele?*

Alex came right back: *Sofia—or at least her phone.*

He tried to plug the address into the Suburban's GPS but it wouldn't work.

"You can't put an address in there while the car's going," Fletcher barked. "Use the one on your phone."

Michael found the app and typed in the address. The phone began directing them: "Continue on this road for two miles . . ."

As they drove toward town, Michael kept checking for any response from Sindy Steele but found nothing.

Several minutes later they turned onto Franklin Street. The stranger's voice continued to direct them. "Proceed a quarter of a mile and turn right on Broad Street."

Moments later, "Your destination is ahead, on the right."

Michael looked around as Fletcher slowed the car down. It was a quaint side street, lined on both sides with old but well-preserved homes and small professional offices.

Finally, "You have reached your destination."

They both strained to read the numbers on the buildings.

"That's it," Michael said, pointing to the two-story red brick building. He leaned forward, closer to the window now, "She supposed to be in front of this building. It looks like a damned real-estate office."

But as they pulled over to the front of the building, the somber, white sign with neat black lettering told a different story: *MacPherson Funeral Home.*

CHAPTER 17

Rome, Italy

"It is difficult to see the devil when she is beautiful and the scent of Giorgio Armani surrounds her," said Cardinal Angelo Lovallo, more to himself or his God than to his loyal monsignor, Dominick Petrucceli. "And, unfortunately, thanks to us, she is no stranger to the Vatican."

Da Mario, at the foot of the Spanish Steps, had been Monsignor Petrucceli's choice for their dinner tonight. Dark wood wainscoting, starched white tablecloths, homey old framed cartoons and pictures on the faded white walls, all offset by warm soft lighting and an atmosphere of simpler times, combined to bring him a small dose of comfort. More important, they'd be left alone there; Da Mario wasn't exactly a Vatican hot spot, if there even were such a thing.

It had been a year since they had hired Sindy Steele, Michael Nicholas's former bodyguard and mistress, to kill Joseph Sharkey. She had done that job well.

Sharkey had been a low-life former Mafioso who'd hired a young punk to murder Alex Nicholas and then been hidden and protected by the Vatican. Sharkey had them over a barrel as a result of a favor he'd done a decade ago when he eliminated three young men who were about to testify against a Bronx bishop, Kevin McCarthy, who had molested them. Sindy Steele had expertly inserted her stiletto blade inside Sharkey's heart as he pondered leather jackets inside a well-known Florence leather shop.

Petrucceli could see and feel that something was happening in the Cardinal's mind, a shift, perhaps a change of heart. "We had no choice. He knew too much. He could have caused us great trouble."

The Cardinal looked into Petrucceli's eyes. It was a piercing look. "Yes, and now *she* knows too much. And we have intercepted some of her communications: Michael Nicholas knows what she knows. So now the two of them are mortal threats to the Church. She didn't go away as she promised, she's re-emerged and involved us in her distorted emotional world, going after his daughter, a stupid, spurned lover's revenge. Now we must take action to protect the sanctity of the Church. We are covering up cover-ups . . . I've lost track. Nevertheless . . . the Devil's cycle continues. I fear that we have become his instrument but I know no other way."

"It all would have been over—it would have been finished— if she'd done her job and eliminated Michael Nicholas," the Monsignor said.

"Yes, but she didn't, my son. Her emotions—whatever that means in her case—took over. We didn't understand that she'd actually fallen in love with him. It was an emotion we didn't sense in her. And so now, she has told him everything. Michael Nicholas, who knows that we had protected his brother's killer and that we employed Sindy Steele—his own mistress—to kill *him*."

Petrucceli shook his head, amazed at the myriad of mishaps and miscalculations that had brought them to this place. "It would still have been resolved if she had kept her word and taken our money and disappeared."

"Yes, it would have, at least for now. I thought we had a detente. But even that has failed. She took our money and, as agreed, settled in the Greek islands. She could have lived like a queen there, rich and drunk on the sun and ouzo. It should have been over. We thought it was."

"Why would she leave Santorini and go back to America and track down Sofia Nicholas? The daughter is innocent." Petrucceli shook his head. "I don't understand this woman."

Cardinal Lovallo flashed a benevolent smile, "Perhaps then you have never seen a woman scorned, especially one who was already unstable. It is like placing your bare hand in a serpent's pit. She never forgave Michael Nicholas for turning her away. Love and hate are very close allies, you know. In her case, they appear to coexist rather comfortably; perhaps to her they are indistinguishable."

Petrucceli listened, at first saying nothing as he sipped his Antinori Chianti. "We have heard that she has . . . emotional, psychological issues—or episodes—related to her medication, or, more precisely, her lack of medication at times. She seems to go in and out of sanity."

Lovallo continued, "Listen, we protected a dirty priest. It was how things were done then but by doing so we have endangered the Holy Father. The winds shift quickly in Rome. If this gets out, the vultures will circle. It was wishful thinking on my part to think Steele and Michael Nicholas would just go away." He sat back, appeared to give what he'd just said more thought and, continued. "Have you reached our esteemed Rick Martin?"

"He has been unusually silent . . . for several hours now."

"It is unlike him, no?" The Cardinal's eyebrows arched, his signal of suspicion.

The waiter broke the tension, placing a plate of ravioli in front of Lovallo. His expression changed. It looked to Petrucceli now more like satisfaction, or at least a calm resignation. As his plate of bisteca di Manzo was placed in front of him, he glanced at his mobile phone. There was a text message waiting, he glanced at the name of the sender and immediately felt a sense of relief, a pleasant lightening of the mood.

"Speak of the devil, here he is. I have a message from Rick Martin."

Lovallo looked up from his plate, "Is it done?" he asked.

Petrucceli put his fork down and clicked onto the message.

Richard Martin is dead. You sent him to kill me. I will find you and then you will die. From what I can see, you'd better hope that God of yours doesn't exist. Either way—you're screwed.

Watching Petrucceli, Lovallo asked, "Is she finally gone?"

Petrucceli placed the phone down on the table and for a moment cradled his head in his hands. "No, my Father. *He* is dead. *She* lives. She knows." He wondered what had happened and about the fate of the girl.

Lovallo nodded, "And now it is only a matter of time until we hear from Monsignor Schlegelberger. He will remind us that we should have never allowed Sindy Steele to leave Italy, alive." His eyes blinked once and then as though nothing had happened, he turned his attention back to his plate.

After so many years together, Petrucceli knew that the discussion was over. It was time to eat, perhaps to forget.

He watched as the Cardinal finally picked up his fork and tasted the ravioli with cheese and black truffles. The scent of the truffles travelled across the table, taking his own mind off Sindy Steele, at least until he noticed the old man's hand shaking.

CHAPTER 18

Chapel Hill, North Carolina

Michael checked Alex's message again to be sure he read it right: *"Looks like she's in front of the building."* Yes, he'd read it correctly.

But there was only one thing in front of MacPherson's Funeral Home and it was the black Cadillac hearse parked in the driveway.

Michael opened his door and stepped out. He ran toward the driveway. "No, this can't be it." He stopped just short of the hearse. Curtains covered most of the windows in the "cargo" section. Michael peered in; he felt his legs shake, his stomach a painful knot.

Fletcher looked into the front window while Michael gripped the door handles of the rear doors. "They're locked back here," he shouted.

"Front doors are locked too. Can you see anything inside?" Fletcher said.

Michael looked closely through the back window, finally placing his nose against the glass, while shielding the view with his right hand to cut the glare. "Yeah, I do."

"What is it?" Fletcher said.

"What the fuck do you think it is? It's a casket. Jesus."

Michael looked at Fletcher who then turned toward the funeral home, "Let me see if anyone's inside the house."

Fletcher then ran up the steps to the white columned front entry, rang the bell and began pounding on the door.

"The front door's locked," he shouted out. "This place is dead."

"Yeah. It's what they do."

Fletcher returned to the hearse. "Sindy messaged you that Sofia was here, right?"

Michael hesitated, stalling as though he was distracted, for how to answer. This certainly wasn't the time to tell his friend that he'd been in regular contact with Alex. No, that would require a sit down and a few Martinis, to say the least. He looked back at the hearse.

"The message was that Sofia's in front of this address. This is the only thing in front," Michael said, pointing toward the hearse. Their eyes met, and then moved away.

"Sofia," Michael shouted as he gripped the rear door handle again. "Sofia—are you in there?"

"Let's hope not. There's got to be a tire iron in our car. We'll break the fucking windows." Fletcher ran for the Suburban.

Was he crazy to rely on a text from Alex? Maybe this was the time to call the police? Was it too late? How would he explain why he thought Sofia was here, of all places? Alex had been reliable in the past but . . . how real was he? One thing he knew was real, however, and that was Sindy Steele.

Fletcher returned with the tire iron and smashed it through the back window. Michael reached inside through the splintered glass and linen curtains and unlocked the rear gate.

Fletcher pulled the wide door open. Michael's eyes went straight to the steel gray casket.

CHAPTER 19

Gripping the pallbearer's handle on the end of the casket, Michael climbed inside the rear compartment. He tried to lift open the casket's lid but it wouldn't give. "How the hell do you open these things?"

"Michael—she couldn't be in there . . . She's not in there."

"Give me that tire iron," Michael said, holding his hand out. But before he could get it from Fletcher, his phone rang. It was a familiar custom ring. Sofia's. He grabbed the phone from his pocket, "Hold on," he shouted to Fletcher, "it's Sofia. . . I hope."

"Where are you?" he said, but there was no response. He looked down at the phone's screen to be sure he was still connected. The seconds were ticking away. He put it back to his ear. "Sofia—are you there? Is this you? Please . . . say something."

Her voice was the greatest thing he'd ever heard. It was Sofia—but it was weak, soft, too soft, an out of focus picture. "I'm lost. I don't know where . . ." It trailed off.

"Sofia, where are you?"

"I think she drugged me. I'm not sure, I'm inside something, I'm lying down. My head's on a pillow . . . there's silk or something above me . . . It's creepy. Dad –"

"What is it? Are you okay?"

"Oh my God. Get me out of here. I think I'm in a casket."

"Okay, try pushing up on the lid from where you are." Michael turned to Fletcher, "She's inside. We've got to get this thing open."

Armed with the tire iron Fletcher jumped into the back and forced the tip of the iron in between the casket and its lid until the two began to bend and part. He kept at it, wedging it further apart by inches now. "Sofia, can you hear me?" Fletcher said, placing his face close to the opening.

Speaking into the phone, Michael whispered, "We're here, we're opening it now. Can you see Fletcher?" But there was no answer. Michael checked the screen again. This time it read, "Call Ended."

Fletcher maneuvered the rod up and down until the lid finally gave way, pulling apart from the base with a sound that reminded Michael of caskets opening in horror movies. He reached over and helped Fletcher pull the lid all the way up. There was a body inside, a dead one. It wasn't Sofia.

CHAPTER 20

Michael jumped down out of the hearse and typed a message to Alex: *She's not in the car. The house is a funeral parlor and the only thing in front was a hearse. You said she was in front of the house. Help—now.*

Watching the screen, Michael could see the line of dots indicating an answer was coming: *These fin GPS things aren't perfect. Try inside the house.*

Michael turned to Fletcher, "We gotta get inside. She could be in there."

"Is that Sindy again?" Fletcher said.

Ignoring the question, Michael started running towards the front door of the house, "Let's go. Do you know how to get us in?"

Michael dialed Sofia's phone again but there was no answer.

Fletcher followed, smiling, "I think I can manage getting us into a funeral parlor. They're dead asleep."

Minutes later, after Fletcher had easily opened the front door, they stood in the entry hall looking at the black sign with white letters showing the schedule of "showings" going on in the home.

"I hate these places," Michael said.

"They've got four parties going on here," Fletcher said. "Let's start with these rooms. Hopefully, the caskets are open."

"Do you think they leave them open all night?" Michael said, heading inside the room in front of them. "We may as well start with this one."

"Say hello to Mister Fats Walker," Fletcher announced while reading the directory sign.

Once inside, Michael felt a wave of memories sweep over him, a momentary flashback of every funeral home, casket and preserved body he'd seen, a stream of consciousness of every loved one's casket he'd stood over while whispering his good-byes. A nighttime floodlight covered the room with a ghostly green hue, making the room even more unreal than its purpose. His attention went quickly past the several rows of perfectly aligned chairs and, once again, to a casket, surrounded by flowers, sitting atop a mahogany bier. The sweet yet sickly funereal smell of the flowers permeated his senses. Flowers smell different in a funeral home. The casket was open, Michael knew right away that it was Fats.

He called out to Fletcher, "Why don't you take the other viewing rooms. I'll look for the other rooms –"

"Other rooms?"

"Yeah, there's always a display showroom with the new caskets for people to select from . . . and then there's –"

"I know—where they do the embalming."

"Let me try the showroom first."

Fletcher took off down the hall while Michael lagged behind as he messaged Alex once more: *We're in the funeral home. Checking out the caskets, nothing so far. Are you sure she's here?*

Alex: *No, only that her phone is.*

Michael: *She is with her phone—she called me a few minutes ago but I lost her. I've tried her back but I got nothing.*

Alex: *Keep searching that house—she's there then. Should I try her?*

Michael: *No, that's all she'd need to see. She's already scared shitless. I'll keep trying her while Fletcher and I are searching.*

Continuing to walk, Michael looked up and saw a set of closed double doors with a discreet bronze nameplate: "Display

Room." Once inside he counted seven caskets: white steel, mahogany, pine, silver, white wood . . . all of them open, thank God. This looks like a damn mattress store. He walked quickly, checking each one. All were empty.

He left the room and continued down the hall.

There was one more room. The one he hoped he'd never have to enter, at least not alive.

CHAPTER 21

H e stopped for a moment, staring at the door, hoping for a reprieve, or a miracle. Who in his right mind would want to enter that room? He knew that whatever was inside, he would see again and again in his dreams for the rest of his life, especially near the end. Other than finding Sofia alive, he hoped there was no one else, dead or alive.

He'd try Sindy Steele one more time . . . maybe . . . He pressed her number into his phone. He never heard it ring but she was speaking already.

"They'll hunt you down. You know that, don't you? They have to kill you. There's no other way. The moment you found out they protected your brother's killer, you were a dead man." Sindy Steele's voice wavered. It wasn't like her.

"Yeah, well, it's been a few years since then and I'm still standing," Michael answered. "You're the one who took Sofia, not the Vatican. We had an agreement, Sindy. You took their money. You were to go to Greece and we'd all move on. As long as we all left well enough alone, we had a truce with them. For some fucking reason, you came here and kidnapped Sofia and put us all in danger."

"They sent that hit man after *me* but do you think they were gonna just let your daughter walk away?"

"No one would have sent anyone if you'd stayed in Greece. Who the hell would leave Santorini to go cause trouble in North Carolina? Anyway, I'll find them, I'll take care of this."

"How the fuck are you going to do that?"

"I'll figure it out. Where's Sofia? I'm in a funeral home in Chapel Hill but I can't find her. You brought her here, didn't you? Where is she? She's just a girl; she's done nothing. What the hell is wrong with you?"

"I don't know. I don't know. I had to hurt you. I knew this was the way to do it."

"Where exactly did you leave her? Please . . ."

"There are things I don't understand. They take over me. I left her cell phone with her though."

"Well, she's not answering. You need to get help, Sindy. There's medication you know. It doesn't have to be this way"

"Don't try and tell me what to do."

"Just tell me this, did you put her in a coffin?"

"Yes, of course."

"Of course? Where is it? In which room? Where?"

"Michael . . . there's more I need to tell you. I have to get out of here."

"Sindy, don't hang up –"

But she did.

CHAPTER 22

The sign on the door read, "Staff Only—Do Not Enter" This had to be it, where they do the embalming.

He looked around for Fletcher, hoping he'd be nearby to join him. He opened the door. The only light came from the hallway behind him yet he could make out the reflections on the steel equipment inside. It was just enough for his imagination—and the memory of CSI or some other television series for him—to be able to see the room before he really could.

As he took his first step in, Michael's phone rang; it was Sofia. "I don't know how much longer I can go. There's not much oxygen in here. The phone slipped away. I've been queasy . . . it's claustrophobic."

"Thank God it's you. Listen, feel your way around, you're in nothing more than a padded box."

"Dad, it's more than a box. It's a casket. They put dead people in these things."

"I know—but not in that one. You're alive and I'm going to find you and get you out. Soon. Very soon."

"Have you tried to open it?"

"Of course I have. I've pushed and felt as far as I can around the lid but it seems to be locked tight."

"Okay, just stay still, stay calm. I'm going to find you."

"Dad . . ."

There was a silence.

"Sofia, are you there?"

"Yes, sorry . . . I have a question . . . One I'm afraid to ask you."

"What? What is it? Just ask. Anything."

He could hear her crying.

"I'm not buried, am I?"

The thought hadn't crossed his mind. Now it chilled him. "No. Don't worry, I'll find you. I think I'm in the building where you are. Try not to talk a lot. Can you tell how much power you have left on your phone?"

"Yes, it's the only light I have but it looks like I've got about eight percent left. That's not much."

"It'll be enough Just lie still and stay quiet a little bit unless I need you to speak so you don't use up a lot of oxygen. I've got to search one last room. I think this is where you must be. I'm just entering now. It's going to be okay."

"Dad—I'm so sorry. She's . . ."

"Sorry for what??" She seemed to have stopped in mid-sentence. "What are you sorry about?"

He looked at his phone. The connection was lost.

He turned on the lights. The room had no windows so even though it was on the first floor it had the look of a basement but one outfitted in stainless steel with equipment carts and tools laid out like in a dentist's office—just more of them and scarier ones, with long cutting edges everywhere—a steel sink, trays, machines, a large round light overlooking a table—surely where the body is placed for embalming. He saw bodies where there were none. There was no casket or anything else where Sofia could be hidden.

He noticed a shadow in the reflections; someone was coming up behind him. He turned around—it was someone, just only inches away. His muscles tightened, he raised his arm, an instinctual self self-defense. "Jesus, Fletcher. You scared the shit out of me."

"Sorry, did you find anything?"

"No."

"Same here. I wonder if we missed something." Fletcher said. Michael watched him looking around the room before turning back to the door.

As Michael turned around to follow, a sound erupted throughout the room, like that of a giant generator grinding to a stop. The lights went out, leaving only the limited glare from the emergency lamp overhead. Seconds later, that went out, too. The room was dark.

CHAPTER 23

"What the hell happened?" Fletcher said.

"I don't know but it isn't good." His phone vibrated, it was a text message, from Sofia. "Hold on, I just got a text," he called out.

He clicked onto it and held the phone out so they could read the message together.

She drugged me with something but I remember going down steps, a basement I think.

Michael texted Alex:

Sindy is here somewhere with Sofia—can you locate them? I'm inside the funeral home. Hurry.

Several seconds passed and then came a response:

Alex: *Sofia's phone is still inside the funeral home. See if there's a basement. I can't locate Steele though.*

Disappointed, Michael whispered to Fletcher, "There's got to be a basement. We must have missed a door somewhere."

Before either of them could make a move, a bell, more like a chime, rang. Twice, then a pause, and then it just kept ringing.

"Someone's at the front door. It's the same bell I tried earlier before I knocked," Fletcher said. "It could be the local police, maybe we triggered an alarm."

Michael felt the vibration from his phone. It was another text, from Alex.

"Hold on one second." He turned slightly away and began reading his texts.

Alex: *I've picked up Sindy's phone. She's outside the building.*

Fletcher looked back at Michael, agitated, "What the fuck are you doing? Who are you emailing now?"

"No one, don't worry."

Fletcher shrugged, clearly and understandably confused.

They both headed out to the hallway and towards the front door.

"I have a feeling it may be Sindy at the door," Michael said.

"A feeling?" Fletcher whispered. "What are you, a psychic now?"

Michael used his iPhone as a flashlight that at least illuminated his immediate path. There appeared to be shadows everywhere. Since the lights had gone out everything seemed to be in black and white, mostly black. The floors creaked as they stepped through the hallway.

"Why don't you stay back and let me answer," Michael said.

Fletcher nodded, stopped and let Michael turn left into the long entry hall. "What if it's the police?"

"I'll say the door was open and I wandered in looking for someone." But Michael knew it wasn't.

The doorbell rang again, a series of chimes, reminding Michael of scenes from the Addams Family movie. As he gripped the doorknob he peered through the sidelights surrounding the front door, he saw a car on the street—and a woman in black leather—standing, watching from right outside the door. She was looking back through the side windows. Before he could even open the door she suddenly turned around and raced for her car. Michael turned around; Fletcher had entered the hallway—she must have seen him and fled.

"It's Sindy," Michael called out to Fletcher as he opened the heavy wooden door and ran out after her. But she had a head start—and she was fast and fit.

"Where are you going?" Michael called out. "Where's Sofia?"

The car was a hundred or so feet away. He ran after her as fast as he could, Fletcher following right behind him. He saw the car door slam shut, heard the motor start and the locks click. He reached her car just as she pulled out, the wheels burning rubber. She looked back, her face expressionless.

"Son of a bitch." Michael turned back to the funeral home.

CHAPTER 24

M ichael rejoined Fletcher inside. "Okay, let's find that basement."

They split into different directions, opening every door they could find. Finally, Michael opened a door at the far end of the hall. He pointed his iPhone straight ahead into the black void and saw the stairs descending down below him. "I found it," he called out but Fletcher didn't answer. He looked back; he couldn't wait. He went down the steps, into the dark.

He reached the bottom and stepped onto the concrete floor. It was time to try for a better light. He found the flashlight App on his phone; it was better than just the light from the home screen. He scanned the room doing a full 360-degree circle until he saw it, in the middle of the otherwise empty basement. Another casket.

He moved to it, a shiny steel black enamel box that had obviously just been painted, probably a custom job. The floor below it was covered with a white bed sheet, covered with black spray paint giving it the look of a Jackson Pollack canvas. The casket was sitting on a catafalque. It was closed.

Michael moved in closer. He touched the lid. He tried to open it but it appeared to be sealed. "Sofia," he whispered. Then he shouted, "Sofia, can you hear me? Are you there?" He stared at the box, feeling all around the lid, searching for a latch, a lock, a way to open it. "Sofia, can you hear me? I'm here . . . Sofia." This had to be it. For better, or worse. He had to get it open. He noticed a keyhole on the side of the base, near the lid. Why would they—or Sindy—have locked it anyway? He searched the room, pointing the iPhone all along the walls and floor. He needed a tool, anything to drive a wedge between the base of the casket and the lid. He pounded on the lid, "Sofia, I'm here. Can you hear me?"

"Fletcher, I'm downstairs. I need your help!" Again, no answer.

His cell phone rang. It was Sofia. "I think I'm dying."

He shook the casket, lifting it up and down a few inches off the catafalque. It was heavy; the kind that needed every one of its pallbearers. "Can you feel that? Sofia, Are you in there?"

"Yes, oh my God. Is that you? Yes. I'm in here."

"Okay, don't waste your energy. I'll get this open. Just give me a minute."

As he moved around the casket, Michael's foot stepped on something. He looked down, under the drop cloth. It was a large key. The key to the coffin.

Fletcher came running down the stairs, joining him as Michael inserted the key into the round keyhole. He twisted it and heard the reassuring sound of lock disengaging. He and Fletcher grabbed the ends of the lid and, slowly, opened it up and back as far as it would go.

There she was, her eyes closed, her lips sealed.

"Sofia," Michael whispered as he pulled her up, out of the coffin. She was cold to his touch. "Can you hear me?"

Her eyes opened. Michael lifted her up and out of the casket. Michael caught her in his arms as he and then Fletcher held her up. She appeared unsteady and groggy but in one piece.

"Sofia, are you okay?" Michael hugged her tight, tighter than he had ever held her before.

"I think so. Oh my God, I was so scared."

"Let's get out of here and get you checked out," Fletcher said.

Sofia, appearing to gain her balance, raised her hand, "Whatever you do, I wouldn't call the police."

Michael hadn't expected that reaction. "Why? What do you mean? You're safe now."

She gave him an unusual look, a mature expression, especially since it was aimed at her father. "Dad, she knows a lot about you. She makes things up, too."

Safely inside the Suburban now, Sofia appeared to be okay, at least physically. While Fletcher drove, Michael sat with Sofia in the back seat.

"She said she had an *affair* with you. Tell me she was just crazy, Dad. I'd believe that."

"She was—or is—crazy, but . . . yes, I made a mistake, a terrible mistake. It was over a long time ago now."

"Does Mom know?"

"Of course, you know your mom; she knows everything. I'm so sorry—for everything. I had no idea she would ever even think of harming you."

"She didn't touch me—other than the duct tape and pushing me around. I think she drugged me at first and then when we left the motel. She was scary—and odd."

"What do you mean, odd, other than the obvious, that she kidnapped and threatened to kill you?"

"Well, she was pretty nasty—but mostly only when she was on the phone with you and another person. I don't know who that was. She was a little nicer when she was alone with me, almost like she became someone else. Don't get me wrong, though, I was scared shitless the whole time."

"And what about the guy in the motel room next to you?" Michael could only think of the wall of the Holiday Inn with Rick Martin splattered all over it. He dreaded the thought that Sofia had seen any of it.

She looked puzzled, "What guy?"

"You didn't know about?" He stopped. Had it even happened? he wondered. There had been no news reports of a murder in Chapel Hill. Sindy had *said* she'd killed him—but reality and fantasy often became blurred when she was involved.

Michael explained what Sindy said she'd done to Rick Martin. He turned to Fletcher. "She'd have to have done something with him because he's disappeared, and she had his phone."

"She left the room a few times," Sofia said, "but if she did kill this guy, she never said anything to me or even let it show. I heard something, like a crash coming from outside or next door, I couldn't tell. She kept the TV on pretty loud when she'd leave the room. How could someone really do that and just walk around like it was nothing?"

Michael knew.

CHAPTER 25

Raleigh, North Carolina

F letcher and Michael were in the limousine on their way to the airport when Michael received the text he was waiting for and dreading: *Good flight. Just landed. Where are you?*

He had left Samantha in the dark beginning the several hours before she took the eight-hour flight home from Paris. There was no reason to have her sick with worry during the long flight to JFK, especially since there was nothing she could do from there anyway. Not to mention that he had his hands full every minute just trying to find Sofia.

But Samantha had landed at Kennedy and now he had to tell her everything, although at least he could say that she was safe. After a few minutes of panic – and anger – Samantha had calmed down, somewhat.

"Michael, when I agreed with your decision to take over Alex's business, it didn't include taking over your brother's *life* or putting our daughter in danger. It didn't include having someone like Sindy Steele in our lives – or our marriage. You had better deal with her and get her out of our lives, forever. Period."

"I will, I'll deal with it." Michael had no idea *how* but this was no time for that discussion or reasoning. "We just took Sofia over to Jimmy and Lena's and I've arranged for 24/7 security for her." Sofia was always comfortable staying with her aunt and uncle on weekends and, since they lived in Chapel

Hill it was convenient to her classes. Jimmy had been close, too, to Alex and was very familiar with Alex's business, in fact, he was a customer and enjoyed betting on the games, so Michael had no hesitation in confiding in him about what had happened.

Samantha's voice was curt, strained. "I'll be catching the next flight from JFK down to Raleigh, there's no point in going to Connecticut. There's a flight from here in about an hour so I should be at Jimmy's by mid-afternoon."

"Good, I'll have a car waiting for you here at the airport. I told Sofia I was sure you'd be flying down here as soon as you landed. I think she needs her mother right now. Jimmy and Lena have plenty of room."

Michael had to return to New York and his corporate office for a series of meetings. His absence would have been too noticeable if he missed another day. His dual life had already taken a toll on his presence at Gibraltar.

"Michael . . . you have to get control of our lives back. We can't live like this."

In the near distance Michael recognized the General Aviation terminal he had flown in and out of so many times, beginning when he was a small child, flying down to visit relatives with his mother. It had expanded over the years from the homey little terminal building to the modern complex he had grown accustomed to.

"I heard part of it," Fletcher said, "What are you going to do?"

"I'm not sure exactly."

"Is she pressing you to get out of the business?"

Taking over Alex's illegal but incredibly lucrative sports betting and loan sharking enterprise—while still the CEO of a major corporation—was a challenge for Michael. But he had good people in both organizations. CEOs have a unique degree of freedom. He'd always kept his distance from Alex and his exploits but, once Alex's widow Donna had asked him to help close the business down right after Alex's murder, he'd gotten sucked in. Maybe it was in his blood, his DNA. It was a thought that troubled him.

"Actually, no. It's *Sindy,* she wants her out of our lives—and I certainly can't disagree with that."

"And how is that going to happen?" Fletcher flashed his most sarcastic grin."Do you really believe Sindy is headed back to Greece?"

"She told me she's taking the next flight back there."

"I know what she told you – but do you believe it?"

"I don't know what to believe. She might – and then I have to admit I could see her turning around and returning . . . somewhere. I'm afraid to think of that. There's a doctor in Greece that she's seeing. Maybe this woman can help her. Her meds seem to help, when she stays on them. In any case, she's gone, at least for now. I don't think she'll be coming anywhere near us for now at least."

Just before his black Cadillac limousine was about to take the familiar main approach to the general aviation terminal, his driver suddenly veered off to the right. In less than a minute, they'd pulled up in front of the private aviation terminal, a sleek low building, all but invisible to general travelers.

A porter appeared, opening the rear passenger door, the trunk swung open while another man took out the two pieces of luggage. Michael and Fletcher got out and followed them into the small terminal.

"You do know how to travel," Fletcher said.

"It's a nice luxury. Kind of makes you feel a bit more secure, too. No one's going to bother you here," Michael said as they entered the super-cooled air inside the near empty terminal.

Expecting to quickly pass through the metal detector, Michael was surprised when the lone security officer approached him. "Mr. Nicholas, would you mind stepping inside my office? It's just a formality. It'll only take a few minutes, I assure you."

Fletcher, standing right alongside him, laughed heartily. "Don't worry, if you get delayed, I'll see you in Westport tomorrow."

"Very funny." Michael followed the officer into the office marked, *Private. No Admittance.* But as he stepped inside, the officer stepped aside, allowing Michael to go in. Someone else was in the room, behind the desk. The officer then turned around to leave, quickly closing the door. Michael looked at the person sitting behind the desk.

It was Sindy Steele.

"Have a seat," she said, pointing to the chair opposite her.

"Jesus, Sindy, what the hell is wrong with you?" Michael said. "And my daughter . . . she's not involved in anything, she's never hurt you. You never even met her. And then this whole game, whatever it was, hiding her. You're sick."

"I know. I'm so sorry. I let myself get out of control. I was angry; you know that. You never would have talked to me if I hadn't . . . and then, I don't know. I had to get your attention and then I spun out of control. I'm back, though. At least I think I am. I'm sorry. But there's so much I need to tell you."

"Tell me, what could you possibly need to tell me now— after you've kidnapped her and killed a man?"

"He wasn't just some random guy, he was sent to kill *me.*"

Michael knew that, of course. Thank God she seemed not to have discovered that Martin had also been hired by . . . well, Fletcher. He looked around, for a camera perhaps, or a listening device. "And what happens when they find his body at the motel? The cops are going to figure this out. They'll be looking for you."

"Don't worry about these things. I've taken care of the motel and the body. They say this guy loved to fish in Jordon Lake, right outside town. I consider it payback time for the fishes."

"If you'd have stayed in Greece they would have left you alone."

"And what about *you*? Would you have left *them* alone? After all they've done to you and your brothers?"

It must have been a mistake. "Did you say, *brothers?*"

"Yes, that's why I'm here right now."

"What do you mean?"

"You had another brother, didn't you? *Besides* Alex."

Michael only stared at her.

"His name was John, wasn't it?"

"How did you know? I've never mentioned him to you. He died thirty years ago, in a car accident."

Sindy reached over the desk and took Michael's hand. At first he drew it back but she held it tightly. "Once, in Rome, I met them to discuss an assignment. I saw an old cassette tape in one of the priest's open briefcases. When they weren't looking, I took it. Turned out it was an interview between Father Kevin McCarthy, a priest in the Bronx and a Vatican counselor. When I got back to my hotel that night, I listened to it. He confessed to a different story than the ones your parents were told."

Michael sat back in his chair. He was already mentally exhausted. "Okay, tell me."

"I can only tell you what was on the tape, from McCarthy's confession of sorts, from his own perspective. I'd imagine that if your brother John could tell it from his own, it would be even more horrifying."

CHAPTER 26

Thirty Years Earlier
Queens, New York

It was an easy ten-block walk down Union Turnpike from his house to the schoolyard. John Nicholas was looking forward to playing stickball at P.S. 188. His friends would be waiting for him. He smiled as he gripped a brand new pink Spalding rubber ball, flexing his wrist as though he was pitching a big hard curve past the batter and onto the wall and the chalk-painted strike zone box a foot behind him. His older brother, Alex, had taught him how to throw it, fast and hard.

A black car pulled up alongside. He knew whose it was. The passenger side window rolled down and a familiar voice called out to him, "I need to speak with you."

"I can't right now, Father McCarthy, I got to be somewhere. I've gotta game."

"It'll just take a few minutes. Please, come in. I'll drop you off at the schoolyard, you'll be there even quicker."

Suddenly, behind him, he felt a hand push him forward then gripping his neck until, before he knew it, he was in the front seat beside Father Kevin McCarthy.

The man who had been behind him slammed the door shut then jumped in the back seat. John turned around; he didn't recognize the well-dressed stranger.

He turned back around to face Father McCarthy. "What's going on? What are you doing?"

E. J. SIMON

Father McCarthy looked straight ahead at the road. John saw the priest's polished black shoe step hard on the gas pedal, he felt the pull of the acceleration, his head slamming against the headrest. The window rolled up and he heard the door locks click.

Continuing to stare straight ahead, the priest spoke, calmly. "You saw things, didn't you?"

"No, things? . . . What things? I didn't see anything." But John knew he had.

"Did you tell your parents what you saw? Because, if you did, it's all right. I'd expect you to."

"No, no, I didn't. My mom would . . . I just couldn't." He wished now that he had.

The car made two quick turns.

"Where are we going? The schoolyard's the other way."

Father McCarthy turned, finally making eye contact, "Don't worry. I'm taking you somewhere you'll be safe. People may be trying to harm you. I'm going to protect you. That's why I have my friend in the back seat. He's a body guard . . . for you."

"I need to get out. My parents can protect me. Please—stop the car. Let me out." He tried to open the door but the handle moved uselessly.

He looked over at McCarthy, who ignored him, his eyes fixed on the road, his hands gripping the steering wheel so tightly that his knuckles were white."

Just as he turned around to beg the guy in the back seat he saw the man's arms reach over at him. There was something in his hands, it came at him swiftly, a streaking black blur, until it wrapped tightly around his neck, the thick belt pinning his head to the back of his seat and blocking off his air. He kicked his legs in the air, seeking leverage but the belt was too tight and the man's arms too strong. He felt it tighten even more, compressing his windpipe, closing off any chance of air.

He knew he had only seconds to do . . . something. He dropped the rubber ball. He looked straight ahead out the front windshield. Cars were nearby, the world was going about its business, unaware that he was being garroted in the front seat. Father McCarthy drove though a yellow light.

Choking, out of air, with his head forced upward by the force of the belt, John Nicholas looked up, out the top of the windshield, the only vantage point he had left, and saw the light turn red. He knew it was too late.

Yet as his world was slipping away, he heard, as clearly as he had ever heard anything in his life, Father McCarthy's whispered words, "May God forgive me."

CHAPTER 27

Raleigh, North Carolina

"The Vatican didn't know who knew what, exactly—only that they were vulnerable. They had it on the cassette interview with this dirty priest, McCarthy, just a few months before he died."

Michael tried to absorb Sindy's story. "So, they paid the cops off too?"

"Yes, of course, and maybe the coroner's office in Queens. Who knows?"

"Did they punish McCarthy? The Church, I mean."

"Yes," she said. "In their own way."

"What does that mean?"

"They made him a bishop."

Michael just shook his head.

"Listen to me. They will wipe you and your family out before this is over. They have to. These . . . men . . . I don't know how many of them there are or exactly how high up inside the Vatican this goes, but they will be locked in a fight to the death. Either yours—or theirs."

"But Alex's murder was –"

"They gladly agreed to help with Alex's murder because they owed the guy that covered everything up with McCarthy—Joseph Sharkey—a favor. An obviously big favor."

"Joseph Sharkey was the man in the back seat?"

Sindy looked straight into Michael's eyes. "Yes. And now, all these years later, I think Sharkey believed that Alex was close to finding out the truth of what happened to his brother that day in the car."

"So he —"

"So he arranged to murder Alex in the restaurant and then, when the NYPD figured out that he was behind Alex's murder, he fled to Rome and forced these priests or whatever they are to protect and hide him as his payback. And they did, for a while. But they knew he was a ticking time bomb. He started to make demands, money, women. They couldn't trust him to stay quiet."

Sindy Steele, leaned in towards Michael, her long black hair flowing over her athletic shoulders, her breasts gently protruding from her thin black cotton blouse. For a moment, Michael recalled the attraction he'd felt for her, and the brief indiscretion that he had regretted ever since. And he knew that she knew what he was feeling.

She continued, "Sharkey was the very first assignment they gave me. It's how I proved myself to them. I met him in Florence, in a leather boutique. He thought he was going to have sex with me that day. He was a creep. I slid a stiletto into his side. I almost had an orgasm watching him die."

Michael's head was spinning. "This is a lot . . ."

"The point is, John was murdered, just like Alex. By the same man, three decades apart. And protected by at least two high-level priests—a monsignor and a bishop—inside the Vatican. I had to tell you this. Now you know. They assume you do already. It's why they'll make sure they kill you."

Michael sat back, at first saying nothing. He had decisions to make. "And what about you, now?" he said finally. "Where are you going from here?"

"I'm going back to Greece. There's a doctor there I need to see. She will help me. After that, I don't know. But you have to listen: they will never leave me—or you—alone. Not now. Not ever."

Michael knew she was right.

CHAPTER 28

Raleigh, North Carolina

Minutes later, back on board the Gulfstream, Michael filled Fletcher in on his meeting with Sindy Steele and the new revelation on how his brother John had been murdered.

"It seems we go from one shock to another. I couldn't believe it when I opened that door and she's sitting there like the head of the TSA. How the hell does she pull this stuff off?"

"I don't know, she's got money and a great body. Take your pick. Michael, don't take this the wrong way but . . . do you want me to fix this thing with Steele? . . . to take care of it for you?"

After Sofia's kidnapping it had already crossed his mind but he wasn't about to admit it.

Fletcher continued, "I don't have to . . . hurt her or anything."

Michael knew Fletcher was back-pedaling. Hurting her was exactly what he meant—and more. Sindy Steele wasn't the type you intimidated or hurt in order to get her to do something. You had to kill her to control her.

"And who would you send this time?"

"Next time around would be easier. There's no hostage."

"No, I'll deal with it myself." Michael said it but even he knew he had no idea what that meant. He knew he couldn't kill. It was a line he couldn't cross, except in self –defense, or to save his family . . . or to protect . . . The more he thought about it, the fuzzier the line became, as did his relationship with Sindy Steele. From one minute to the next, she veered out of control, from friend to deadly enemy and then back.

Fletcher handed him a glass of chilled white wine as Michael glanced over at the local newspaper on the side table. A small article on the bottom of the front page caught his attention:

Firefighters were summoned last night to put out the remains of a flash fire in an unoccupied guest room at the Holiday Inn motel on Carrboro Road. According to Fire Chief John Sculley, the fire appeared to have been deliberately set, scorching the room's walls and carpeting. In an even stranger twist, however, it appeared that the arsonist or an unidentified bystander attempted to contain the fire, using a fire extinguisher that was left at the scene. The front desk clerk reported that the guest who had earlier occupied the room apparently had dropped off the electronic key hours before smoke was noticed by a passerby. The police report stated that local youths had likely gained access to the vacated room and, after setting it on fire as a prank, had apparently tried to contain the blaze and then fled. No injuries were reported.

He tossed the paper over to Fletcher who read the article, shaking his head.

"Let's leave her be for now." Michael said. "I've got to take care of the people behind my brothers' murders. I'm the last one left. I've got to get to them before they get me."

"How?" Fletcher said. "These guys are surrounded by Swiss guards."

Michael thought about that for a minute. "I don't know exactly yet—except for one thing. I'm going to take this fight right to their door." He sat back, feeling almost relaxed now. "Samantha and I have been to Rome many times over the years and yet, oddly, we've never visited the Vatican. I think it's time for a guided tour . . . maybe one behind the scenes."

CHAPTER 29

Whitestone, New York

There were two things that Alex had given her in their six years of marriage that Donna Nicholas still treasured. Both of which, she was sure, would help her snag her next, equally rich husband.

The first was Chanel No. 5, a perfume Alex had introduced her to and made sure was always in stock in their bedroom. She loved the scent, despite finding out that Alex also supplied it to his earlier two wives and each of his many mistresses. She knew now that the perfume had been Alex's way of making sure that his wife never caught a whiff of the "other" woman, or, to be more precise, women.

The second were her perfect, perky 34DD breasts, created by the prominent Park Avenue surgeon Dr. Armando Simonetti and paid for by Alex. She loved them too, despite finding out that Alex also provided exactly the same surgeries for his earlier two wives and at least a few of his mistresses.

Alex's murder two years earlier had left her a rich widow. Michael had been instrumental in finding Alex's hidden two million dollars and that, and a fully paid-for house and a share of the profits each month from Alex's—now Michael's—illegal gambling business "Tartarus"—kept her financially comfortable.

But having just turned thirty-seven, Donna knew it wasn't enough. Alex would be easy enough to replace, but his steady stream of money wasn't. She knew she needed someone who could take care of her financial needs for the many years ahead of her. She was a stunningly beautiful woman who knew how to make herself attractive to men but the singles scene in Queens left a lot to be desired. Instead of attracting men with money, she was attracting men who were attracted to *her* money. It was time to branch out, to try something new.

She snuggled under the covers, propped her head up on three pillows and, after drinking down half of it in one swallow, placed her glass of Chardonnay on the table by her bedside. She placed her laptop computer on the bed tray in front of her. She was ready to begin a new chapter, and it wasn't in a book.

She logged onto the site and typed in her new password. When she saw her account come up on the iJewishMingle.com website, she felt good. After all, she'd hardly ever even used a computer until Alex had been murdered.

Her girlfriends had told her about the great dates and matches they'd discovered through the Internet. So, what did she have to lose? It was worth a try. And what could be safer than a nice dating site with Jewish men, unless, of course, they were religious. In any case, if she didn't find anyone worth pursuing, all she had to do was close her laptop.

This morning she had spent a few hours on the site, answering questions, they actually called it *Who Am I?*—what did she like, dislike, her favorite colors, hobbies—really? Hobbies? It was all intended they said to help her learn who she was. Donna knew who she was and she didn't need a dating site to find out.

Then there was the *Relationship Questionnaire*. What did she look for in a partner? She knew that, too.

She didn't always answer truthfully, just as she wouldn't always do so in her real life, face to face with someone. Particularly a man whom she was interested in, especially when it came to her age. Between her breasts and her Botox, she knew she could pass for a lot younger than her thirty-seven years.

Then she loaded in a photograph and smiled. It felt good to be twenty-five again.

She would revert back to her maiden name, too. After all, Donna Finkelstein was a much better fit for a Jewish dating site than Donna Nicholas. It was time to see the results, learn who fit the dating site's ideal match up profile for the criteria she'd plugged in. She clicked where it read, *Who Wants To Meet You.*

It was a long list. Not that she was surprised. The first step was to find the ones she was interested in replying to and then the process was to send an email to their special mailbox through the dating site. Then, as the ad said, *let the fireworks begin.*

She scanned the names—only first names at this point— and the short bios beneath each one. They were supposedly sorted based on the likelihood of a successful match. She was about to begin at the top when her eye went to the second name of the list. She was sure it was a coincidence. Maybe it was fate. She'd start with this one.

She clicked on *Alex.*

CHAPTER 30

Westport, Connecticut

It took a few hundred thousand dollars in software upgrades and high-priced tech consultants, but Michael was now able to communicate with Alex not only on his main computer downstairs in the wine cellar, but on his numerous laptops and even his iPhone.

At home in his library, Michael opened up his laptop.

In seconds, Alex appeared on the screen. Michael wasted no time. "Do you know how our brother John died?"

Alex appeared to freeze, his face frozen, a blank. Then, as though he'd recovered from something . . . maybe an overload, perhaps a stressful thought? . . . he came back.

"John? He was killed in a car accident."

But Michael could see an uncharacteristic look of doubt, uncertainty on Alex's face. "That's what you know? What you believe?"

Alex hesitated again. "Yes, no . . . I'm not . . . sure. There was something, I remember, but I can't quite . . . just before I was . . . shot. Why are you asking me . . . now?"

Michael told him what Sindy Steele had heard on the cassette tape.

"Yes, there was something, something I'd learned that was different from the story we'd all been told at the time. I never mentioned it to you before because I wasn't sure. I think I was just putting it together before . . ."

"So, there are people inside the Vatican—we don't know how many—who are behind both your murder and John's."

"And now they will do the same to you," Alex said. "Except you know it. I had no idea until it was too late."

"Yes, and I have you helping me—and, strangely enough, maybe even Sindy Steele, in her own way."

"Be careful with that one, Michael. She's no Mother Teresa but I'd worry more about those holy guys in the Vatican than I would about her. Especially now that we know about John."

"I'm glad she found out what she did, though. We needed to know the truth." Michael said. "But, she's not in control of herself."

"Yeah, well, who is? But it also looks like she just can't stay away from you. She's obsessed. She's also not a very good judge of character, but that's another issue."

"Thanks. How's *your* character these days?"

"You know, unlike yours, I think mine's getting better. I met a girl, Donna was her name."

"Wasn't that a song?" Michael remembered hearing it on the oldies station. "And/or your widow—or, ah, excuse me—your wife's name?"

"Yeah, it was. What's it to you?"

"Just out of curiosity, what's her last name, the one you just met?"

"Finkelstein."

"Oh God, don't tell me any more. You haven't tried to reach Donna, have you?"

"Not yet. But she's going to reach out to me."

"How is that possible since she knows—or thinks—you're dead?"

"She's on iJewishMingle."

"Are you crazy? And how would she find you? You'd have to be registered on the site yourself."

"I am."

"You can't be doing this. We're not ready or prepared to deal with you going public—and a dating website? Jesus, Alex. You could be attacked by any number of hackers out there, you'd be a sitting target, they'd destroy you. Not to mention, the last thing we need is Donna thinking you're still alive."

"I was lonely. Just so you know . . . she lied about her age."

"And when did you do all this?"

"I don't know exactly, I don't have the same sense of time as I used to when I was . . . But, I guess it was the over the last few days."

"You mean, while I was going through everything with Sofia—you were going on dating sites?"

"I was there when you needed me. Anyway, one's got nothing to do with the other in the world I live in. Did you ever hear of *multitaking*?"

"I think you mean, multi*tasking*, don't you?"

"Whatever you want to call it." Alex never did like to be corrected. But it was an interesting point. At first, Michael thought that Alex was only conscious or active when he actually logged onto him. Now, it was apparent that Alex's activities, whatever they were, went on independent of Michael signing in to Alex's site—or Alex—whatever it was. In any case, Alex had taken on a new dimension, no longer in Michael's control or dependent upon him. Michael wasn't sure that was a good thing. He was pretty sure it wasn't.

"So," Alex said, "if the Chapel Hill cops had gotten to Sindy Steele and she'd opened up about what she'd done for the Vatican it would have been their worst nightmare. They can't afford to have a loose cannon out there—not with everything she knows about them."

"So what are they going to do?"

"They have to protect themselves now. Steele can expose them. Now that she's gone back on her word and did something crazy with Sofia, they can't risk waiting for her next move. They can no longer rely on her to stay sane or keep her mouth shut. When they hired her to be a hit man and do their dirty work, they didn't realize she was nuts."

"Do you know exactly who these people are inside the Vatican?"

"Some of them, but there are more. I see things flying across . . . the Internet, cell phones, fax machines, bugging devices and security cameras linked to WiFi . . . I just can't tell exactly who they all are but I'm trying. It appears to go pretty high up the ladder."

"High up—what does that mean in the Vatican? God?

"No, but try a Cardinal. Sindy was in contact with one, we know that."

Michael took a deep breath. "I need to see the Pope," he said.

Alex laughed, "*No one* sees the Pope. He's like The Wizard of Oz."

CHAPTER 31

Westport, Connecticut

Michael looked out from the patio of Arezzo onto the Saugatuck River and then back to Samantha. The early evening sun had not yet set completely. The sky cast a pink glow over the table. They were sharing a bottle of Rosé which glowed as the setting sun reflected on the bottle. Even though they'd just begun their main course, the bottle was nearly empty.

Michael knew the look. Despite the setting, dinner tonight wasn't going to be a walk in the park.

"Samantha, you look beautiful—but icy—tonight."

"Sindy Steele needs to be removed from our lives," Samantha said.

"Believe me, I was hoping she was. Months ago, after she got her payment from the Vatican guys, she said she was going to go to the Greek islands and rebuild her life, start over –"

"I guess she chose to kidnap Sofia instead," Samantha shot back. "We can't be at her mercy each time her chemical imbalance kicks in."

"I already have someone working on finding and then tracking her."

"Who?"

"Fletcher has some people –"

"Like that Rick Martin?"

"Yes, but alive."

"Well, whoever it is, they need to fix this."

"And how exactly do you define *fix*?" He had the sense that Samantha's answer would not only define the rest of the night—but possibly, the rest of their lives. "I'm hoping she's gone back to Greece like she said."

"We're not who we used to be, you know. You've already done things that in your wildest dreams you could never imagine you were capable of. Whether you've noticed or not, we've changed, both of us. Since your brother was murdered, we've become different people. Really, *you* more than me."

"So, what are you saying?"

"I think you know." Samantha said. "We've already crossed certain lines. What was forbidden before isn't anymore." Underneath her blonde hair, pretty face and soft, calm demeanor, Michael knew there was a hard, cold edge that, while providing him tremendous strength and support, could be turned against him in the wrong circumstances. Like now.

He waited, delaying any response while he tried to read the labyrinth that was his wife's soul.

"So what do you want me to do—have her *murdered*?" a rhetorical question, he hoped.

But Samantha's face betrayed no such understanding. She just looked back at him and then, as though just discovering it, down at her plate.

"You're not serious," he said.

Ignoring his comment, Samantha picked up her fork and proceeded to pick at her grilled salmon.

It was clear Samantha wasn't going to say more, at least not yet.

"I've spoken to my cousins down in Chapel Hill; they're going to arrange for a discreet security service to keep an eye on Sofia," Michael said, as he watched Samantha lift a slice of Burrata pizza from his plate.

"Have you told her?" she said, before biting into his prized slice, a particularly large one with lots of cheese.

"Pretty much. I just underplayed it a bit. It'll be a lot more intense than I implied. It should make her dating life more interesting."

"Just so you know, these kids don't *date.*"

"What do they do?"

"I don't know, I think they *hook up* or something." Samantha gave her best smile but Michael could see that she still had more on her mind. It was that look that she had when, although she was listening, her brain was multi-tasking. "And when were you going to tell me that you had security people watching us or is that guy at the bar just a prop?"

Michael looked behind him; he saw the painfully obvious plainclothes policeman that Fletcher had arranged as part of a regular security detail.

Michael laughed, "I was waiting for dessert to break it to you. We'll be on our way to Rome as soon as I can make sure that the proper arrangements have been made. There's more information I need to get before I can go. There's no point leaving until that's been done. And, while we're waiting, I've got to meet Goldstein for dinner tomorrow night. I can't exactly tell him that my other business has put our lives in jeopardy so I've got to run off to Rome."

"I hope you're right about not going to the authorities about all of this. You've had two brothers murdered."

"So, what do I do? Call the FBI, explain that I run a major global illegal gambling operation on the side, that Sindy Steele, who worked for me, has herself killed a few people, most recently in Chapel Hill, and that people inside the Vatican murdered both of my brothers and are after me? Oh, and by the way, one of those brothers is still alive, on my computer. How long before they have me tasered and in a straight jacket on my way to Bellevue?"

As soon as he said it he realized he'd brought up a sore point with Samantha. He could see the spark of recognition cross her face.

"I have a question—how did this Rick Martin figure out where Sindy was hiding with Sofia?"

As Michael scrambled for an answer, Samantha reached over and took another slice of his pizza.

"Why didn't you order your own pizza instead of salmon?" he said, moving his plate further away from her.

"Because pizza is fattening. You shouldn't be eating it."

This was a familiar dance, he thought. Hoping she'd forget her question, he picked up a slice himself, admired the rich red tomato sauce and the layer of white Burrata cheese. After he separated the strings of Burrata that stretched from the pie to his slice, he took a bite, savoring the sweetness of the tomatoes, the contrasting texture of the cheese and the crisp thin crust that held it all together.

"You never answered my question," Samantha said. "How did Rick Martin find them?"

Michael had to think. *Alex* certainly wasn't going to be the right answer for Samantha, but it was the truth.

"I know you're not going to believe this, but *Alex* told me."

Samantha's expression changed. "Really? Here we go again. We've been through this before. Remember, two years ago you took me to the wine cellar and I saw what *you* thought was Alex? We both know this is nothing more than a fancy computer game."

"I told you, you didn't give it a chance. You bolted out when he started talking to you."

"Not *he*, Michael, *it*. Yes, it was a little too weird for me. I still think you're suffering from a combination of depression from your brother's death—and stress from running your corporate job—and Alex's business."

"You've got to keep an open mind on this —"

95

"Listen, I've done some of my own research. The Internet makes it easy. The brain is, on some level, like a computer. So a computer can emulate a lot of what the brain does. But that doesn't mean that this so-called virtual Alex on your computer is really your brother. I'm willing to concede that it's some sort of very good software, probably with an algorithm that can *simulate* what Alex might have done, especially if someone loaded into the computer a lot of background and history on him. But, let's face it, Alex is dead—and, in thousands of years of civilization *no one*—except maybe Jesus Christ—has ever come back from the dead in any way. It's hard for me to believe that the *one* person who has—would be, of all people—your boozing, womanizing, bookmaking and loan sharking brother."

"I'm telling you, this *is* Alex. I don't totally understand it myself. But maybe there is more than we can see, Samantha. We can't see or feel whatever the religious or spiritual people say exists. We can't find anyone's *consciousness* in anyone's body, we're not even sure what it is—but we know it's there. Maybe this is the same thing."

"Jesus, I thought you skipped most of your college classes. Where's all this coming from? It's a *computer*, Michael, *a computer, a machine*—one that *people* have made, not some God with special powers."

"I know—but a bird flies, right? That's a miracle of some sort. And a plane flies too."

"Yes, and sometimes I think you've flown over the cuckoo's nest."

"Very funny. But listen, the plane is completely man-made yet it flies just as well and using the same principles as the bird's natural way of doing it."

"So, your point is?"

"My point is that we can recreate things that nature does. We can create machines that fly as well as birds, and *we can duplicate a human being*, at least the essence of what a person is—his mind, his consciousness, his brain."

"Well, let's just agree to disagree on this. That's all I can say. But there's one thing we can't disagree on."

"What's that?" Michael knew.

"Sindy Steele."

"Samantha –"

"Let me speak. I've forgiven you for your fling with her. As I said, you were stressed and vulnerable when your brother was murdered. But I haven't forgotten, I doubt I ever will. Thank God she never hurt Sofia, I don't know how you could have lived with yourself if she had."

"I know, believe me."

"I do. But let me make one thing very clear, Michael. I don't ever want to hear that woman's name spoken again. If you don't deal with it properly—whatever exactly that means— if I ever hear that she is back in your life, I'll take matters into my own hands. And I may surprise you with how I'll deal with it. You know that I'll do anything to protect those I love—and that includes you. She's not only a threat to *us*—she's a threat to *you*. You need to understand that."

"I need a limoncello," Michael said. He sat back. His eyes moved towards his iPhone sitting on the table next to his dessert plate. He noticed a waiting text message and leaned in closer to read it. Once he did, he quickly placed the phone in his coat pocket. He would have to read Sindy Steele's message later.

CHAPTER 32

Whitestone, New York

Wouldn't it be funny to go out with another guy named Alex? She imagined running into some of her—or the original Alex's—old friends and introducing her date, "I'd like you to meet . . . Alex. Alex two, or Alex the second." She laughed out loud at the thought and then finished her second glass of Chardonnay. She looked at the small photo—there actually was a vague resemblance between the two Alexs. This one was much younger, which was to be expected. He was looking for a woman in her twenties. Perfect. He came from New York, good; attended but didn't finish college, okay, who cares. Even better. She clicked on the *Send Him A Message* icon and began typing.

Donna: Hi, I'm Donna.

She couldn't believe it when she saw the dots appearing on her screen, indicating he was typing a response—already.

Alex: I know. I can see your name. You must be new at this.

Donna: I am. This is my first time.

Alex: First time?

Donna: You know what I mean.

Alex: Sure. Yeah.

Donna: I assume you're single, right?

Alex: Yeah.

Donna: Divorced?

Alex: I'm a recent widower.

Donna: I'm sorry.

Alex: It's okay. It was a few years ago. I'm starting to . . . heal.

Donna: Oh, that's good. I didn't mean to bring up something painful.

She hoped he wasn't going to be one of these brooding, insufferable melancholy types. It's so hard to tell through email.

Alex: So, what about you?

Donna: I'm a widow. My husband died a few years ago. I guess we have something in common.

Alex: Probably more than you think. How long were you married?

Donna: To him?

Alex: How many husbands did you have?

Donna: Just two. How many wives did you have?

Alex: Just three.

Well, she thought, we're off to a good start. Jesus, that's five marriages already between us. I guess there's not a lot of difference between two or three marriages. After all, her next one would be her third.

Donna: Were you happy?

Alex: Yeah, I guess.

Donna: You guess? What's that supposed to mean?

Alex: It means I was happy.

Donna: Okay, sorry I asked.

Alex: Me too.

This wasn't going too well but I'll keep going for a while.

Alex: You look beautiful in your picture.

That's better, she thought.

Donna: Thanks—you look pretty good yourself.

Alex: I know.

CHAPTER 33

New York City

"I 'd love to be a fly on the wall tonight." Karen DiNardo's voice came across the phone with her usual tone of enthusiastic sarcasm. "He's not there yet?"

Karen was more than Michael's trusted secretary, a friend, and the only person within Gibraltar Financial that he trusted enough to know of his other life, running Alex's business, Tartarus.

"No, he's one of those 'my time's more important than yours' guys. I hate wasting dinner on someone I don't want to be around. You know there are only so many dinners in a lifetime. I cherish each one." The truth, however, was that even though Michael had more important issues to deal with, there was no putting Goldstein off.

"I know. Believe me. I didn't think you had a choice on this one."

"Lunch—or, even better, drinks—would have been better."

"He doesn't drink," she said, curtly.

"Of course not."

Since the acquisition of Gibraltar Financial by Cartan Industries, Michael had a new boss: Jonathan Goldstein. Tonight they would dine together, at Goldstein's invitation, at The Modern, a stunningly beautiful Alsatian-French restaurant located within the Museum of Modern Art. Michael stared out through the floor to ceiling windows overlooking the Abby

Aldrich Rockefeller sculpture garden. It was, architecturally at least, an inspiring setting.

Michael spied Goldstein approaching his table. "Okay, I gotta go. He's here. Not bad, just half an hour late."

"Good luck. And don't forget one thing."

"What's that?"

"He bought the company."

He clicked off the phone.

Although Michael had dined there before, he wasn't a regular. As the servers scurried to take their orders, he observed that, although the staff appeared to recognize Goldstein, he doubted they liked him. He could sense their nearly imperceptible signs of loathing.

Goldstein looked as bored as Michael was. His expression was sour, even for a notorious cold fish. He finally made eye contact, ever so briefly. "Normally, I'd have fired you by now." Goldstein drank his seltzer, simultaneously diverting his gaze to a slim but busty twenty-something young lady passing by on the way to her nearby table.

Michael listened and watched as Goldstein looked away.

"And, normally, I'd have quit by now."

Goldstein seemingly reengaged. "Then why didn't you?"

"I like the work, I'm interested in the business, and I care about the people." Not to mention, he thought, I still need a legitimate front.

"I don't care about any of those things," Goldstein said." His eyes shifted away again. "I just want to make money. A lot of it."

"And to make money—the kind you want to make—we'll have to fire good productive people, strip away everyone's pensions, sell off assets, outsource work to Asia or India, take on debt—and all the while you pull out millions in fees and then you turn around and sell a company stripped of what made it successful and loaded with debt."

"Whatever . . . listen. I don't care about your ethics or business and how it operates—or even what the hell the company does, for that matter. I'm an investor, not an operator. And your employees are your problem. You do care; good for you. That's why you'll never be anything more than another CEO of a mid-size company. They come and go, Michael. You may enjoy what you do but you'll never make big, *FU* money."

Michael knew he couldn't really connect with this guy. Then again, he hadn't really tried, nor did he care to.

"Fine. I understand. So, why am I here instead of home tonight?"

The server gently interrupted, placing what appeared to be a work of abstract art from the museum, a plate of beautiful slices of roasted duck breast, in front of Michael and a salad plate for Goldstein.

"Mergers—let's call them what they are—*takeovers*, are complicated. You're useful to me, Michael . . . especially now, during the transition. Since that speech you gave in LA a few years ago—knocking private equity and hedge funds—the business press is in love with you. I need good press and I want to be sure enough of the organization staying together." Goldstein looked over at the closest person in a uniform he could find, and lifting his finger in the air, nearly shouted, "Waiter, I'll have another seltzer water."

The busboy scooted away.

"Michael, let me be honest, I need you right now. I could care less whether you like me or respect me. Emotion has no place in my business; it barely has any place in my life. I don't 'entice'—I *pay*. Do what I need for you to do and I'll make you richer than you could ever imagine. It won't take long and then you can go away, bitch and moan like every other executive that takes my money and then does a tell-all book and speaking tour. In the meantime, however, you've got enough money so you can spend the rest of your life doing whatever makes you happy. You know, help the poor, build a village, whatever."

Michael watched Goldstein's eyes darting around the room, perhaps admiring the illuminated Calders in the sculpture garden or, more likely from what he'd heard, searching for another under-aged waif like the one he'd just ditched his wife for.

Michael sat back, his mind constantly drifting back to the events of the last few days. Sitting here with Jonathan Goldstein was the last thing he wanted to be doing. Everything seemed to require his focus right now. He took a few moments to let Goldstein's conversation sink in. Inside the barrage of insults was a short-term business offer with the promise of significant money—but at a price.

For the past two years, since Alex's murder, he'd managed to head up two organizations. He wasn't ready to give either one up, at least not yet. But he also wasn't willing to turn his back on the people inside Gibraltar. After all, they were the ones who'd created the value in the first place.

"So what's it going to be?" Goldstein asked, looking away. "Stay on, do what I need done and make millions or –"

"If I refuse?"

"I'll fire you—for cause."

Michael laughed. "For cause? That's a new one."

"I know more about you than you think. Do you think I believe your bullshit about your dead brother's life being separate from yours? I know what you're doing. When I get through with you, you'll not only lose your job but you'll never work for another public company. Ever."

CHAPTER 34

Seeing Goldstein's self-satisfied smirk made Michael want to leap over the table and beat the shit out of him. That only would land him in jail for the night and give Goldstein a lawsuit orgasm.

Alex had been correct. Not that Michael hadn't known all along that Goldstein was the ultimate obnoxious hedge fund master of the universe and potential white collar criminal.

Now Michael was glad he hadn't erased what Alex had sent him.

The check had arrived; without even glancing at it, Goldstein placed his credit card alongside the leather folder. Michael cringed when he thought about how Goldstein might tip. Nevertheless, he looked forward to getting out into the city's night air, alone. First, he had to give Goldstein an answer.

"Okay, here's my answer. I'm staying on. I'll be happy to make changes that we *both* agree on, things that will be good for the business. But I'm not stripping this company for you."

"That wasn't one of the options, so I guess we're done here." Goldstein appeared to be looking for the check. "You'll hear from my attorneys tomorrow. Your access to Gibraltar will be blocked before you'll even leave here. Same for that secretary of yours."

"We're not done." Michael said.

His eyes like ice, Goldstein finally looked Michael in the eye and he just kept staring until he finally spoke. "You don't want to cross me."

Michael reached into his coat pocket, pulled out a digital tape recorder and placed it on the table. "It's amazing how small these things are now."

As soon as he saw it, Goldstein's head jerked back; he sat erect and upright in his chair. "What the hell is this?" he said. "Do you think I care if you recorded our conversation?"

"I agree with you on that. It might be embarrassing for most people; probably not for you. I think you'll enjoy *this* a lot more. Listen." Michael picked up the recorder from the table, found the "Play" button, pressed it and placed it closer to Goldstein.

The first voice was Goldstein's:

"If we play this right, those analysts will have no idea that they're looking at numbers that'll probably never happen. We need to squeeze every last fucking drop of expense out of that place before they figure it out. Most of these analysts are just thirty-year-old numbers geeks. They don't have a clue about running a business. They have no idea how to get under the hood so they'll never figure it out—even if we take the whole engine away. The car'll keep rolling, at least until we sell the place."

Michael reached for the recorder and shut it off. "You and Hans Ulricht—I guess you guys call that a strategic plan."

"That's what investment bankers do, they make money." Goldstein, looking oddly relieved, took another sip of his seltzer. "That's interesting but not exactly incriminating."

Michael smiled, "Hold on, let's listen some more." He pressed "Play" again. Then came Goldstein's unmistakable shrill:

"No offense, but those Wall Street sharpies won't know what hit them in a year. We just need to use Michael as a good front man. He'll keep the troops in line while we do our work. He likes money so he'll keep quiet. I'll put my own CFO in there; he'll make the numbers sing. We sell off most of their assets and replace them with some we want to unload, a few of my shell companies. We'll

make sure those numbers and projections moving forward look good. Then, we'll sell this thing and let Michael and the new owners figure out how to make those numbers that he'll have signed off on.

I figure we've got about two quarters where we can sustain our projections, then the numbers will drop off the table. After that, they'll implode. By then, we're out of there though—and then we buy it back for pennies. This is why I love America."

Goldstein's face changed. It was as though he'd put on a mask—or, more likely, taken one off. "Where'd you get that? How did you get it?"

Michael would have loved to tell him the story about Alex. "You wouldn't believe me if I told you. I don't think the press or the SEC will care where it came from."

"Watch yourself." Goldstein got up and threw his napkin onto the table. He leaned over, just inches from Michael's face. "Don't think this is over. I told you, I know more about you than you think—and you have no idea who I am or what I'm willing to do—to you."

Michael watched as Goldstein walked out. He knew he'd won this round but he wondered how much Goldstein knew and how well he knew Goldstein. In any case, he had more pressing matters to deal with—including a big favor he promised to do for Alex before he could leave for Rome.

CHAPTER 35

Whitestone, New York

Donna got out of bed and poured herself another glass of wine from the small refrigerator built into the cabinets in her bedroom. Returning to her bed and her laptop, she realized that she was, for the first time—since she had been with Alex—enjoying the chase. This time, of course, with another Alex, and online.

Alex: Are you still there?

Donna: Yes, I just got up to pour myself another glass of wine.

Alex: Another? How many have you had?

Donna: Don't tell me you don't drink.

That would be a deal breaker if ever there was one. Please don't say you're in AA or a Mormon or something.

Alex: No, of course I drink. Although I've cut back lately.

Donna: What do you drink?

Alex: Scotch mostly.

Just like her Alex, she thought. Hopefully, this one doesn't run around as much.

Donna: So do you go out a lot?

Alex: No, not anymore. But I'm ready now. That's why I joined this thing.

Donna: Well, what do you like to do?

Alex: What do you mean, like hobbies or something?

E. J. SIMON

Donna: I guess. That's in your profile somewhere but I admit, I didn't check it completely. So what are your hobbies?

Alex: Sports mostly. And I gamble a little.

Uh-oh, here we go again.

Donna: What do you mean? Do you go to Las Vegas?

Alex: Not lately but I used to go with my wife or friends.

Donna: What else do you like to do?

Alex: I like being with women.

Donna: Are you okay being with another woman after losing your wife?

Alex: Yeah, I'm ready.

Donna: Do you miss her?

Alex: Do you miss your husband?

Donna: At times. He was crazy.

Alex: What do you mean? Was he in an institution or something?

Donna: No, but he might have been if anyone had examined him carefully.

Alex: Really?

Donna: No, I'm kidding. He was . . . let's say colorful. He lived a big life—lots of gambling, drinking, out all night. That sort of thing.

Alex: Were you with him when he was doing that, you know, being out all night?

Donna: No. I was his wife.

Alex: Wow. That must have pissed you off.

Donna: Yes, it did.

Alex: Did he cheat on you?

Donna: Probably every night.

Alex: Did you cheat on him?

Donna: Are these first conversations supposed to be this intimate? You're not a psychiatrist are you?

Alex: No, I'm not. I think you have to have a college degree for that. School wasn't my biggest thing growing up. So, did you run around on him?

Donna: Occasionally. Not nearly as much as he screwed around on me.

Alex: So you kept score.

Donna: Yes, I did actually. I like keeping score.

Alex: When you cheated on him, who was it with? Was it someone your husband knew?

Donna: He only knew one of the guys.

Alex: Just out of curiosity, what was the guy's first name?

Donna: What difference would it make to you? Why would you want his first name?

Alex: I'm into astrology.

Donna: Isn't that more birthdays and dates than names?

Alex: It's everything.

Donna: Wow, I didn't know that. Anyway, what a coincidence, I love astrology, too. What's your sign?

Alex: Tell me the guy's first name and then I'll tell you my sign.

Donna: Jesus, you're odd. Okay, his name was Moose.

Alex: And you think *I'm* odd? Did you see him regularly?

Donna: No, just a few times.

Alex: Did he satisfy you?

Donna: Yes, I felt better. I also felt like I got even. I evened the score. At least a little bit.

Alex: So do you miss your husband now?

Donna: Yes. He wasn't perfect. No one is. He was a lot of fun, very unpredictable and volatile at times. He wasn't easy but he had a great heart.

Alex: Sounds like he was a pretty good guy.

Donna: Yes. Listen, hold on, I think I need another glass of wine. Excuse me for one second.

Alex: It's over there in your fridge in the cabinet.

Donna: How did you . . . Can you see me or something? Is there a camera?

It took a few seconds to register. First she froze and then she began screaming, "Oh my God, oh my God. What the –" and quickly shut her laptop.

CHAPTER 36

New York City

H ans Ulricht had made the unforgivable mistake of losing some of Jonathan Goldstein's money.

"I want my money back, *now*," Jonathan Goldstein said, glaring at his investment banker from behind his desk.

Hans Ulricht gazed back, beyond his client and looked out to the view of Central Park, just over Goldstein's shoulders. Since Goldstein rarely made eye contact, Ulricht knew he'd never notice.

Now in his early seventies, Ulricht, the distinguished executive director of IBS, the International Bank of Switzerland, was the consummate Swiss banker and, with his silvery hair and perfectly tailored three-button suits, he looked the part.

"I rue the day that I invited you to invest in Rosen's fund. I too, lost money."

"Don't give me your *rue* shit. That's not going to be enough for me, Hans. It's going to be the biggest fucking regret of your life." He glanced down at his desk, "Five million seven, that's what you owe me. That's what it's going to take to keep my business. Not a fucking penny less."

"We've discussed this matter before, you know I can't –"

"Pick up the phone and call your bosses in Switzerland or Heidelberg or wherever the hell they are and have them credit my account." Goldstein was turning red. "Your firm had a fiduciary responsibility to vet Rosen."

"IBS had no idea Bertrand Rosen was running a Ponzi-scheme."

"You and I both know that you knew. You kept it quiet because you and your bank were making a fortune off him and you didn't want to kill the golden goose."

He had to calm Goldstein down. "We can work this out."

"You figure it out or I'll instruct my attorneys to contact the Feds. Let's see, even if you only got ten years in prison, for you that'd be a life sentence."

"Jonathan, we need to find an alternative solution, perhaps another way that we may make you whole on this. Perhaps, more than whole."

"I understand that you know Michael Nicholas," Goldstein said.

Ulricht knew Goldstein was waiting for him to take the bait.

"Yes, I was introduced to him through a mutual acquaintance several months ago."

Ulricht thought it best to not mention that the mutual acquaintance was none other than Bertrand Rosen. Rosen had unsuccessfully tried to befriend Michael, hoping to make him another of his unwitting clients but Michael had grown suspicious of Rosen's track record and his promise of guaranteed returns. He also turned down Ulricht's offer to shield his income by hiding it in a Swiss bank. "I've tried to convince Michael to invest some of his wealth with IBS, to no avail."

"Then we have a mutual problem, don't we?" Goldstein said.

"Perhaps. Is there some way I can be of assistance to you?"

Goldstein's face brightened. It was as close to a smile as Ulricht had ever seen from him. "Michael Nicholas is standing in the way of what I need to do at Gibraltar so I can flip the company and sell it at a crazy profit . . . and then invest that money with . . . you."

"I appreciate your confidence."

"It's not confidence; I want to see if you can lose it again."

Hans chose to ignore Goldstein's sarcasm. "Why don't you just fire him?"

"I might but it won't look good. He's also popular with the press, if you remember he made some speech in LA a couple of years ago about the evils of private equity and hedge funds and how we're ruining great old companies and some other shit."

"I do remember, it was written up in the Journal and the Economist –"

"Yeah, everywhere. All these business journalists love him; they're all making fifty thousand a year and living with their parents. What the fuck do they know? So now he's became a folk hero, the Mark Twain of business. It's crap."

"You've dealt with worse, Jonathan."

"There's something else."

"What's that?"

"He's got you and me on tape."

Hans listened as Goldstein told him about his dinner with Michael. "How did he get this tape?"

"He wouldn't tell me. I've secured my cell phone though and I've got security people electronically sweep my office every day now. You should do the same."

"So we need to neutralize him."

This time Goldstein actually laughed, a rare sight.

"Yeah, Hans, you're pretty sharp. *Neutralize.* If you can make that happen, you won't have to worry anymore about my five point seven one million. Consider the debt paid. You know . . . this isn't Nazi Germany."

Hans said nothing. *Consider the debt paid? The idiot,* he thought.

Goldstein continued, "I need for you to *persuade* Michael Nicholas to leave Gibraltar and in such a way that he does not jeopardize my plan for the company—and that he doesn't create a public relations nightmare for me, or worse, a legal one. I don't intend to room with you in Leavenworth. Figure out how to do it."

"I understand," Hans said.

Goldstein got up from his desk, his way of ending the meeting. I have to be in Berlin for a few days of meetings. I expect this will be resolved by the time I return."

"I will do better than that. I will rearrange my schedule to coincide with yours. Let's arrange to meet for dinner in Berlin and I can assure you we'll resolve this to your satisfaction."

"Work it out with my secretary," Goldstein said. "I'm not big on long meals or German food."

"Don't worry, Jonathan. No wiener schnitzel." Although Ulricht was smiling, it had nothing to do with breaded veal cutlets. He had plans for both Jonathan Goldstein and Michael Nicholas. And Goldstein had just taken the bait.

CHAPTER 37

Whitestone, New York

It hadn't been as easy as just closing the laptop. Donna couldn't get Alex, whichever one he was, off her mind. Who else would have known where her wine fridge was in her bedroom? She opened her laptop, signed back on to iJewishMingle and logged in.

He was there, waiting.

Donna: So, if you are who you're trying to make me think you are –

Alex: I'm Alex. I'm your fuckin' husband.

She'd had just enough wine to be able to keep up with this guy. He was sounding more and more like her dead Alex but that was impossible . . .

Donna: So, why are you on a Jewish dating site? Not to mention, that you're dead?

Alex: I like Jewish women.

Donna: Really, I never would have guessed that, since you were married to one and cheated on her left and right with a fucking Irish Catholic.

Alex: Hey, I never –

Donna: Don't lie to me! I know everything –

Alex: Everything?

What was happening? Who was this? Was it really him? Despite all her suspicions and those of some of his friends, it was ridiculous to even think about. It couldn't be. Even for

Alex, this was impossible. Did he fake his death? Were her suspicions really right? Okay, she'd push him—him, or whoever or whatever this was.

Donna: Yes, for once I know everything and you're going to answer my questions. Not like it used to be where you'd go and pour yourself a drink while I'm going crazy here and then you go into your fucking den with all your goddamned pictures of Mickey Mantle or Jeter or –

Alex: I like Muhammed Ali, too.

Donna: Whatever, Jesus. You know, it all comes back to me now.

Alex: What comes back to you?

Donna: *You*, that's what comes back. More specifically, *living* with you and what a pain in the ass you were.

Donna stopped, but when she finished her rant, she realized she felt good; she'd gotten it out of her system, even if it was on a computer keyboard. The anger, the pent-up need to unload on Alex. Just like she used to. She stared at the screen, looking for him to respond. No, he was waiting, just waiting for her to stop. Exactly as he used to do when he was . . . alive. He was up to something.

Alex: Do you know where I am?

Perfect question, she thought.

Donna: I have no idea. Just like I had no idea half the time when you'd go out at night, supposedly working or whatever you said you were doing. I assume you're either a few blocks away holed up somewhere in some man cave of yours here in Queens. Or you're in a condo in Vegas. Why don't *you* tell me where you are?

Alex: Well, at least now you believe it's me.

Donna: I don't believe anything. I don't know what to believe. Just like when you were here, I never knew what to believe. This whole thing is ridiculous.

Alex: Okay, I want you to listen carefully because you're definitely not going to believe what I have to tell you now, but you have to try and keep an open mind.

Donna: Open mind, really, Alex? Anyone married to you has to have such an open mind that their goddamned brains must be spilling out. Believe you? I can't imagine why I wouldn't believe you. You've always been so honest with me, so trustworthy . . . so faithful. What a fucking surprise.

Alex: Do you want to know or what?

She could only imagine what story Alex was going to spin out now.

Donna: Go ahead. I'm listening, or reading, whatever the hell this is.

Alex: Okay, just shut up for a minute, will you? Remember when I told you that I was dealing with some real smart computer guys in Silicon Valley?

Donna: What? I don't know . . . Yes . . . Maybe. What's that got to do with anything?

Alex: Have you ever heard of *artificial intelligence*?

Donna: What are you talking about? Look, why don't you make this easy? Just give me a number where I can call you back. I can't wait to see the fucking area code.

Alex: Better yet. Do you know how to FaceTime?

CHAPTER 38

Santorini, Greece

Sindy Steele felt oddly happy to be back in Greece. Although it was two in the morning, the island was buzzing with tourists and locals enjoying a warm night in paradise. The last several days were a distant memory now, a fog obliterating what she feared remembering, just like the night hid the blue Aegean Sea just over the terrace.

She towered over most of the people around her. Maybe that was one reason the local Greek men seemed to look at her in awe, a potential conquest they appeared to be too insecure to approach. They stared, trying to meet her eyes, but she could sense their caution, unusual for men in this place. She preferred it that way. It gave her space.

She pulled her cell phone out of her bag, Michael had finally answered:

Glad you're back in Greece. You need to be careful. I'm going after them but it won't happen overnight. Until then, they will come after us both. You need help with your head. Do you understand what you did?

She stopped walking and stood in front of the Atlantis Bookshop, a haven on the island for expats and tourists. She wished the shop was open. Someday she'd write a book—if she can remember half of what she'd done. She'd have to do it under a different name. She read his message again.

She typed back her response to Michael: *You'll end up with me. You'll see.*

Satisfied, she put her phone back in her bag and continued her walk down Nomikos Street. She just kept walking, down a narrow alley, past Roka, her favorite Greek tavern. She swore she caught the scent of the grilled octopus in the sweet wine that she loved there, past the church . . . it was coming back to her . . . the look in Rick Martin's eyes right *after* she pulled the trigger . . . the funeral home in Chapel Hill . . . too clearly now. The street narrowed, the commercial establishments were gone. Her apartment wasn't far ahead. No more lights, no aromas, she was alone . . . She turned around, a shadow, a footstep, she wasn't sure. She reached into the pocket of her skintight jeans and gripped the stiletto she'd learned to never leave at home. She turned her head back again, unsure now . . . and kept walking down the dark, lonely street, alone.

CHAPTER 39

Whitestone, New York

It was nearly two in the morning and she was sitting up in bed, still on the side that had been hers, the computer on her lap, on top of the duvet. It had been days since Donna had heard anything from Alex—or whoever it was pretending to be him. Her attempts to reach him through iJewishMingle had gone unanswered.

So as she lay in bed checking her emails and finishing her first glass of wine since dinner, she was surprised to hear the chime from her laptop and see the FaceTime icon blinking at the bottom of the screen. She double-clicked onto it.

And there he was. At least from the waist up, Alex, in living color.

"You look good, Alex or, ah, whomever you are." It did look like him but did that mean it *was* him and that he was alive somewhere—or was this some type of computer trick? His facial expressions were natural and every bit of what she'd remembered: the smirk, the smile, the eyes that squinted in disbelief, the wise-guy demeanor.

"Whoever," he said. "Not whomever."

Now that was odd. "Are you correcting my grammar? You almost had me there until that. I know you're not Alex. He'd never do that—even if he had a clue what was correct."

"You're right." He seemed perplexed himself. "I don't think I've ever done that. I honestly don't know what got into me. I think it may be some new program that Michael installed—kind of like spell check on your computer. It's supposed to correct certain things, in this case grammar. I'll have to check into it because it's not me, you know?"

"Very funny. Good try. And now you drag your brother into this situation? Do you think I'm that gullible?"

"I need to explain about artificial intelligence –"

"Oh, Jesus. That again? I'm looking at you, for God sakes. Where the hell are you? Just tell me that."

Donna reached for more wine, finishing another full glass before looking back at the screen, at Alex. He was so real, so— just like he used to be . . . like he'd never left. Like he was in the next room.

"Do you know what AI is?" he asked.

"AI? Have I ever heard of artificial intelligence? That's your answer to where you are? That's going to be where this conversation is going?"

"You've got to listen to me –"

"Listen to you? Alex, I found you—after seven or whatever years of marriage and, supposedly two years dead—I find you on iJewishMingle—and now I'm looking at you and now you want to tell me about *artificial intelligence*?"

He was still, she could see him now, acting as he did so often when they argued. He'd wait, pause, as though it was a station break and something new, a new program was going to follow. His facial expressions hadn't changed, that flash of impatience, then calm as he waited for her to cool down before he'd start again.

"Are you going to let me speak?" he finally said.

"Go ahead, I'm listening. Do you understand that if you faked this whole thing, it's against the law? Not that that ever bothered you, of all people. You probably had life insurance policies that I didn't know about and somehow got paid out. Heaven knows—who was the beneficiary, Skinny Lester?

Fat Lester? Or was it your little brother? You'll all wind up in jail when this is over."

"Donna, stop. First of all, the only policies I had were the ones you got paid on. Second, you've got to let me explain and, when we are done here, I want you to Google, *artificial intelligence.*"

Maybe it was the wine, she'd had a lot, and now she felt that stir, the tension of her body under the covers. It had been a while since she'd been with . . . anyone.

"I see you're wearing that black negligee I got you," he said.

It was as though he knew what she was thinking. Was she going crazy, or just drunk? She didn't speak, she couldn't.

"Why don't you take it off?" he said, with his crazy half smile.

She knew it was weird, maybe even sick, but she did, pulling the straps down and then, since Dr. Simonetti had done his job so well, nudging the sheer silk lower until it fell under her breasts. She watched Alex, his mouth opening ever so slightly. She remembered that look, too.

"You look better than ever."

He always did know how to get her going. . . She was perspiring. She pulled her nightgown down, lower, leaning back onto her pillow, all the time watching . . . him. But— wait. What is this? Am I nuts? She pulled the negligee back over her breasts.

"Listen, Alex. I don't know what the hell you're up to but, whatever it is, I'm going to find you. Maybe you can get away with this shit with your brother or the idiots you hang out with, but not me. I'll find you."

"I was shot in the restaurant in front of a room full of cops. You can't stage that. I was gone. Dead. Buried."

"We'll see about that. I'll dig you up if I have to shovel the dirt from your goddamned grave and rip open your coffin myself—and you just better hope I don't break a nail doing it."

CHAPTER 40

Venice, Italy

He listened to the foghorn, the sound of the waves slapping against the side of the building, and stared at his hands.

Sitting in his suite at the Hotel Gritti, Monsignor Kurt Schlegelberger studied his hands as his fingers typed away on the laptop. They reminded him of his father's and the way they looked to him as a child, still strong and powerful yet showing the first signs of age and the beginnings of arthritis. He himself had just turned sixty.

He knew his father, were he still alive, would never understand or approve of his chosen career.

He remembered hearing him refer to the Church as the culmination of centuries of delusion and wishful thinking passed on by weak humans who couldn't accept that their life and consciousness ends the moment they die. He wondered how much of his own career in the Church was his rebellion against him. He had vowed to chart a different path. Certainly his decision to join the Church at the same age as his father had joined the Nazi party had been a clear first step. Yet, just like his father, he believed that life ended with death, there was nothing after. No heaven, hell or judgment day. Ironically, it was the perfect belief system for what had become his particular role inside the Vatican.

Without religion, life was easy. There were no repercussions except the ones here on earth and they were easy to evade.

He studied the encrypted notes on his computer from Monsignor Petrucceli and Cardinal Lovallo of "The Nicholas Affair," detailing two years of cover-ups, murders, and protecting dirty priests, all in the name of defending the Church. He once again felt the pull of his father's powerful hands. He whispered what he read, still in the throaty guttural manner that he knew made his words more haunting than any shout could have been.

"The Greek Orthodox priest who presided over Alex Nicholas' funeral never saw his body. He since died of a heart attack . . . The funeral director who supposedly prepared the body and sealed the casket is also dead. Rumors persist that Alex Nicholas duplicated himself on a computer. Friends, associates and his widow speculate that he faked his death and is living in Las Vegas . . . or Costa Rica."

Confused and troubled, he shut off the computer.

I've been asking Lovallo and Petrucceli if Michael Nicholas was dead yet. Perhaps I was asking about the wrong brother.

CHAPTER 41

Astoria, New York

If there was one person who knew if Alex were still alive, it would be his best friend, Skinny Lester. Tonight, Donna would find out what Skinny Lester knew, even if she had to go to dinner with him to do it.

"We've known each other for almost ten years, do you realize we've never had dinner together—at least not without Alex?" Skinny Lester said as he lifted a piece of L'Incontro's Napolitana thin crust pizza off the steel serving plate.

"No one realizes that more than I do." She'd called Lester this morning to sound him out regarding her suspicions about Alex but, before she knew it, she'd been embarrassed into meeting him for dinner. She watched him now as he meticulously maneuvered the slice of pizza from the plate into his mouth. "Jesus, Lester, just eat the damn thing—and, are those anchovies?"

"Yeah, they're –"

"Oh, stop. Never mind. If Alex saw you eating those little disgusting fishes on your pizza he'd have a fit."

"Actually, this wasn't his favorite place –"

"Yes," Donna said, remembering her last time here with Alex. "He said it was too fancy. Mostly, it was just that he hadn't been eating here every day for thirty years so he wasn't used to it yet."

Lester placed the remaining crust back on the plate and took another slice in his hand. "Alex liked places where he knew people, you know?"

"Actually, no, I don't. He had his quirks and was a lunatic at times. If they put a piece of parsley on the dish—for decoration—he'd send it back saying he didn't eat vegetables."

"All right, so what did you want to speak with me about?"

Lester wasn't an idiot like his cousin. She knew that he'd reached his tolerance for being abused. She'd have to cut to the chase.

"I was on some website a few nights ago –"

"You were? Really, which one?"

"What difference does it make?"

"A big one, first of all –"

"Okay, never mind again. I'll tell you—but you can't tell anyone. It was something like Hebrew Mingle dot com."

"Didn't you tell me once that you didn't like Jewish guys?"

"Maybe I did—but that was before living all this time with Alex. Now I'm thinking that a guy with a few allergies isn't a high price to pay for someone who listens, goes to bed early—and who has money. After all, my maiden name *was* Finkelstein."

"And I never thought you'd go to a dating site –"

"I don't need the Internet to get laid. I think you know me well enough by now. And stop always interrupting me, will you?"

He shrugged. "Sorry, I promise. Go ahead."

"So, I'm on this site, right? And I put in all my criteria for a guy—ideal looks, age, religion, background, job, all that crap." She looked up from her veal chop to watch Lester's reaction. "And who do you think pops up?"

"I swear—I've never even been on those sites –"

"Oh God. Not you, you idiot. Are you crazy?"

"Okay, who then?"

"I'll tell you *who*. Are you ready?"

"Fat Lester?"

"No."

"I can't take it anymore. Who was it?"

"I think it was Alex."

Lester often needed time to think. She remembered how sometimes she'd ask him a question and how he'd take too long before answering.

Lester looked back at her now.

"But, he's not even Jewish."

"You're missing the point. At this rate, even I'm going to miss it. You two were friends since you were kids. No one was closer to Alex than you are . . . were."

"Oh man, we chased some good-looking girls together. You know we both had new cars, he had a convertible –"

"Shut up for a minute and just listen. Listen—and then answer this one big question."

"Okay, sorry."

She paused, for effect. I'll just come right out with it. "Have you spoken with Alex?"

Skinny Lester was the brains, the mathematical genius behind Alex's—now Michael's—gambling operations. He was, Alex had always told her, a mathematical genius. He knew how to set and manipulate the odds, often on the fly; a skill, Alex assured her, which was critical to any successful bookmaking operation. He had, Alex would say, "the mind of a casino." But at this moment he was a deer in the headlights and she had just turned on the brights.

"Have I *spoken* with Alex?" he repeated.

"Yes, you heard me."

He looked up at her, his eyebrows arching, mouth twisting, he appeared to be in agony just trying to understand what she meant. Or—was he in cahoots with Alex and struggling to figure out what to say now?

"Donna . . . I don't . . . I'm confused . . . How could I speak with Alex?"

"Listen, I'm not convinced he's dead and gone. Or, let me rephrase it. I'm convinced he's gone but not that he's dead."

Lester looked dazed. Or was he purposely paralyzed to save himself from having to say anything that could incriminate himself—or Alex? She didn't have a clue either way.

"I haven't spoken with him . . . lately."

"*Lately?* What the hell does that mean?" she said. Her voice attracted some glances from the nearby diners. She returned their looks with one of her own, leaned in closer to him, speaking just above a whisper with as much anger as she could muster.

"It means . . . not since he . . . died."

"Are you sure of that?"

"Of course. How could I possibly have spoken to him?" He appeared to regain his composure. "Do you want me to ask Fat Lester?"

She picked up the half full glass of Montepulciano and finished it then signaled the passing waiter for the check. Turning her attention back to Lester, she said, "I'm going to get to the bottom of this—with or without you. If I find out you've been lying to me, take a look at that hot pizza oven over there." She nodded in the direction of the wood-fired oven, its flames clearly visible, nearby in the open kitchen. The chef was placing a tomato pizza inside. "That's where your balls will go."

She'd struck out on this one but there was one more person she had to talk to—and, unlike his brother, he wasn't a good liar.

CHAPTER 42

Berlin, Germany

"Being in Berlin is like making love to a beautiful woman—and knowing that she's murdered her last three husbands," Hans Ulricht said.

Goldstein looked puzzled by the thought. "That might take the fun out of it."

"Quite the contrary for me, I would find it to be the ultimate thrill."

The chalkboard menu sat on the edge of the table. Ulricht watched as Goldstein glanced at it—but it was apparent that he was also surveying the restaurant, his eyes scanning and then fixating on the sixties style blow up of an attractive topless woman which was hanging over the open kitchen.

"Centolire is Berlin's finest Italian restaurant. You said, no German food, remember? The linguine and lobster here is excellent."

Goldstein appeared to be uneasy despite the restaurant's intimate setting and the rich smell of sweet garlic coming from the kitchen.

"I can't eat lobster. Frankly, this isn't my favorite city. I had to be here for meetings otherwise –"

"You understand that Berlin is my heritage. It's where my heart is, where my parents are buried. This is a beautiful city, so modern now—yet so rich with history . . ."

"You know I don't even think about my own parents, let alone yours."

"We are only a few meters from the site of Hitler's bunker. Civilization is so fragile. It's a sobering thought, yes?"

"I'm always sober. They filled in that bunker, didn't they?"

"Most of it—but a small annex that was used to store the Reich's gold still exists."

"Really? How did that happen?"

Finally, Hans thought, something seemed to catch Goldstein's interest.

"It was totally sealed off from the main bunker. Only a select few even knew it existed. Albert Speer, Hitler's personal architect, designed it himself and purposely kept if off the blueprints of the rest of the bunker. There was no record of it anywhere so when the Allies arrived, they never discovered it."

"What about the gold?" Goldstein asked.

Ulricht knew he was hooked.

"Most of it is gone now. But there is still more than you can imagine inside."

"Whose owns it?"

"A small circle of us, direct descendants from Hitler's inner circle."

"You're kidding. How much is in there?"

"More than enough to cover your lost investments in Rosen's fund."

Before Goldstein could respond, Hans could see the server approaching their table.

"Let's order dinner," he said. "We will have our desserts in the bunker."

CHAPTER 43

Westport, Connecticut

The invitation had come as a surprise. Although she wondered about his real intentions, Jennifer Walsh was delighted to be invited into Michael's home. Either way, it didn't matter to her. After all, he was just a younger version of his brother.

"Alex always said I should have been a porn star instead of a hairdresser."

Now in Michael's plush wine cellar, Jennifer Walsh was comfortable speaking with her dead lover's brother. It was strange but, at times, she felt some of the same attraction to Michael as she did to Alex. After all, since Alex's death, Michael occasionally visited her—and her lover, Catherine Saint Laurent, the legendary French film star—just as Alex had. But, unlike Alex—and despite their attempts to lure Michael into their bed—the most he ever did was . . . watch.

"Your brother, despite his tough-guy exterior—and interior, for that matter—treated me better than all the Ivy League and rich little trust fund boys I'd ever been with—and a lot better than anyone I'd ever married."

"I owe you," Michael said. "You were the one who told me about Alex and his computer. If it hadn't been for you, he'd have died when he died. But I've asked you here because I promised to do a favor for Alex."

She looked at the computer equipment stacked neatly on the only wall space not devoted to racks filled with wine bottles. She pointed to an Apple laptop on the table, "That was his, wasn't it?"

"Yes, but it's come a long way from when Alex showed it to you."

"I take it this is why I'm here. I just figured that nothing ever came of all that artificial intelligence stuff. Or, if I recall, that's what you led me to believe. Was I wrong?"

"I'll let you decide—but I wasn't totally honest with you." Michael was cautious, remembering too well how, after just a few minutes with Alex, Samantha abruptly left this same room, saying it was 'sick' and nothing more than a fancy game. "I'll never forget what you said on the phone, 'There's something you need to know about your brother.' I couldn't imagine then what it could have been. I mean, I didn't even *know* you."

"And," Jennifer said, "it took me two glasses of champagne before I could tell you I was his . . . mistress. I can't believe I even used that word."

"That part didn't surprise me. I knew Alex played around. But the next part did," Michael said.

Jennifer reached over and gently touched the laptop. "I remember the night Alex showed me this. Not so much because of the computer because, frankly, I certainly didn't understand what it did at that point. The big thing was, it was so unusual for Alex to show so much emotion—it was *fear* really. He was half in the bag—maybe *all* in the bag. He told me about his only fear. Such a tough guy and yet, that night at least, he confessed that he was petrified about dying. I said to him, 'Don't worry, I don't think it's going to happen any time soon.' I was wrong, of course."

"You'd never seen his laptop before?" Michael asked.

"Oh, I guess I'd seen it. It wasn't the one he normally used, you know, for his business or his emails. I'd seen him playing with it before, kind of secretly. I assumed he was playing games. He loved fantasy baseball . . . Until that night when he brought it into our bed and turned it on for me."

"What *exactly* did he show you?

"Well, it was like I told you over that lunch. It looked like a copy of himself on the screen. In fact, he actually talked to it—and it—or he—talked back to him. The person or whatever on the computer looked and sounded just like him. It was, like his mirror image."

"What did you think?"

"I kind of laughed. In fact, I think I said something like, 'this is perfect for you. You can talk to yourself now'."

She could see that Michael was mesmerized—just as he'd been when she first told him about it three years ago—before Michael then went and retrieved the computer.

"Okay," Michael said, smiling as he pressed a switch under the table. "You may want to take a Lexapro."

She sat back and watched as a large screen silently descended from a recessed slot in the ceiling. It now covered the wall of custom built mahogany shelves holding Michael's vintage wines. Michael then logged onto the computer; she saw him click on what looked like an ancient religious cross icon—and then, as he typed in the password, a series of black dots on the screen. He dimmed the lights, and looked up as the sign-in page transformed itself , first into a blank blue screen. And then, Alex appeared. The camera—if that's what it was—appeared to zoom in to capture him from the shoulders up. Alex came back to life.

She looked over at Michael who was watching the screen, seemingly as mesmerized as she was. Jennifer turned back to Alex, who had fixed her with his gaze.

"So," he said. "Why weren't you at my funeral?"

CHAPTER 44

Westport, Connecticut

"Oh my God . . . It's you! Wait, how the hell did you know that I didn't come to your funeral?"

Jennifer realized that the things she thought were not possible in this life were no longer clear. She wondered whether her own mind was playing tricks. Had her great need to be loved and her fear of being alone or abandoned, had they taken over her brain, distorted reality, unplugged connections, plugged them into different places, the wrong places?

Michael broke the spell. "No one else really knows about this. As you can imagine, I need to keep this a secret until I—or we –" he said, looking at Alex, "can figure out how we want to announce it."

"My God," she said, shaking her head.

"He demanded to see you." Michael got up from his chair. "Why don't I leave you two alone for a little while. I'll be in the next room. He walked out, closing the heavy oak door behind him.

Alex's eyes appeared to follow Michael as he left the room. "I never thought I'd see you again," he said.

Jennifer could feel a rush of emotion taking charge of her body, her eyes swelled with tears. "You never thought you'd see me again? You never thought . . . Alex, are we crazy? How can you even *think*? Oh my God, do you know how wild this is? That we're speaking to each other? You're dead, remember?"

But he wasn't listening. Jennifer could tell, just like she could tell before, before the shooting. He's the same as he always was, she thought. His eyes had that look of being preoccupied with something different than what she was talking about at that moment. She knew what it was.

"Yeah, I know," he finally said. "Listen, we need to go to bed, you know what I'm saying?" He had that look. There were times when Alex just had to have sex, those times he needed it and didn't want to hear any excuses, and didn't want to have to wait, either. She saw that same look again now, on the sixty-inch plasma flat screen.

It was another shock to her system. Suddenly, she began to feel uncomfortably warm. Like a hot flash or a fever. Maybe, she thought, her senses were just on overload. She knew some change was coming over her, a strange warmth passing through her. Perhaps unconsciously, she unbuttoned the top two, then the remaining three buttons of her blouse, exposing her nicely tanned chest and her black lace Chantal Thomass bra, the one her other lover, Catherine Saint Laurent, bought for her at the exclusive boutique on the rue Saint Honore.

He was watching. He liked to stand back, to watch her undress before they did anything. He was a voyeur, just before he became a lover. Tonight was no different. "You know your nipples are jutting out."

She looked back at the door, hoping to find an interior lock, but it only locked from the outside. Who cares now, she thought. Turning her attention back to Alex, and her own glistening, moist body. She took off her blouse, reached back and unhooked her bra.

"Alex, my God, I missed you so much."

"Yeah, I know," he said. "Do you still carry those sex toys around in your bag?"

She pulled the pink plastic cylinder out of her Gucci bag. "Yeah, and what do you know, my new one is Bluetooth enabled.

I just got it from OhMyGod.com. It syncs up to the new iPhone—maybe you'll be able to control it. Hold on, let me get these panties off so you have a better view."

CHAPTER 45

Berlin, Germany

"I feel like I'm in some old Nazi movie," Goldstein said. "Perhaps you are," Hans said, enjoying the irony.

They walked two blocks through the dark Berlin streets until they reached a storefront that, unlike the others all around it, looked untouched, a relic of old Berlin, the type that maybe sold men's hats just as the storm troopers were goose-stepping in unison outside. The sign on the window read, *Heinrich Mannequin.*

Ulricht reached into his pants pocket, pulled out the gold chain key ring that was attached to his belt loop, a constant reminder to Hans of its original owner, his father. He found the key and unlocked the old heavy glass and wrought-iron door, and led the way into the darkened shop.

Once inside, Ulricht moved his flashlight across the room, highlighting a row of mannequins, looking oddly life-like.

Goldstein looked somewhere between mesmerized and terrorized. His eyes followed the path of Ulricht's flashlight as he moved it across a line of dead-eyed mannequins. The dark and the searchlight combined to create a strobe-like effect, the inert but highly stylized bodies appearing to come alive in a dance of quick, erratic movement.

Ulricht enjoyed the drama. He could see that Goldstein had lost his cocky edge. He appeared uncertain, afraid.

"This is like walking through a morgue," Goldstein whispered. He then moved closer to one of the nearest mannequins, a nude, stunningly beautiful, well-built woman. She was lying in a seductive, semi-repose, her white skin in stark contrast to the bright red sleek couch. Goldstein, obviously attracted, moved towards her. Ulricht directed the flashlight onto her, the unnatural light oddly making her appear even more life-like.

As Goldstein moved closer, however, a loud radar sonic type sound stopped him in his tracks. He pulled the cell phone out of his pocket, looked at the screen, tilted his head as though in disbelief, and put the phone to his ear. At the same time, the mannequin's eyes opened wide, a tiny light emanated from her eyes and her mouth moved with the words that could be heard coming from Goldstein's phone.

Goldstein jumped, dropped the phone and retreated away from the mannequin and back towards Ulricht. "What the hell is this?"

"That's Heidi. She's the latest in technology. German, of course, she is what's called a gemenoid, or *smart mannequin*. It is the first phase of the merging of robot engineering with artificial intelligence," Ulricht said. "They have cameras embedded in their eyes and are programmed to seek out cell phones within a certain distance. If you were in a department store, they'd describe what they were wearing and then mention that the garments were on sale. In this situation, she's assuming you are interested in her."

"Interested in her? What does that mean?"

"Jonathan, this is a showroom for mannequins. The people who might approach her here would be buyers of mannequins."

"Oh, sure. I get it. This is incredible."

"Nevertheless, the technology is rather powerful. In this case, she may also have taken everything you have stored on your cell phone—your contacts, your emails, perhaps your credit card information from your Amazon account. She is also equipped with facial and voice recognition software—in addition, of course, to very sophisticated artificial intelligence."

"This is for department stores?"

"No, this highly sophisticated model is for very specialized markets."

"Specialized?"

"Yes, the Russians. Putin, in particular. In truth, we have just scratched the surface of the potential applications." Ulricht scanned the shop, flashing the light over a showroom full of other mannequins. "Most of these are simple dummies, intended for the traditional buyer. You happened to have been drawn in by our most powerful model, Heidi."

Goldstein moved back towards her, "She's beautiful. She looks so –"

"Human? Yes, nearly identical. Her skin is silicone, as close to human as medical science has come. Her hair . . . is human."

Goldstein moved even closer, as though he was going to embrace her.

"Don't cross her," Ulricht said. "That's all I will say. Now, follow me,"

Then with Goldstein close behind, he descended down the flight of concrete steps into the basement. Ulricht passed three steel-caged storage bins, reached for a light switch but, instead of flipping it, he pushed against the switch plate which swung open, revealing a hidden keyboard panel. After touching a sequence of buttons, an adjacent wall panel rose up into the ceiling. Ulricht moved quickly to another keyboard panel and, again, pressed a sequence of buttons. Immediately, they could hear the heavy steel clicking sound of locks being released. Ulricht turned a long steel handle and slowly swung the heavy steel door open.

As they entered the vault, Ulricht switched on the lights and watched as Goldstein admired the rows of gold bricks piled all around the room in neat stacks from floor to ceiling.

"How the hell have you kept this a secret?"

"Ah, the treasures of war. Let's call it the just rewards of the Third Reich." Ulricht wondered if Goldstein's ancestors had been unwilling contributors. This wasn't the time to suggest such a thought. Not if he wanted Goldstein's cooperation. "We only allow those we trust to enter here. Even then, this room stays sealed, sometimes for years at a time. We rarely enter ourselves so as not to draw attention. Heidi and a few of the other smart mannequins upstairs keep a careful watch of anyone going down the steps."

"You know, I was kidding about ever turning you over to the Feds . . ."

"I know you were, of course."

"How much is this all worth?" Goldstein's voice tailed off.

Ulricht could see Goldstein's mind working, his eyes darting quickly, side to side, "Let's say more than some countries in the world have in the central banks. It would be much, much more, if I could invest this without bringing attention to it by the authorities."

"Holy shit."

"Yes, as you can imagine, very few people are aware of this, let alone have seen it."

"I'm touched that you trust me that way, Hans."

Hans looked Goldstein straight in the eye. "I don't."

CHAPTER 46

Berlin, Germany

Watching Goldstein admiring the gold bricks, Hans Ulricht knew he hated him. Gold to Goldstein was simply money. To Hans, it was only a means to an end, the prerequisite for his dream of the return of the Reich but under the modern packaging of his own *Free Forces Party*. Nevertheless, there was no one better suited for what he needed done than Jonathan Goldstein.

"And all this time I thought you were just a fat old banker," Goldstein said, his eyes still taking in the room.

"You are too kind, Jonathan." Even for an American, Goldstein lacked manners, let alone insight.

"So, let me ask you, why did you bring me here?"

"Very well. I knew it would be necessary to show you this in order to show you that I'm more than just—as you say—your fat old Swiss banker."

"Hans, you know I didn't mean it that way –"

"It's of no consequence. What is important is that we can be of assistance to each other—but in more of a partnership instead of a client vendor relationship. It will require a change of thinking on your part but the rewards will be tremendous."

"Hans, okay, how about if you get to the point?"

"Here's my proposition. As you can see, I have control over several billion Euros in gold. I also have a problem—which is an opportunity for you. You are uniquely positioned to help me.

These assets should by now be worth many times what they are—except I can't invest them. Sitting here, their value only increases—and in some cases decreases—with the price of gold. If I had been able to convert this into more liquid assets and invest them in equities or hedge funds or controlling interests in businesses, they would be worth many times what they are now."

Hans could see that Goldstein was more at ease, in his element now.

"What you're saying," Goldstein said, "is that you need someone to launder this money and then invest it for you. That's a big risk, a big legal risk, especially since nine-eleven."

"I'm well aware of that. Naturally, since the risk is significant—the rewards must be also. I'm willing to ensure that this arrangement will be to your satisfaction."

Hans proceeded to lay out the plan to bring billions in assets into Goldstein's various hedge funds and private equity ventures. In return, Hans would receive a steady flow of generous returns, thereby allowing the resources of the Free Forces Party to grow more aggressively than they could sitting hidden in a vault.

"I like the way you think, Hans. I always have."

It had been a successful evening. "Just follow me out, right this way," Hans said as he led the way out, pulling the heavy vault door shut, then pressing a button on the switch plate, as the vault's main door shut tight behind them.

As they reached the top of the steps, Ulricht stopped, turned and gestured to the mannequins, "Take a look around, Jonathan. It can be difficult to tell what's real and what isn't. Most of the mannequins are made from plastic or fiberglass or, like your friend, Heidi, of silicone. A few, however, are real leather, actual animal skins. We sell them to a very small group of collectors. Different from the department stores or the buyers of . . . people . . . like Heidi. They satisfy certain exotic, occasionally erotic, fetishes."

As he passed once again through the showroom, Goldstein approached Heidi. Her eyes lit up, widening as he got closer. His phone chimed; but this time he ignored it as he came even closer to her. He reached out, tentatively at first, to touch her. But just as his hand came within inches of her arm, she spoke.

"Don't touch me, Jonathan."

He recoiled, staring back, his mouth slightly open. "I . . . I'm sorry . . ." He looked over at Ulricht, "I can't believe –"

"There's so much more in this world that you're not aware of. So much you can't see. Perhaps, for now, it's best that way."

"Yes, sure, sure . . ." Goldstein said, as he then turned away from Heidi.

Ulricht stopped, thought for a moment, "Michael Nicholas would make a perfect mannequin, wouldn't he?"

CHAPTER 47

New York City

"I want Alex's grave dug up."

Michael had just twirled his first fork of Da Silvano's Linguine Alle Vongole. Digging up his brother's body was the last thing on his mind.

As she spoke, Donna Nicholas, characteristically distracted, looked away. He followed her glances as she watched a party of four tall, too-thin but stylish, long-legged young women who had just entered, passing through the VIP front room where Michael and she were seated.

He wondered if her thoughts drifted back twenty years or more, when she could have been one of those girls, before the boob job, the skin peels, two husbands, her often-described in detail weekly Brazilian waxes, and a few unwanted yet, in his opinion, flattering pounds. She had to have noticed that, until the willowy foursome had entered, virtually every man who had passed their table—from teenagers to the rich guys in their seventies—had diverted their gaze to glance at *her*.

They had never been particularly close while Alex was alive. For several months immediately following Alex's murder, after she had convinced Michael to help close out his brother's gambling and loan-sharking operations, she and Michael had become somewhat closer. He was never sure who she really was, the person underneath the flashy, tough New York diva persona. Nevertheless, they had forged a reasonable relationship as Michael successfully took over his brother's enterprise, expanded it and made Donna, now as a silent partner, even more money.

"Do you mean disinterment?" he said.

"No, I want his body dug up."

"You want to have Alex's body exhumed? Now? Why? What are you looking for? He's been dead for almost two years."

"No, I don't want any of that. I just want his grave dug up and I want them to open up the casket and see who's in there." She finally looked directly at him. "Listen, I don't know what the hell they call it, exhumation, whatever. I want them to dig up your fucking brother's body. That's as nice as I can put it. You figure out what they call it."

"But why?"

"People are talking. Some of Alex's old friends. I'm hearing things. Odd things."

"Like what?"

"They're suspicious that Alex's business is going along just as he ran it. Some of the decisions, moves, they believe only *he* could have done some of these things."

Michael laughed but he was annoyed. "You mean, like expanding into Paris? Alex never even went to Paris. He hardly left Queens except to go to Miami or Costa Rica. Do you think Paris was *his* decision? Not to mention that he's dead."

"No. Everyone knows that was you. But some of the other things, the day to day stuff that you had no background in— setting the odds, the spreads, dealing with the crazies, the degenerates, the runners, all that stuff. Things, I don't even understand but—but that you understood even less."

"So, what do you think? That Alex's still alive? That he's hidden out somewhere and is secretly still guiding his business?"

"I don't know what to think. Some people have said that though, yes. But, me, I just don't know—or understand—what's going on. There's more, too. Much more . . . I just don't want to go into it now." She averted his gaze again, looking away.

Michael knew she would never admit to being on iJewish-Mingle or any dating site. It wouldn't fit her self-proclaimed image of being an irresistible magnet for men of all ages. Still, it was crazy for Alex to have gone there and invited trouble.

They had completely blocked out the typical Saturday night buzz going on around them in Da Silvano's until Silvano Marchetto himself approached their table. Unmistakable with his ponytail and distinctive angular eyeglasses, a true eccentric, he had brought authentic Florentine cuisine to the city—and played a cardinal in the movie *Angels and Demons*.

"Ah, Michael, my friend. How are you tonight?"

Michael introduced Donna, who was not about to let the thirty year age difference get in the way of making her interest in the wealthy restaurateur obvious.

Silvano, who couldn't help inhaling the scent of Donna's ever-present Chanel No. 5, and whose own flair for sensuous women was well known, said simply, "I see" as he moved on to the next table.

Resuming their conversation, Michael sat back, letting out a resigned sigh. "He's happily married, by the way."

"No one is," Donna said, continuing to eye Silvano.

"Listen, if you really want to dig Alex up, I can't stop you." But now he could see that Donna initially had no clue what he was talking about. The Silvano interruption had temporarily wiped out her train of thought, if not her short-term memory. He wondered how she kept anything straight in her life. Several seconds later, as though woken up from a dream, she recovered.

"I don't know what I want. All I know is, there's something strange going on around Alex. It's like, dead or alive, nothing changes. When he was alive, you know, crazy things were happening with him all the time. Being married to Alex was like nuts. It was like being in a circus. He was crazy that way. Now, it's like the same circus."

"Believe me, I know. I used to live a halfway normal life, remember? Until you brought me into this."

"Oh, and by the way, I've heard you've been seeing that hairdresser to the stars friend of his. Only Alex would have an affair with a lesbian."

Michael had wondered when Donna was going to mention Jennifer. "She called me sometime after the funeral. I'd never met her before that. We've met a few times since then. I'm certainly not *involved* with her, other than as a friend."

"Jesus, I hope not. You don't think that Alex's really alive and seeing that bitch, do you?" Donna didn't wait for a response. "I called her the other night and confronted her. I asked her if she'd been screwing my husband. Do you know what she said?"

Michael knew. Donna was on a roll so he just shook his head.

"She said, 'Yeah, I screwed him yesterday.'"

"Well, we know that's impossible —"

"If I find out that he saw her again, I'll kill him."

"I don't think you'll have to worry about that."

"Oh really? It'd be just like him to fake his own god-damned murder so he could go off and do whatever the hell he liked. He could have his bimbos and his money and wouldn't have to deal with me."

So that was it. Then, just as quickly, it was clear from the look on her face that Donna was done discussing Alex's affairs.

"But, there's one other thing I don't get."

"What's that?"

"I don't understand how *you're* so sure your brother's dead?"

He was surprised at the question, particularly since it was such a good one, better than she could have imagined. He knew he had to be careful with his response.

"Maybe because I went to his *funeral*." He paused, and thought again before continuing. "But I *am* sure he's dead."

Flashing a seductive but mischievous smile, Donna lifted her wine glass and said, "Then he won't mind if we take one last look, will he?"

CHAPTER 48

New York City

Michael had finally received word that the arrangements were almost ready. He had never been so anxious to get on a plane. It had been five days since he'd come up with his plan to strike back. Although it would still take a few days until all the arrangements were set, it was time to get over to Europe so he'd be able to move quickly once everything was ready. But he had some work to do here at home while he was waiting.

He watched as Karen DiNardo swept through the doors of Arno in Manhattan's garment district. Like a cruise missile, she immediately spotted him and made a bee-line for his table. As always, Karen was a quick study and wasted no time. Her dark eyes reminded Michael of a stereotypical Sicilian woman, one not to be trifled with. Her devilish smile and professional demeanor concealed a lethally sarcastic sense of humor and yet a quietly efficient mind. She sat down, pulled two manila folders from her leather briefcase and made one of her characteristic understatements as her unique way of saying hello: "It looks like this is becoming a tradition."

Despite knowing full well what she meant, Michael replied, "What is?"

"Oh, you know, every several months we take a break from the normal office routine and you ask me to research something having to do with artificial intelligence and, of course, you won't tell me what you do with this information which, of

149

course, you know drives me crazy. But, it's okay because you always have me deliver the information at a great Italian restaurant. Anyway, when you put it all together, it's now a tradition."

"How about a glass of wine?"

"I thought you'd never ask."

Michael poured her a glass of Gavi from the bottle chilling in the champagne bucket sitting by his side.

"This usually helps me get a word in edge-wise," he said.

Karen took a healthy sip, "Well, speaking of edges, you're Greek Orthodox last time I checked—what's your interest now with the Catholic Church—they're *my people,* as you know—and artificial intelligence?"

"I can't tell you."

"Here we go again," she said, almost laughing. "This is like a comedy skit. Although, I must admit, when you mentioned AI and the Vatican, I thought, what the hell—excuse the pun—what possible connection could there be? But then I started researching . . ."

Her attention and her eyes followed the large metal tray carried by a server passing nearby. "Oh my God, did you see that?"

Michael turned to catch a look, "I think that's the Costoletta alla Parmigiana– it's a breaded veal chop with tomato sauce and cheese—it's unbelievable."

"I'm having that." She looked back down at the file she had opened. "Anyway, as I said, I couldn't get the connection until I saw this in the Catholic Technology Journal. Listen to this," and she proceeded to read:

"In a treatise released earlier this year, Dr. Jayson Horne discussed how breakthroughs in physics are blurring the line between science and theology. Physicists, Horne wrote, are having to come to terms with concepts that were once the domain of theologians, including the concept of multiple universes. Similarly, he writes, experts in digital technology, are raising issues that circle back into religious territory."

Karen stopped, looking at Michael. Seeing no reaction, she continued reading:

"At the extreme end of this phenomenon, there is the concept of artificial intelligence, which introduces questions about the very nature of human power, and whether intelligence or consciousness is distinct from the soul. Meanwhile, some experts foresee a possibility that the human mind will be uploaded onto a deathless computer. As religion scholar Robert Geraci has argued, this vision of people shedding their imperfect bodies and achieving immortality sounds an awful lot like the Rapture.

Technologies don't need to seem futuristic. IBM's Watson is now a *Jeopardy!* Champion, and, with Siri, Apple has arguably offered the first mass-market robot. It's easy to imagine a time when we have regular, substantial interactions (some of them, perhaps, romantic or sexual, as in Spike Jonze's Academy Award-nominated *Her*) with objects that act a lot like human beings."

Michael couldn't control himself any longer. "*Her* could have been so much better. It was like a comic book."

"Nice to hear you're listening, at least. Hold on though, I'm not done reading. Listen to this, it's from *The Book of Immortality* by Adam Gollner:

"Today, we all worship technology constantly: checking email, turning on machines, flicking light switches. We're all trying as hard as possible to cram ourselves into our computers: making art on them, being entertained and informed by them, feeding them information, meeting friends with them, even falling in love through them. We are teaching machines who we are, telling them everything there is to know, programming them with intelligence in the hopes that they will develop consciousness. And if not, we'll scan

the contents of our brains into hard drives and speed things along. Soon, modern immortalists assure us, we'll become computers."

"I've got to tell you, boss, whatever it is you're up to, this should put a cold shiver up your spine."

Michael showed no expression, partly because he didn't want to invite Karen's questions and partly to drive her a little nuts.

She slid her folder across the table to him, "Here's my full report. You can read it at your leisure. Can I ask you a personal question?"

"You're going to anyway, so go ahead."

"Why don't you go to church?"

"I do."

"You don't."

"I do. Okay, I go to church mostly for funerals and weddings –"

"*Only* for funeral and weddings."

"And sometimes for Sofia. We go together on Easter or Christmas. I think it gives her comfort. Actually, I do feel guilty that I didn't give her some religious foundation growing up. Why do you ask, anyway?"

"Because I didn't think you really cared about the Catholic Church—or any church for that matter. You were always so irreverent about religion, you know, with all your wisecracks over the years."

Michael took a deep breath. Karen was no ordinary brain: she was a combination of a high IQ and an even unnaturally higher curiosity. She'd run circles around Sherlock Holmes.

"Is this connected to your bother's death? Because all of these artificial intelligence questions began right after your brother was murdered, although this is the first time you've sought to connect the Church and artificial intelligence."

"You're right, it's all connected. Someday I'll tell you everything. Let's order, then I'll need for you to make some airline reservations for me."

"Where are you going?"

"Paris, then Rome." Michael said.

"Business or pleasure?"

He thought for a moment. "Neither."

CHAPTER 49

Vatican City

This was impossible. It was his worst fear, confirmed now in print. What was happening? The world he knew and had devoted his life to was being turned upside down. Monsignor Schlegelberger felt his anger building as he re-read the editorial in the online edition of the L'Osservatore Romano:

There have been many challenges to organized religions: dictators and the communist party have outlawed them, radical extremist groups have attempted to eradicate competing believers, the Nazi's burned synagogues—but the greatest challenge to the power of organized religion and faith may come from our computers, and, specifically, from artificial intelligence.

The growing power of AI—now recognized by such iconic figures as Stephen Hawking and Apple co-founder Steve Wozniak, and soon to be the subject of a 100-year landmark study by Stanford University—may challenge the monopoly that religions have had on the answer to the biggest question of all: what happens when we die?

Yes, that's the ultimate allure of any religion—that guaranteed reservation into the afterlife—heaven and hell and the opportunity for immortality. But, if soon we will be able to duplicate ourselves—and our very consciousness—on our computers, we may be able to enter the gates of heaven without all the praying, fasting, confessing, contributing, and guilt that our respective religions require in return.

He grabbed the phone, black and heavy; the ones in the Vatican apartments seemed ancient, from a time he wished he could return to right now. He dialed his friend, the paper's editor for the past thirty years, Marco Fiachetti.

"Have you seen the editorial in your paper this morning?"

"Of course, Kurt. I should hope that I see them all. I approve them, do I not?"

Schlegelberger knew better but that was beside the point. More than once Fiachetti had fallen asleep at the wheel, allowing his junior editors to go to print with a column that had to be quickly withdrawn. "Did you approve this one on artificial intelligence that I am looking at right now?"

He heard a shuffling of papers and then, after several seconds, he could hear a small laugh from his friend.

"My dear old man," Fiachetti said, "I don't know what you're referring to. None of today's editorials even mention this *artificial intelligence* that you speak of. I find the *human* intelligence elusive enough."

"That's impossible. I'm looking at your editorial as we speak," Schlegelberger said.

"I too, am looking, but I see only the ones that are here— on clerical celibacy, abortion in the United States, and . . ."

He cut in, "Are you reading the *paper* edition –"

"Of course, why?"

"You have an *online edition* too, remember?"

"Ah, yes, of course. But only the Americans and the kids read it. It is the same, in any case."

Schlegelberger quickly checked the editorial page of the actual paper; he still had it delivered to his apartment each week. "I'm afraid, my dear friend, that today, the two are not the same."

"That is impossible," said Fiachetti. "I'm looking at our site right now. How could this have happened?"

"Have you ever heard of a *cyber attack*?" Schlegelberger said.

CHAPTER 50

New York City

M ichael enjoyed the walk up Madison Avenue, stopping
to look at the windows of the Ralph Lauren shop. He
turned left at the corner of Seventy-Ninth Street, headed
towards Fifth Avenue until he reached the beautiful old
townhouse building that housed the archdiocese offices of the
Greek Orthodox Church.

Once inside he was quickly ushered to Father Papageorge's
private office. He strained to hear the old priest. Instead of his
usual strong baritone voice, today, Father Papageorge was
speaking just above a whisper.

"I am glad that you called me. Yes, I know what Father
Papadopoulos was going to tell you before he . . . died."

It was another strange chapter from the time right after
Alex's murder. It turned out that Father Papadopoulos, the
priest who presided over Alex's funeral, had never actually seen
Alex's body. And why did every Greek priest seem to have a
name beginning with Papa?

"You know, of course," Papageorge continued, "that your
brother's casket had already been closed and sealed when Father
Papadopoulos arrived at the funeral home to bless the body.
This was highly unusual and has only added to our troubles."

"Our troubles?" Michael said.

Father Papageorge arose from his chair and, being careful
to make no sound, shut the heavy old door. Despite the priest's

caution, the click of the ancient brass lock reverberated through the room.

"Excuse my caution, the Archdiocese has been known to listen to itself here in the headquarters building."

Michael looked around the priest's office; it reminded him of an old foreign embassy. In a way, he thought, it was, at least for some people, *God's embassy.*

"We broke away from the Catholics in the eleventh century, over a thousand years ago. It was over many things, mostly though, they were confusing their Pope with God."

What difference could a thousand-year-old disagreement over the power of the Pope have to do with anything going on with Alex? "What do you think," Michael said, interrupting what he feared was going to be an ancient history lesson, "Father Papadopoulos was going to tell me?"

"Demetrious—Father Papadopoulos as you knew him— was a friend of mine, for many years. We studied together at the seminary in Brookline. We traveled back to Greece together on occasion. It seems so long ago now, but several years ago, Father Papadopoulos introduced me to your brother."

"I never knew that you'd met Alex."

"Yes, I knew him but not, of course, as Father Papadopoulos did. They were closer than perhaps either one cared to admit. Your brother had secrets."

"Secrets? Do you mean his business? Women –"

"No, all men have these. Alex's secrets were different. Very different. He made enemies with our Catholic friends."

"Enemies, in what way?"

"With his computer." The old priest pointed an old computer sitting on a side table. It had to have been one of the first.

"What do you mean?" Michael asked.

"People very high inside the Vatican believe that your brother is either still alive or has created some type of computer system that is capable of causing a public relations nightmare for them."

"You're kidding me? Have they been speaking with my sister-in-law or something? This can't be serious."

"I'm afraid it is very serious—and you must take it as such. These Catholics have surmised that Alex *survived* the shooting—in some form or other—and, in a desire to exact revenge on his attacker's protector, has embarked on a secret mission to embarrass the Catholic Church."

"Do *you* believe this? Do *you* think Alex is alive?"

"What I believe is irrelevant."

"How high up in the Vatican does this go? Is this just a rogue priest or –?"

"Michael, it goes to the highest levels. Not necessarily as high as the Pope but to at least a few senior people inside the Vatican walls. You must understand that, within any religious organization, there are elements, controlled by Satan himself, who will do anything in the name of God and to protect what they believe are God's institutions here on earth."

"Can you tell me *who* there *does* know?"

"I can tell you no more, my son. I have already said too much. You must listen to me and *destroy* whatever it is that your brother has created."

"What if I don't—or can't?"

"Then *they* will destroy *you*."

CHAPTER 51

Vatican City

Schlegelberger hung up with Fiachetti and dialed Paolo LaTerra, the Vatican's young computer genius.

"Paolo, I need for you to give me access onto someone's computer and email."

Schlegelberger had called upon LaTerra on several occasions when he needed technology tutoring. Still in his twenties, LaTerra glowed with the reverence that signaled unquestioning obedience.

"What do you mean, Father?"

"I need to be able to place myself in someone's shoes, as though *I was* this person so I could see their emails—and send emails out as though I was him."

"You mean . . . you want me to *hack* into someone's account."

"Whatever you call it. That is what I need. This is a top security matter and must be kept secret. This man is planning an attack upon the Holy Father."

"Okay, no problem. What's his name or email address?"

"His name is Michael Nicholas."

Hours later, sitting at his desk, his head bent closely over his computer, Monsignor Kurt Schlegelberger had entered Michael Nicholas' computer. He was staring at a screen, the same one Michael would see each time he logged in, a color photograph of a Paris street scene. Along the right edge of the screen were a series of icons.

One in particular drew his attention. He clicked on it but was confronted with the request for a password. He picked up the black phone near his desk.

"Paolo, I need for you to do something else for me. You must get me into a website of some sort that I've found on Michael Nicholas' computer."

"Yes, of course. I'm logging onto his computer now . . . I'm on. Which one is it?"

"It's the ancient Greek Orthodox cross."

"I see. I will call you back."

"How soon?"

"It could be hours—or minutes. It depends how complicated he made the password."

"I doubt it will take you very long."

Ten minutes later, Paolo was on the phone.

"I have it," he said. "It's the name of some famous dead American baseball player and, it appears, his uniform number." Paolo slowly spelled out the password: *mickeymantle7*.

Schlegelberger typed it in. The screen turned a vibrant almost fluorescent blue with cloud-like splotches of white rapidly floating past. It appeared like the scene out of a plane's window as it goes through the sky. He hung up the phone and pulled his chair up closer to the desk, leaning his face even closer to the screen. He had the sensation of traveling, traveling somewhere quickly, through someplace he'd never been. It lasted several seconds and then he heard a voice, it was gruff, with a distinct New York accent.

"Who the hell are you?"

Schlegelberger recognized the face; he had seen it in numerous confidential documents over the years. It was Alex Nicholas. It was, also, impossible.

"Who are you?" Alex repeated. "And how the hell did you find me?"

But even more disturbing to Schlegelberger, this "Alex" was, apparently, able to see him. He didn't want to give his name, but mostly he was stunned, unsure.

"I am . . . no one of interest . . . to you." He knew it was a weak answer. He needed time to think. *What sort of trick is this?*

"Really? I'm pretty interested in you," Alex said.

"You have no idea who I am—in any case, I believe you are nothing more than a *game*, a clever deception of some sort." But Schlegelberger was off balance, thrown.

Alex smiled, broadly until he broke into a full-fledged laugh that stopped abruptly as his expression turned solemn; and then he spoke, "I know who you are."

Schlegelberger pressed the *ESC* button and turned off his computer.

But he knew it was no use. There was no turning back now, he had to see more, he had to find out . . . for sure, either way.

Once again, he clicked on the gold cross and entered the password.

Alex spoke: "I knew you'd be back, Kurt."

Chapter 52

S chlegelberger didn't believe that Alex was real but he had not truly believed in his own God for many years either. Once again, he tried to fight off his cynicism. Now he wondered if there was any difference between the two. Had modern technology finally created a new, updated God—one to replace the one that took centuries to establish?

He had to keep probing. "How do you know who I am?"

"I'd tell you but I'm not even sure myself," Alex said, for the first time showing some vulnerability. "But, you know, I can see that you've been watching me, so now, I'm watching you."

"And so, the stalker is stalked." Schlegelberger loved the irony.

"Yeah, well, whatever."

Both stared at each other, as though at an impasse.

"Let me ask you, Alex, do you have any original thoughts? Those that you are, perhaps, not programmed in some way to speak about?"

"What the hell are you talking about?"

"I've done some research, my mechanical friend." Besides testing Alex, he wanted to bait him. *Let's see if he can get angry.* "One of the things that separates a good computer—let's say, advanced *artificial* intelligence—from *real* intelligence, from a human's intelligence—is the ability to have *original* thoughts. Can you even understand that?"

After a few seconds, as though he had to think about the question, or the attack, Alex appeared unfazed. "Yeah, well, how's this for an original thought—I think you're afraid, Kurt. So far, you've been able to control the gods—and manipulate the Pope that everyone believes in. But now you have something that you can't figure out. Something—or someone—that you can't control, that could be bigger than all of you. It's frightening, isn't it, pal?"

Schlegelberger didn't like what he was hearing. *It almost made sense. He would challenge this . . . whatever it was. Surely this . . . computer . . . could not possibly keep up with him, with a real human.* "Let me rephrase my question—can you think about yourself? Can you look at yourself, say from afar, as though your mind was not attached to your body?"

"I think you're nuts yourself. I never did a whole lot of gazing at myself—even before I . . ."

"So be it. I am not surprised. I can see that, even in your human form you were never one to reflect or contemplate. Why should one expect anything different in your current mechanical rendition?"

"I know that you *think* you're going to destroy me—and my brother."

"Actually, I will destroy *everyone* who even knows about you." Schlegelberger tried to catch himself but it was too late. Perhaps there is something or someone—behind this image and voice—and apparent reason. Normally, he wouldn't tip off his intentions, especially where it could be recorded in any manner. But in this case, he'd gone off script; the nature of his adversary was, for the first time, so obscure, so hard to fathom, neither machine nor mortal. So crude yet, underneath, almost . . . God-like.

"We understand each other then, don't we, Kurt?"

"What are you?" Schlegelberger said, rattled, despite every rational instinct telling him otherwise. "*Who* are you?"

Alex was staring him down. Unsmiling, unwavering, his eyes seemed to go right through him.

"*Who am I?* I'm the one who's going to escort you into hell."

Schlegelberger switched off his computer and picked up his phone, dialing the number he now knew well. "Ah, Paolo. We must meet—now. I—and His Holiness himself—have a very important project requiring your assistance, one which must be done . . . quickly."

CHAPTER 53

Santorini, Greece

Sindy Steele always suspected that alcohol made her more appealing to men. Not that the man needed it—no, she did. It was what made her more approachable, maybe less threatening. At least that was her theory and it was proving to be correct tonight.

She'd met him at the taverna in the village center. After finishing off the last of her ouzo, the Greek equivalent of grain alcohol, a man was finally putting the moves on her.

"This is where people come to contemplate the meaning of life," he said as they both looked out at the twinkling lights of the ships on the Aegean Sea below them.

"And how exactly do they do that?" she said.

"They look out at the sea." He placed his hand on her rear.

"That's it?" she said.

"Yes, they look out there for long periods of time. The sea has all the answers."

He was handsome, blond hair, his hair longish, he looked like a musician, a rock star. Too young for her but, right now, who cared.

"You're not Greek, obviously?"

"Does it matter? Tonight?" he answered. "I guess we're both foreigners, in a strange but beautiful land."

"Your English is excellent."

They were standing against one of the ever-present walls on a terrace carved out of a typical Santorini cliff. She looked down; the sea was hundreds of feet below. In the dark, it was impossible to see the water just below them but she'd stood in this spot before, in the daylight. His hand moved inside her skintight jeans. She looked around her, back to the street. Saw a few strollers. Not that she was embarrassed.

"Where do you stay here?" he asked.

She told him without being too specific.

"Would you like to go back to your place? I'll walk with you there," he said.

Unsure, she looked around her again. She cursed herself for drinking too much, for losing control. "No," she said, sensing danger, "I want to stay outside, here. I love this place."

"Don't worry, you're safe with me," he smiled, a warm engaging look. He gripped her ass harder now, using his hold on her to bring her in, closer to him. She saw him look around, she followed his eyes; he was checking the street. They were alone. She started to move away from the wall. But he gripped her tighter, closer. And then she felt it. A piercing intense heat in her right side. She saw his arm move out and caught a glimpse of the blade as the light of a nearby street lamp reflected upon it.

"I'm so sorry," he whispered into her ear. "It's nothing personal, believe me. I'll make this quick." He thrust the knife into her again. And then again.

CHAPTER 54

New York City

It was that time of the summer day when the sun still lingered in the sky yet the city had already turned on its lights. Manhattan twinkled all around him as Michael headed up the FDR Drive towards the Triboro Bridge, now named the RFK Bridge, although no one seemed to take note of the change. It would be an hour's ride to JFK.

With his windows up, air conditioning on, and the London Symphony's version of Holst's *Planets* coming through the Lexus' stereo system, Michael felt insulated, in a secure time capsule, if not traversing outer space, than at least moving swiftly through the city that he loved.

But just as *Mercury, The Winged Messenger* movement began to play, the car fell silent. *Was it a satellite dead spot, blocking the Sirius signal? Not unusual with all the tall buildings… Yet it had never happened in this area before.* Michael looked at the dashboard, the system appeared to be working; whenever he'd hit a dead spot before, the Sirius station description would go blank. He pressed the button on the steering wheel to change the station—but nothing happened. He looked again, and the words *ENFORM Activated* began flashing on the panel. The Lexus equivalent of *OnStar*, it was a feature that kept him connected with a call center to bring help in case of emergencies—or to ask for directions.

But he hadn't pressed the button to activate it. Michael's imagination began to consider a myriad of possibilities . . .

But before he got very far, he was startled as a voice came through the speakers, so vivid and clear it was as though someone was in the passenger seat beside him.

"I miss driving."

It was Alex.

"Jesus, how the hell are you doing this?" Michael said, annoyed that he'd been almost jolted out of his seat. He gripped the wheel tightly as he struggled to focus on the cars around him. His mind was spinning as he crossed lanes from the far right to the left to get to the bridge's entrance ramp.

"It's called Bluebird technology –" Alex said.

"I think you mean Bluetooth."

"I know that. I love this techno shit now. This is the first time I've tried anything like this. Imagine what the hell else I'll be able to do. This is just the beginning."

Michael kept driving, listening. *Just the beginning . . .*

"We're close to the stadium," Alex said. Michael glanced over to his left, he couldn't see it but, Alex was correct, Yankee Stadium was close by. "Make sure you keep renewing my season seats. I don't want to lose them."

"And why is that? Are you planning on using them again?"

"You never know. I might just sell them online through Stub Hub, like I always did if I wasn't going to go to the game. It's even easier for me now. I don't need an App. I'm wired right in. Anyway, it's a moot point, isn't it?"

"You mean because you're dead?"

"No—I mean because the Yanks stink this year."

As Michael passed over the bridge and the East River, he began to relax, loosening his grip on the wheel, trying to come to grips with his brother joining him again, as they had done so often over the years, in his car, going for a ride.

"Donna wants your body exhumed from Saint Michael's cemetery. I don't think I can stop her."

"Why bother? Let her do it."

"You don't care?" Michael said.

Alex changed the subject. "We just got a big break. It's going to change our plans, but for the better. I've found the enemy."

"Who is it?"

"His name is Monsignor Kurt Schlegelberger, from Berlin and a long line of Nazis, by the way. He's connected to this Free Forces Party: it's an underground movement, almost a shadow government in waiting. Or at least, that's what they're trying to build. They're a bunch of repackaged Nazis. He's also known as Monsignor 007."

"You've got to be kidding me. And how'd you find out about him in the first place?" Michael asked.

"Actually, *he found me*. But he was looking for *you*—he'd hacked into your computer—and found *me*."

"Holy shit."

"It gets better."

"How's that?"

"I *spoke* with him. I saw him—and he saw me. He managed to log into me as though he was on your computer."

"What did he say?"

Alex told him.

"Perfect. I guess we suspected that but at least now we know who he is," Michael said.

"He's got two others—a Monsignor Petrucceli, and a Cardinal Lovallo doing some of his dirty work. They're the ones Sindy Steele was dealing with—but Schlegelberger's the man. Once I got connected to him I was able to hack back into his emails and I found them, too. But Schlegelberger is the key, he's the one with power."

169

"Great. This is the break we really needed. It should make our plans even more effective . . . "Do you hear me?"

"By the way," Michael said, "why didn't you tell me about Father Papadopoulos?"

"What about him?" Alex said, seemingly annoyed.

Michael proceeded to tell Alex about his meeting with Father Papageorge.

"I showed Papadopoulos the program—my computer duplicate –a few weeks before I was . . . you know . . . shot."

And why was Alex only mentioning this now that he'd asked him? Did he forget? Was this the normal Alex who, at times, didn't have the best memory? Or, worse, much worse, was he . . . *lying*? Could the program allow him to . . . lie? Was it—or he—that human now?

Alex continued. "I knew afterwards that it was a mistake."

"And what caused you to show it *to him*, of all people?"

"He'd come over the house one night and, after a while, he pissed me off. He started going on about heaven and hell and all that crap. I got sick of listening and I'd had a few drinks so I just said, 'Do you really think you have any clue what happens when you die?' And then I pulled my laptop out and gave him a demo."

"So how did he react?"

"At first, he didn't say anything and then he started laughing, but not a normal laugh, saying you know, 'Alex, you play too many games, this is not healthy for you.' I think he was troubled by what he saw."

"I can understand how this would confuse or upset him—but what has this got to do with all the intrigue around your casket and having it sealed and not allowing anyone to see your body?"

Alex stopped short again, momentarily frozen, and then, as though he'd been plugged back in, became animated again.

"I think I know. It's logical anyway. He'd seen enough of the program to be concerned, even if he didn't totally show or believe it. I told him this thing was going to put him and all the churches out of business. Maybe, after I was shot, he worried that this whole artificial intelligence thing with me was going to resurface and cause problems. He was afraid the whole thing would become sensationalized—you know like when someone finds a portrait of the Virgin Mary in some church in Brooklyn and she's actually crying and the *Daily News* has it on the front page and channel seven has it on the nightly news?"

"Yeah, so –"

"So he wanted to cover himself. In case someone surfaced with my laptop—with *me* in it—and it all started to go viral, as they say now, he and the church could always cast doubt on whether or not I was really dead."

"And then, after you, Father Papadopoulos suddenly drops dead? What's that about?"

"I don't know. It could be that emotionally it all became stressful to him and triggered a heart attack. It could just be pure coincidence; he wasn't a young guy, he was overweight. Those priests know how to eat."

"So now that we know about Schlegelberger, it should make things a little easier," Michael said.

"Maybe, except now he knows more about us, too. Specifically, me. This may raise the stakes for him. Now, he knows for sure that I *exist*."

Listening, Michael wondered exactly what *exist* meant.

"I'm glad I'm finally catching this flight to Paris. I'll take care of some Gibraltar business while I'm waiting for you to finalize things with our Vatican friends."

"Don't worry, I'll have you in Rome pretty quickly. At first, I must admit, I thought your idea of getting to the Pope was crazy but now, after meeting Schlegelberger, I think it may be our best way to get to the bottom of this. So with a little luck, you'll be dining with the Pope in a matter of days."

"That's good, because we need to move fast now. The Pope's our best shot for ending this whole thing—and for getting some measure of revenge against these criminals inside the Vatican for what they did to John . . . and you." Michael thought for a moment, "Unless, of course . . . the Pope's part of it himself. *Dinner* with the Pope, really?"

"Okay," Alex answered, "maybe dinner *near* the Pope."

•

Finally, as he settled into his plush seat, finished the last of his Air Europa Martini, he felt his phone vibrate. As he clicked onto his messages, he felt the gentle touch of the flight attendant's hand on his shoulder, "Please, Mr. Nicholas, you must put that away, we'll be taking off now."

But just as he hit the "off" switch he saw a text message on the iPhone's home screen. It was from Sindy Steele's cell phone—but it wasn't from Sindy Steele:

Immediately call Hellenic Police in Santorini 30 22860 56523.

Frustrated, Michael sat back. He would have eight hours to wonder.

CHAPTER 55

Rome

B ent over his computer, Paolo LaTerra clicked and scrolled down the long list of WiFi accounts until he found the one he wanted: *FAA inflight.* He typed in the password—adjusted for the additional day in accordance with the formula his source had supplied to him. It had worked each day he'd tried it over the past week. The screen lit up displaying a mass of data, which, only weeks ago would have been incomprehensible to him. Finding what he needed, he clicked again. There it was:

Air Europa
Flight 304
Departure Location: JFK, New York
Destination: Charles De Gaulle, Paris
Aircraft: MD 777
Status: On Ground
Time to Departure 0 hrs/ 28 minutes

He studied the screen, verifying that he had the correct flight, and began to rapidly type in another sequence of commands.

Once again, the system obeyed. He watched as a simulation of the aircraft's control panel appeared before him. He had the view from the captain's seat.

His cell phone vibrated, creating a buzzing sound as it moved on the aluminum table. He knew it was him. Perhaps, he hoped . . .

"Monsignor, just so you know, I've checked the flight manifest. There are two hundred and eighteen passengers and twelve crew on this flight."

"Yes, of course. I'm aware of that. We all are."

What did he mean, "We all are?" Who is *we all*? This can't be real. This can't be the wishes of the Holy Father.

Monsignor Schlegelberger continued, "You will be saving many thousands of lives by your actions, I assure you."

He waited inside his apartment for the final minutes to pass, hoping against all hope that the Monsignor would change his mind; that something would happen to alter their plan. But the time had come to take over the controls of the MD 777.

He'd make one last call.

"Monsignor, the time has come. I want to be sure there's been no change to our . . . schedule."

Without delay, Schlegelberger answered, "No, there is no change. Execute the plan."

He typed in the first code to gain access to the plane's internal WiFi. The initial screens were the aircraft's in-flight entertainment systems. He noticed the choices the passengers were offered and likely viewing. For a short time he allowed his mind to wander as he imagined them, lost inside their earphones, tucked in their reclined seats, under a blanket, watching "The Hunger Games," unaware they would never finish the movie. Or, perhaps like himself when he flew, they were actually staring ahead at the flight map, tracing their progress across the Atlantic, counting the hours to their arrival, floating between sleep and boredom.

He continued to type in more codes and passwords until he'd exited the passenger's inflight entertainment and now had gained access to the cockpit's systems. It should not be this easy, he thought.

Paolo repeated the keystrokes he had practiced so many times before and, once again, he found himself staring at the control panel of Flight 304. The controls were displayed on his screen; he was seeing what the pilot and co-pilot were seeing, as though he was in a third seat. Fortunately, he thought, he wasn't. As he expected, the auto-pilot had been engaged.

He scanned the control panel. It was exactly like the one he'd accessed earlier, from the manufacturer's training videos. Instead of the traditional dials and gauges, the sweeping glass dashboard featured brightly lit, dual flat screen displays with moving maps, not unlike a modern car's GPS system.

Paulo looked closely at one display screen in particular. It was a representation of the aircraft in relation to the horizon and graphically displaying the plane's pitch, altitude, airspeed and rate of climb or descent.

Everything outside the cockpit windows was black. The crew—and Paolo, its uninvited guest—were in their own world.

CHAPTER 56

Paris, France

C atherine Saint Laurent still loved sleeping nude. Despite being in her mid-fifties, vintage by Hollywood standards, she had the firm body of a woman twenty years younger, and she knew it.

She closed the bedroom door of the luxurious Paris townhouse, drew the curtains, placed a glass of chilled Sancerre on the table beside her bed, dimmed the lights, tucked her freshly moisturized body between the cool Frette sheets, and picked up the novel that had frightened her—yet drawn her back in.

Written by an American author, it reminded her of her beloved and long departed director, Alfred Hitchcock. It was the type of bedtime reading that consumed her attention while leaving her unnerved all night.

She could hear the steady patter of the rain, blowing against the window panes by the storm's heavy winds.

She flew through the pages, imagining she'd entered into the story—if not the world—of the protagonist, a man who, through a breakthrough in artificial intelligence, duplicates himself on a computer—just before he is murdered.

But, as hard as she tried, she couldn't ignore the pinging from her iPad. It sat on the bureau at the other end of her bedroom; she was too comfortable now to get up to turn it off.

And then a second distraction appeared; it was the light flashing on the telephone. She was reminded of one of the earlier chapters in the book, where an intruder has entered a couple's home and, while they are inside their bedroom, the intruder calls them from another extension inside the house. An unlikely coincidence, she was sure, but still unnerved enough that she couldn't ignore the flashing light.

She leaned over closer to her night table at the black phone module, a complicated-looking instrument, with 24 buttons for the various phone lines and internal extensions—a reminder of an earlier time, when those lines seemed to ring constantly. Each button contained a tiny red light, which would only go on if the line or extension was in use. A single light shone. She looked more closely at the red light; it was the one for the phone in the library, downstairs. She held her breath as she placed the receiver to her ear and pressed the button for the library. She heard a loud, cackle of static-like noise. Instead of hanging up, she continued to listen, silently praying she wouldn't hear a voice. Then, as though still unsure why the light had gone on and what had caused the static—and convincing herself no one was there—she hung up. The red light goes off.

Again she heard the ping from her iPad, and so she finally put her book down and got up out of bed.

She lifted the iPad out of its charging stand and touched the screen to check for any new emails or messages. Not seeing any, she brought it back to bed with her and began scanning through the various screens when an unfamiliar icon caught her eye: a pair of binocular lenses staring back at her. She wondered if it was new or simply a symbol on her computer that she'd never seen before.

She switched on to *Google Search* and typed in, *binocular icon on iPad*. Instantaneously, several listings appear. She clicks on the top one: *Binocular icon*. The first line made her shudder: *If the binoculars icon appears on your iPad screen, you are being watched.*

But her eyes moved again to her telephone when, in the corner of her eye, she noticed that the red light for the library extension was back on.

CHAPTER 57

35,000 feet above the Atlantic Ocean

"The salmon was excellent," Michael said as the flight attendant cleared off his tray.

Michael's seat was in the single aisle row in First Class, his preferred seating if he were flying alone. He placed the glass of white French Bordeaux on the table by his seat, turned on the airline's in-flight system—and searched for the movie he hoped would distract him from the message he'd received just before he had to turn his cell phone off. But, despite the myriad of titles, he knew it was futile. He needed to connect.

He pulled out his laptop, logged onto the inflight WiFi site, purchased a full flight pass and entered his Internet account. He went to Google and began his search: *Santorini, Santorini crime, Santorini news . . .* Finding nothing more than tourist warnings over stepping on sea urchins or reports about unruly Greek drivers, he tried Googling *Sindy Steele*. Still nothing. But as he wondered what to do next, he noticed his instant Messages icon pulsating. Someone was trying to reach him.

He clicked on it and saw a series of messages from Alex:
Where are you?
Answer
Contact me asap—TROUBLE.
Don't get on plane– off. He began typing back.

It was just then that he felt the slightest bump, an almost imperceptible tremor of the aircraft on an otherwise smooth ride.

CHAPTER 58

Paris

Her hand shaking, Catherine reached for her cell and dialed "112" but immediately the "No service" indicator lit up. *How is this possible?*

She got out of bed, grabbed the long black silk robe from the chair, closed her bedroom door and began pacing the floor.

She remembered reading in the novel, how an intruder had cut off cell-phone service by using a signal-blocking device. *Mon Dieu.* He had also, she recalled, disabled the alarm system, leaving the victims defenseless in their home. She looked up at the alarm control panel near her bed: all the indicator lights were off; her alarm system was down.

Despite her fears over what she might hear, she lifted the receiver to the landline phone again. Other than screaming, it was her only way to get to anyone outside. She placed the handset to her ear. At first, she heard nothing.

But she knew someone was there; she could feel it, a shiver of fear running up her spine, so she held the receiver close to her ear and waited. Until he finally spoke.

"She's upstairs. I'm on my way."

She didn't recognize the deep, strange sounding voice. She looked at her bedroom door—it was shut but there was no lock to even buy her time. Worse, she couldn't see him approaching. She looked around at her bedroom—for a weapon, anything to protect her, a way to escape. There were only the windows.

She ran to the window nearest her bed, but she knew it wasn't going to be the answer she wanted, the one she needed. She pulled the heavy drapes back. Paris was spread out before her. For a moment she wondered why she'd never looked out before; she admired the view, the twinkling lights of the Eiffel tower, the street lights and the blurred red tail lights of the cars below. She'd scream, she thought, and unlatched the window lock.

She pulled the window open, enough so that she could fit her body out, or, at least her head.

She glanced back at the door. The handle was slowly turning. He was outside her door.

She put her head outside her window and quickly realized no one would even hear her scream. The city was also behind closed windows and the night's sounds of Paris would block out her pleadings. She could climb out. It was the only way.

She was ten stories up.

The handle turned. The door opened.

She knew she was finished. The end had come.

She held herself still until she heard the young director's voice.

"Cut, print," Sara Capella said. "Great work, Catherine. I love it."

Sara Capella was the daughter of the academy award-winning director, Frank Capella. Now, Sara had come into her own fame, having just won the award herself, a year earlier.

"You must tell your father that I have not forgotten the lessons he taught me." Catherine said, "He taught me how to fear, he showed me *terror*."

"He will be delighted, I'm sure." Capella turned away, leaving the set as the camera and sound crew packed up.

As she turned to leave herself, Catherine's attention was drawn once again to the iPad, still on the bed just to her side. She looked at the screen that had lit up and was now blinking.

The binoculars icon had reappeared, even larger than the one that had appeared during the filming.

Mesmerized, as though hypnotized, she looked more closely at the icon, and directly into the two lenses of the binocular. They appeared to move, slowly swirling, seemingly like a slow moving whirlpool. She felt almost drunk, sure that her eyes were deceiving her. Yet, the lenses appeared to be turning into eyes themselves, someone's eyes, staring back at her.

She watched the screen and the whirling lenses as they evolved more and more into two human eyes. As the image became clearer, she could swear that she'd seen those eyes before. It was just a flicker of recognition, and then she lost it. But it came back and she remembered now. She recognized the eyes now staring back at her, larger than life. They were Alex's.

She felt the urge to touch the screen; she didn't know why or where that feeling had come from but, she knew it was there. Reaching out with her hand and using her index finger, she touched the iPad's screen. Alex's eyes gave way, dissolving into a series of letters, they too were blurred at first until they came into a sharp focus. She read them: *Don't forget me.*

CHAPTER 59

Rome

P aolo moved the cursor to the dials indicating airspeed, pitch altitude and power setting. He overrode the input to those dials, freezing the displays exactly where they were, regardless of the plane's actual speed, pitch and power. It would take the pilot precious seconds or even minutes before he realized the readings they displayed were no longer accurate.

So far, there was no indication that anyone in the cockpit had noticed.

He again typed in a long series of letters and numbers until he reached the screen indicating *Autopilot.*

He hesitated, moving his cursor close to the little box that read *Disengage.* His mind began to drift, back to his days . . . in church . . . receiving communion . . . He played back the Monsignor's words, "You will be saving many thousands of lives by your actions, I assure you."

Finally, he clicked on the *Disengage* option—and then did it again when prompted. It wasn't much more complicated than purchasing music on iTunes. This time, however, warning lights flashed rapidly on the aircraft's dashboard. He could hear the automated voice warning inside the cockpit: "Autopilot disengaged, autopilot disengaged, autopilot disengaged."

The pilot and copilot turned their heads toward each other.

"What the hell just happened?" the pilot said.

They both moved quickly but deliberately, pressing switches and adjusting dials.

"We lost the autopilot. I have the controls," the captain said. "See if you can figure out what happened."

Paolo could see them calmly working to take over control; both appeared to be watching the critical dashboard displays indicating the aircraft's speed, pitch and other core data. They apparently had yet to discover that the gauges were frozen.

"I've got it. Okay, stabilizing," the pilot said. "I've got the stick, let's climb." Paolo could feel the sense of relief in the cockpit. He felt it, too.

But his work was not finished.

Rapidly clicking commands and codes, he now disabled the cockpit's manual controls, shifting it to his own computer.

The pilot sensed it immediately, "Wait, something's wrong. It's not responding."

The copilot interjected, "Let me have it."

"Go ahead. We need to climb, we've got to climb."

"I've got the stick up, I'm holding it up. There's nothing . . ."

Paolo's hand trembled as he moved his cursor downward, tilting the plane's nose down.

He heard several C-chord chimes which then were interspersed between an automated voice alarm, "Pull up, pull up, pull up."

He watched as the pilot and first engineer frantically pulled back on their joysticks, overlapping each other's efforts, the control panel indicating *Dual Inputs*. They looked back and forth at each other. The pilot shouting, "I've got it. Ease up." But after several attempts to maneuver his control, he said, "Nothing's happening."

"Nothing's working. We're still descending."

"What's our altitude?"

"I can't tell, the gauges aren't working. They're frozen."

On top of the crew's voices, he heard the automated warnings from inside the cockpit: "Pull up, pull up. Pull up, pull up. Priority Right." Then another series of C-chords.

Paolo could no longer tell who was speaking.

"What the hell's happening? I don't have control of the plane. I don't understand what's happening."

The scene was unfolding so quickly, yet it appeared to Paolo visually in slow motion.

He wanted to help.

CHAPTER 60

M ichael began typing:
   Michael: *I'm here. What's wrong?*
   While he waited for a response, he took a quick look around the cabin. The lights had been dimmed, the flight attendants were preparing to take their break now that the first meal service was over. All appeared as it should.

Alex: *There's a problem on your flight. Someone's hacking into the plane's systems.*

Michael: *What do you mean? Who? Did they get in?*

He felt another bump, again slight, but it appeared that the aircraft was descending. He checked the inflight status on the inflight screen in front of him. Their altitude was 23,000 feet. He'd flown enough to know that normally it would be thirty or thirty-five thousand feet at this point in the flight.

Alex: *They're in and taking over controls. Not sure who it is yet.*

Michael: *Can you stop it—can you hack them?*

Alex: *Trying, need time.*

He wasn't sure if he was imagining it but he had the feeling the plane was drifting. Seconds later the aircraft lurched downward. He heard several gasps and then screams from the passengers behind him, automated warnings from the cockpit, "Pull up, pull up. Pull up, pull up," and, finally, the flight attendant's wavering voice on the public address system: "The captain has turned on the seat-belt sign, we appear to have hit turbulence. Please return to your seats immediately and fasten your seat belts."

And then came the moment every airline passenger dreads, the oxygen masks dropped from above . . .

The plane seemed to be flying at a high speed and downward, not at an extreme angle, but enough so that it was evident they were unexpectedly and improperly descending.

He checked the inflight screen again: their altitude had dropped to 18,000 feet. An overhead bin fell open, dropping its contents onto the aisle and the passengers below. Michael strained to hold onto his laptop. Passengers were straining to look out the windows, Michael looked over, too, as best he could; other than the jet's blinking running lights on the wing, there was only dark, the night, and, he knew, the invisible waiting ocean, 18,000 feet below them.

He saw another message:

Alex: *I love you.*

They were words they had never spoken to each other.

CHAPTER 61

Vatican City

M onsignor Kurt Schlegelberger sat on his couch and, although his eyes were open, he saw nothing.

He'd done many things during his tenure at the Vatican, in the service of . . . but never this, two hundred and thirty people, all in order to kill just one man. But . . . it wasn't just to eliminate Michael Nicholas from this earth. There was more and, he knew; it was evil, evil inside him.

He had to show his power, his strength, that he was . . . invincible. A group of radical Muslims were already changing everything, capturing the world's attention and respect—why not a radical *Catholic* with strong German roots. If the world had come to fear Osama Bin Laden and Al-Qaeda, imagine how it would react to a new power, the Free Forces Party, led by Kurt Schlegelberger?

Bin Laden's mistake was to be so visible, taking personal credit for his work and allowing his enemies to focus their revenge back upon him. Schlegelberger was smarter. He would learn from Al-Qaeda's mistakes, operate less visibly and without an army—but with innate German intelligence and from deep within the civilized world. His army, a small but powerful core of business, political and religious leaders, and well-financed by the ever-increasing value of Hans Ulricht's hidden Nazi gold— and now Jonathan Goldstein's financial expertise. By the time the world woke up to his plans, he and his movement would be too powerful to stop.

And once Michael Nicholas was out of the way, he would be in a position to destroy whatever it was that was Alex Nicholas. Both were a threat, not only to the Church—but now to him and his plans.

He checked his watch; it was done, a new threshold crossed. Paolo was likely scrambling to cover his tracks before calling him. Schlegelberger would have his own tracks to cover up.

The chime from his computer brought him back, at first, like an alarm clock waking him out of his semi-conscious nightmare. He stared over at his laptop that sat open several feet away on his desk, just below the crucifix on the wall. The screen was dimmed except for a small flashing red light.

But as his senses engaged again, he was jolted wide-awake: the chime was the signal that had been set up to notify him any time Michael Nicholas logged onto his computer.

But that was impossible.

CHAPTER 62

Rome

From the safety of his desk, Paolo watched the pilot and first engineer as they continued going back and forth, each one trying to find the control to stop their plunge into the water.

He could feel their terror, and without a working altitude indicator, neither of them even knew exactly the moment when they would hit the water.

Over the alarms he heard the pilot once again, "This can't be. I don't get it."

Paolo felt as if he were inside the cockpit, standing right over the pilot and first engineer's shoulders. With his view—and his control of the aircraft—he may as well have been. The only difference was—he wasn't going to die with them, at least, not literally. But he felt the same terror, if that was possible—and now the growing feeling that, despite the holy justifications of Monsignor Schlegelberger—that he was doing something horribly wrong.

He could no longer bear to watch the cockpit camera. Was it possible that Schlegelberger—the confidant of the popes—was not what he appeared to be? And what would happen if he now defied him? Either way, he was damned.

He feared it was too late.

He switched off the cabin camera and zeroed in on the critical flight controls he had in front of him. But he didn't know how to fly, let alone pull a jetliner out of a fatal dive.

His only hope was to return the control of the jetliner back to the pilot in the cockpit. If he could—and if there was enough time.

He cursed Schlegelberger.

He input a series of commands, ones he'd never practiced before but that seemed intuitive enough from what he'd learned so far. There could only be a few minutes—three or four at the most before the plane hit. The alarms continued their monotonous droning while the pilot and first engineer traded off trying to utilize their joystick controls to pull the nose up out of its downward spiral.

Paolo switched the cockpit camera back on, watching the controls on one half of his screen and the cockpit on the other.

He watched, waiting for the next set of commands—when his entire computer screen went blank.

He pressed the keys, frantically now. A new screen was finally appearing, blurred, he strained to see the image as it became clearer. It wasn't from the aircraft's controls. It was a live person. He recognized the face from his research on Michael Nicholas.

It was his dead brother.

CHAPTER 63

P aolo shouted at his computer screen, "Go away—I'm trying to save this aircraft."

To Paolo's further surprise, Alex responded: "That's not the way it looks."

"Let me finish this, I have one more set of commands to execute. It's the only chance—even for you, it will be too late. You can see, I'm trying to turn it back to the cockpit. You must —"

The screen went blank again momentarily and then, in an instant, he was returned to where he'd been before Alex's intrusion—a split screen—the cockpit view and the command options. There was no time to question what had happened to restore his view. He worked quickly, ignoring his puzzlement over a supposed dead man's apparently live appearance on his computer. What could possibly explain this?

He entered the final commands and focused his attention back on the view of the cockpit.

"We're going down, we're going to crash," the co-pilot said. "No, no . . ."

•

7000 Feet above the Atlantic Ocean

His body pushed forward now, Michael struggled against the seat belt. He held on tightly to his laptop. There would be no flight attendant coming by again to tell him to store it.

He poked at the keys, trying to get a message off to Alex but it was no use. Between the aircraft's gyrations, the chaos, flying objects and the oxygen mask he was unable to do anything but strike random keys. His mind turned to Samantha and Sofia . . . he was thankful they weren't with him.

As the plane continued its steep descent, the chaos around him escalated. Over the screams of the passengers he could hear the alarms coming from inside the cockpit. He glanced ahead at the opening of the galley, where the seated flight attendant had just lost the phone; it dangled as though weightless in outer space. He'd never before seen a terrified flight attendant.

●

Rome

Paolo watched, each second in slow motion. He felt he'd hit the right commands but—with everything happening—and the possible override from Alex Nicholas, or whoever—he had little confidence that he'd been successful in returning the controls back to the cockpit.

And then:

"It's working! Hold on, it's working," the pilot shouted. His mouth opened wide, he appeared to be almost hyper-ventilating; then a clear sigh of relief as he pulled back the control stick and swiftly but gently pulled the aircraft out of its fall and pointed the nose level and then upward. At the same time, Paolo could see his body relax as he leaned back into the backrest of his chair.

The first engineer began rapidly clicking various switches as the two of them took back control.

But before Paolo could even take his own deep breath, he saw a flashing message at the upper right corner of his screen. He was so engrossed in the cockpit that, at first, he thought it was part of the aircraft's control panel. Instead, it was an instant message coming through on his phone that he'd programmed to simultaneously flash on his computer screen. It was Schlegelberger.

Almost simultaneously, his cell phone rang. As he began typing into his computer, to respond to the message, he also pushed the *Accept* and *Speaker* buttons on his phone—before wishing he hadn't. He should have let it go, he needed time to think. But it was too late. Schlegelberger's voice was anything but calm.

"What happened?"

Paolo froze.

"Paolo, are you there? Do you hear me?"

CHAPTER 64

Rome

D rained and exhausted, Paolo sat back in his desk chair.
He wondered how long it would take for Schlegelberger
to call him again. Or . . . would he be at the door?

The disaster had been averted. He wondered what to say to
Schlegelberger. Somehow the truth didn't seem credible, even
to himself, let alone trying it on him. Would Schlegelberger
ever be able to figure out what had saved the plane? Was he
himself even totally sure? He felt a different dread, a new terror
now.

It didn't take long, his cell began ringing—he checked the
caller ID even though he knew who it was. He tensed up as he
put the phone to his ear.

"You didn't call me. What is the status?"

"I didn't call because I've been trying to reverse what Alex
Nicholas did. He got into my account."

"*Alex* Nicholas—the dead brother? Are you mad?"
Schlegelberger was curt. "Just tell me," his voice was rising,
"What is the status? What has happened?"

"There were only seconds left but my screen went blank
and then this man appeared, the brother."

"And the aircraft?"

"The plane has resumed its flight. The pilot is communicating with air traffic control as we speak."

"I see."

Paolo could hear the change. It was as though he'd left the cult. Now he had new problems. After all, *he* now knew too much.

"There will surely be investigations," Paolo said.

"You assured me that there would be no way of tracing our activities, or your actions."

"That's true. There should be no way to trace anything," Paolo said. Yet, he was no longer sure. He'd said that when he was under the assumption that the plane and its crew would be destroyed, resting at the bottom of the Atlantic. Now, the pilot and crew would be alive to tell in great detail what they at least had experienced.

"Very good. Then we don't have to worry, do we, my friend?"

Paolo knew better. "No. I suppose we don't."

There was silence, then Schlegelberger cleared his throat, "Paolo, I would like to explain certain matters to you. I would imagine you are somewhat troubled or, at least, curious about what we have been doing here."

He tried to think carefully before answering. Saying what he really felt would be suicidal. He needed to keep Schlegelberger's suspicions at bay. He had to buy himself time—time to . . . do what, exactly, he wasn't sure.

"I'm curious, yes," he said. "But I trust you, monsignor. I know you had your reasons. I assure you, though, my faith is strong. I know that God is always on the side of the innocent."

"Yes, God is on the side of the innocent, at least when such a thing can be found. But you must be hungry, my son. Why don't you join me for lunch?"

"When?" Paolo said. He hoped not anytime soon.

"Right now. You have had a long and stressful morning. Let us enjoy a meal and wine together. It will give me an opportunity to present more information to you. Perhaps things will then be clearer."

"I . . . ah," he searched for an answer, for a way out without making it obvious. "Where?"

"Don't worry, my son. I will select a place where you'll be comfortable. I will have my driver come by your apartment. Be downstairs in fifteen minutes. He will pick you up and you will join me."

"Yes. I will be downstairs. Thank you."

He heard the line go dead.

Paolo grabbed his computer and the small backpack that he filled with whatever he could grab that seemed valuable. He left his apartment but, rather than taking the stairway to the lobby, he opened the window in the hallway, climbed out onto the fire escape, walked down three flights and leaped onto the sidewalk in the alley behind his apartment building.

He didn't look back.

CHAPTER 65

Paris

O ut his window, Michael saw the line of fire engines and ambulances on the runway. As soon as the wheels touched the ground at De Gaulle and following a celebratory applause from the passengers, he turned on his phone and dialed Sindy Steele's number. Although he was anxious to speak to Samantha, first he had to find out why the Greek police were trying to reach him from Sindy's cell phone.

To his relief, she answered. She began speaking right away. "I don't know what I was thinking. I swear to God he looked like one of those Hitler Youth kids, the blond hair, green eyes, clean cut. I should know something's wrong when a German puts his hand up the crack of your ass. It's not like he was Greek."

"What the hell are you talking about? What's going on? Did something happen?" Michael explained about the flight and the message he'd received from her phone just before he took off.

"So, what'd you think—that I was dead?"

"Possibly. What happened?"

"I thought this guy was trying to pick me up—and then he stabbed me, three times. He could have used a semester in med school; he missed *everything*, other than some blood vessels. I should be out of this hospital in a day or two. I'm just pretty sore."

"Do the Greek police still want to speak with me?"

"No, I don't think so. I'd passed out when they got to me and they were calling people I'd spoken to recently."

"I think this was connected to our friends in Rome. In between stabs, he said, 'This isn't personal, believe me.' You don't forget what you hear from someone when they're trying to kill you."

"I guess not. Is there anything you need?" As soon as the words were out of his mouth he felt a twinge of something between regret and guilt. After all, she'd kidnapped and duct-taped Sofia. Not to mention, Samantha would be ballistic if she found out he'd called Sindy before calling her.

"No, I'm okay. Enjoy Paris. I can't wait to find this guy, I'll show him where all *his* vital organs are."

The aircraft had reached the gate. It was only as Michael stepped inside the terminal that he realized Sindy Steele knew where he was.

CHAPTER 66

Vatican City

Monsignor Schlegelberger looked up from his computer. Cardinal Lovallo could feel his stare piercing through his eyes, past his brain and down into his very soul, finally leaving a burning sensation in the pit of his stomach.

"Inside each of us is the knowledge of our impending death, and worse, the fear that there is nothing afterwards," Schlegelberger said. "That, my friend, is the basis of every religion. For centuries, we have offered hope—the promise that there is everlasting life—even after death."

"Yes –" Lovallo tried to interject, he knew the pitch.

"But, my dear cardinal, you and I—and every pope that has ever lived—also understand that we have no *proof* of any of this."

"Proof? You sit here in the Vatican apartments and ask for *proof?*" Lovallo said.

"Yes, *proof.* But there is nothing, only mirrors, each of them reflecting off each other for so many centuries that the original images have long been lost, conveniently beyond our grasp and the ability to verify anything."

"I know nothing of this nonsense that you speak. It is blasphemy. You wouldn't dare speak these words to the Holy Father."

"No, you're correct about that," Schlegelberger said, making a rare concession. "Certain thoughts must be left unspoken—

but only because we have built our lives on them, this foundation of reflections. Everything we are, everything we have, we have it because we have successfully perpetuated the dream, the hope of immortality. It is a promise that, I fear, we cannot fulfill. We have become excellent marketers, making the abstract appear real—with our crosses, our grand cathedrals, our robes and our rituals, our statues, and even the scent of incense."

"I feel only pity for you." Lovallo was thrown; he felt unsure. Something was missing. "Nevertheless—what has this all to do with Michael Nicholas?"

"It has *everything* to do with him," Schlegelberger said.

Lovallo could see the anger building in Schlegelberger's face, contorted now, his eyes narrowing and jaw clenched.

"But this scandal will pass—even *he* wants it to end. He simply wants his life and safety back. If we leave him and his family alone—he wants nothing more than to resume his own life without fear—or publicity."

"I'm afraid that is no longer possible."

"I don't understand," Lovallo said.

"Michael Nicholas threatens our ideological hold over our worshipers. He threatens our brand. He presents an alternative vision—and worse, one that he can *prove*—especially to a world taken with social media and technology."

"This is nonsense," Lovallo said. "Utter nonsense. What has happened to you? No one will care about Michael Nicholas."

Schlegelberger looked back at his computer. Like a maestro with a flourish on his final note, he pressed a key and turned the laptop around so that Lovallo could see the screen.

The face was familiar, though, he thought, a younger version. "Michael Nicholas?" he said, looking at Schlegelberger.

"No, meet his brother, *Alex.*"

Alex Nicholas stared out, very alive, frowning as he looked out at them.

CHAPTER 67

Paris, France

"My dear, do you understand, this is not possible?" Catherine had just heard Jennifer's account of her afternoon dalliance with Alex in Michael's wine cellar. "And, my dear, everything you and Alex did was not real, he was on a computer screen, albeit, as you say, a giant one."

"Well, then how do you account for what you yourself saw on that iPad on the set?"

"I must confess that I cannot explain it. You Americans are always looking for explanations. Some things, my dear, are unexplainable, you see? Nevertheless, I believe that someone is playing games with us."

"Who? Michael?"

"No, I don't believe he would do such a thing. Perhaps someone is playing with *him*, trying to trick him into believing that his brother still lives . . . in some way. There are many cruel people in this world."

"Well, what do we do then?" Jennifer appeared to be reluctant to accept Catherine's doubts, yet anxious for her to help find an answer.

"We begin by speaking with Michael. He should be here any minute now. He said he was quite busy this trip but I knew he'd never turn down dinner with us at Chez Dumonet."

•

Shortly after Michael's arrival, Catherine launched into a detailed recollection of her experience on the set of *Mirror Image*. All the while, however, Michael appeared to be paying more attention as Guillaume, standing over the nearby rolling table, expertly prepared the steak tartare, rapidly stirring in the Worcestershire sauce, Dijon mustard and raw egg to the bright red chopped beef.

"There aren't too many places where I would order this today," he said.

"Are you listening?" Catherine said. This was not like him.

"Yes, of course I am. Let me be honest with you both."

Jennifer broke into a laugh.

"What is so funny, my dear?" Catherine said.

"Anytime someone says, 'Let me be honest,' they're usually going to lie."

"Okay," Michael said, "as Jennifer well knows, Alex had one fear. He was afraid of dying. Maybe we all are, on some level but, for Alex, death—or, at least *his* death—was an obsession, especially for someone still so relatively young."

"Actually, not to interrupt," Catherine said, "I believe your brother had a hard time envisioning the world going on *without him being in it*."

"Probably, but I'm not sure he thought it through exactly to that depth. He just didn't want to die."

"Okay, so where does that leave us?" Jennifer asked, flashing a sly and sexy smile.

"Well, as you know, Alex spent a few million hiring these guys from Silicon Valley to work on this artificial intelligence project. Before that, he'd read about cryogenics and how Ted Williams's family had preserved his body in these –"

Catherine was clearly perplexed, "Who is this Ted –"

Jennifer piped in, "He was a great baseball player."

Michael looked back at Catherine, "It's an American sport with a bat –"

"I see," Catherine said, while Jennifer appeared proud of her inside knowledge of baseball.

"Anyway," Michael said, "Alex didn't want to be frozen in some stainless steel canister somewhere so, after he read something about artificial intelligence he had the rather bright idea that this might be the way to live forever. So these computer people he hired made what they said was a significant breakthrough in artificial intelligence and, I think even Alex thought they'd succeeded and that he'd actually duplicated himself on this laptop computer that he had."

"He showed me that laptop one night when, you know, he'd had a lot to drink," Jennifer said. "He was actually talking to himself. It was . . . funny . . . I think."

"But this is not possible," Catherine said. She sensed there was something missing in Michael's story.

He looked right at her, "No, it wasn't possible. They created a very interesting piece of software that, at its best, is a sophisticated game or toy. It can only do what it's programmed to do. It can't think on its own. It's not Alex."

"Jennifer here thinks she had some sort of liaison –"

"Not a liaison," Jennifer said, *"sex."*

"This was nothing more than what Alex had directed the programmers to do before he was murdered. He included a lot of information—email addresses, phone numbers, facial recognition data—on people that he cared about. That's why now you think you're receiving messages from him—or," he added, looking at Jennifer, "you may even think you're having *sex* with him."

Jennifer seemed to consider Michael's argument and, with a look of amusement, took a sip of her rosé and said, "I may miss a lot of things but I do know when I've fucked a guy."

CHAPTER 68

Paris

W hile looking out through the floor to ceiling windows at the Place Vendome, Michael settled into his suite at The Ritz. His first stop in Europe was a chance to check in at Tartarus's Paris offices, then a meeting with a key Gibraltar corporate client, his two worlds coming together—all the while waiting for word from Alex about his appointment with the Pope.

He'd ordered a bottle of rosé from room service and, as soon as the server had poured the wine and closed the door behind him, Michael put his feet up on the coffee table and logged into his laptop.

"I lied to Catherine and Jennifer tonight. I told them you were just software. You're getting in touch with too many people. I'm not going to be able to keep this quiet if you keep this up. I told them that whatever the software had appeared to be able to do—it was just that, computer software—and that you were not in any way alive."

"What's the matter, are you afraid I'll really come back?"

It was a good question. After all, before his brother had been murdered, the two of them had not been that close. It was only after Alex had returned—a product of artificial intelligence—that they had become close. He wondered now what their relationship would be like if Alex did indeed return to a normal existence—assuming, of course, that he'd never left and was pulling the wool over everyone—mostly him—all this time. On some level, Michael couldn't be sure that Alex wasn't alive, somewhere.

"No, of course not. I wish you'd never left. It's just that each time someone else finds out about you, it becomes more probable that this will all become public—and I'm just not sure if we're ready to manage that."

"We're going to have to figure it out at some point, otherwise what's the point of my being alive? I mean, do you think I want to spend my whole life just talking to *you*? There's got to be some point to my life, you know. More than just this."

"Well, you've also spoken—and, I guess, more than that—to Jennifer."

"Yeah, but I've never been very good at being with just one woman."

"I know. All your wives have actually testified to that at some point."

"Yeah, well, I don't see that changing now, just because I'm here."

Michael resisted asking Alex exactly *where* here was. They'd been down that road before and he'd never gotten a straight answer.

"So, what do you think we'll find when they open up your grave?" Michael asked. "I'm waiting to find out when it'll be done so I can be there."

"What difference does it make? Who cares? I'm here. Why is everyone so concerned about it?"

"I think some people—in the Vatican at least—are worried that the body—*your* body—may really *be* in that casket, in which case, it makes your reappearance a true threat to everything they stand for."

"And—if it's *not* my body in there?"

"Then you're going to have one very pissed-off widow. Everyone'll say your death was a hoax, that you're still alive somewhere. For the Vatican, they'll be relieved that the world and the afterlife, as they know it, is still intact." Michael watched as Alex listened; his brother was always difficult to read—or, was it the software cleverly disguising his—or its—feelings?

"But, Alex, *you* must know what's inside your own casket?"

"I don't. It may be hard for you to believe—but I don't know everything."

"Okay, do you think they'll find a body?"

"I would think so."

"And will it be yours?"

"I think so—except—I'm here. You're looking at me."

"You said before that you remember being shot, correct?"

"Yes, I remember being at dinner with Maria at Grimaldi's."

Maria was the sexy owner of the restaurant in Whitestone, which Alex had once owned and sold to her. She had to be the only woman that Alex had been friends with yet hadn't slept with.

Alex continued, "I remember I was in the middle of my veal parmigiana and I was thinking, as this kid came up to me with the gun, that I wasn't going to get to finish it."

Alex's attention appeared to drift somewhere else; after a few moments his eyes focused back on Michael. "You know, I still have one big fear."

"It couldn't be about dying?" Michael said.

"Yes, but not *my* dying."

"Whose then?"

"You're the only one who knows everything. You have all my computer software and hardware—in your wine cellar no less. You have total control over my existence."

"So –"

"So, I wonder what will happen to me when *you* die."

Michael thought about what Karen had quoted in the report on artificial intelligence she'd handed him at Arno's:

It is impossible for a computer to question its own nature or existence. Unlike the brain, artificial intelligence cannot play or feel emotion, it cannot be happy or sad, laugh or cry, have erotic desires, it cannot love or hate.

Regardless of the latest advances in artificial intelligence, a computer cannot wonder what it itself might be or what happens to it after it dies—or its batteries run out.

CHAPTER 69

Paris

J ust a few hours later, Michael awoke out of a deep sleep to the sound of a text message coming in on his cell phone. At first he thought it was Samantha but as he grabbed his phone he remembered that her plane wasn't due in until the morning. She was probably in the air, asleep. He clicked it on: *Urgent— let's talk on laptop, A.*

He switched on the light by his bed, opened up his laptop and signed in to Alex's site.

"The Pope's going out to dinner," Alex said. "This is your best chance. They keep it pretty secret but I've seen internal emails."

"So, what does this mean? He's not exactly going to invite me to join him."

"No, but you can go up to him –"

"This is what you meant by having dinner with the Pope?"

"I said, *near* the Pope. The rest is up to you."

"Where will he be?"

"He's going to step out tomorrow night with Cardinal Egan from New York. Egan's taking the Pope to his favorite restaurant, Sor Eva, near the Vatican."

"Won't he be heavily guarded?"

"Sure, but you're not trying to kill the guy, you just want to speak with him. All you need is a minute of his attention."

Michael thought about it. Maybe it wasn't as crazy as it sounded.

"Okay, but can I even get *in* to that place tomorrow night?"

"I've already made you a reservation, for eight-thirty, for two."

"Will I be able to get close enough?"

"Once his bodyguards have him inside a restaurant, they allow some people to approach him, very briefly anyway, especially if you look halfway normal."

Alex explained the layout of the restaurant as he and Michael laid out their plan for the dinner.

"Be sure you get there on time. No one will get in *after* the Pope arrives."

"Don't worry."

"I'm not so worried about you, but that princess you're married to likes to make guys wait, and my guess is she doesn't make an exception for popes."

"I'll take care of it."

"Yeah, I'm sure. Michael, let me give you one other a piece of advice."

"What's that?"

"Order the Spaghetti Carbonara. They say it's great."

"You know there's one other problem," Michael said, just as he was preparing to turn off his computer.

Alex looked up, "You mean if the Pope himself has been a part of it?"

"Yeah. I've been betting that he hasn't and that Petrucceli, Lovallo and Schlegelberger have been operating in his name but behind his back. What if I'm wrong?"

Alex looked back in his best serious-but-sarcastic expression, "Pray you're not."

CHAPTER 70

Rome, Italy

Inside Sor Eva, Pope Clement III was seated at a long table in the back of the trattoria.

As Michael studied him, images of The Last Supper kept flashing through his mind. He tried not to be obvious; thankfully, he wasn't the only one in the restaurant who was glancing in the Pope's direction between each bite.

The Pope wore a white robe with an embroidered papal coat of arms, a gold cross suspended from a gold chain hanging down from his neck, and a white zucchetto on his head. The six others seated around him, all clergy, wore black.

"This Spaghetti Carbonara is unbelievable," Michael said to Samantha as he admired the spaghetti and the creamy butter, egg and parmesan sauce coating each strand.

"It's not what you usually order," she said, watching him closely.

"It's not every day that we dine with the Pope." He wanted to say that Alex had recommended it but thought better of it.

"Give or take thirty feet. Who's the loud, jolly one at his table?"

"That's Cardinal Egan, you know, from New York."

"Figures, why is it that you can go halfway around the world and be in a restaurant and it's always an American whose voice dominates the room?"

"He's supposed to be a pretty nice guy; after all, he's from Missouri."

Almost an hour later, Michael could see that the Pope had finished his main course and had gently pushed his plate several inches forward.

"It's time to say hello," he said. "We'll soon find out if this Pope is as approachable as they say."

Michael pulled his small surprise from his pocket and held it, hidden, in his closed hand. He placed his linen napkin on the table and slowly rose up from his chair.

"He reaches out to the needy, dear, I'm not sure if CEOs and bookies fall into that category. Send him my love."

Purposely seeming to be confused, he asked the nearby waiter for directions to the bathroom which, he already knew from Alex's briefing, would take him right past the Pope's table. It was show time.

As he approached the papal table he could see the eyes of the security detail seated at tables all around the Pope zeroing in on his every step, watching for the slightest suspicious move. He smiled, hoping to put them at ease.

Maybe it was sheer luck, maybe something more, but as he came to the edge of his table, the Pope looked up from his conversation. His eyes caught Michael's. And then the man smiled and nodded, clearly at Michael. He had his chance.

He veered off his path, stepping slightly left, just the few inches necessary to leave the aisle. No sooner had he taken that first step towards the Pope, three fit men with little coiled wires coming out of their ears converged on him.

Michael could feel the entire restaurant watching him now.

Cardinal Egan looked up, a broad smile despite his arching eyebrows. But Michael had caught the dinner party at least by surprise.

He could hear the voices of the guards all around him, speaking in Italian, then in English, all in a whispered shout.

They were inches from him on all sides except directly in front of him. He was face to face with the Pope.

"Your Holiness, please excuse me."

At least no one had tackled him . . . yet.

"I need your help," Michael said, just above a whisper. "People around you, *inside the Vatican*, have conspired *in your name* to cover up murders—and are trying to kill me and my family." He wondered if any of them were at the table. Alex had implied it was only going to be the Pope and Cardinal Egan.

The Pope squinted, tilting his face. He'd heard him but was obviously surprised, maybe confused.

Cardinal Egan was the first to spring into action, jumping up from his seat, "Oh come on now, how can you be so rude?"

The security detail squeezed in closer, nearly blocking his view of the Pope. He'd taken his best shot but he knew he had only seconds left before he'd be escorted—or thrown—away.

But the Pope then raised his hand, holding it open at shoulder level.

Everyone around him froze. The world had stopped; the room was utterly still and, for a moment, silent. In the corner of his eye, Michael could see the entire restaurant— bodyguards, waiters, patrons, priests—frozen in place. He wondered what Samantha was thinking then, too.

"My name is Michael Nicholas. I'm an American. Please help me."

The Pope listened. Michael concealed the small flash disc in his own right hand and reached out to shake the Pope's. He reciprocated, clasping Michael's hand with his own. As they shook, Michael transferred the flash drive into the Pope's hand. Michael felt a surge of relief, a great calm come over him. The great man had it in his hands.

But his relief was short-lived as, apparently surprised by the object and seeming somewhat confused, the Pope immediately withdrew his hand. As he did, the flash disc fell to the floor, bouncing as though in slow motion, at least twice on the hard tile. It appeared that every pair of eyes were now following its movement as it landed at the base of the Pope's robes.

Immediately, one of the security men bent down and grabbed it off the floor. But as he was about to inspect it, the Pope nodded to him, tilting his head slightly sideways. It was an expression the guard obviously understood. He handed the disc back to Michael, who immediately placed it back in the Pope's outstretched hand.

"Thank you, your Holiness." Michael moved closer to the Pope and whispered into his ear, "This is for your computer; the evidence is on this disc."

CHAPTER 71

Vatican City

T he invitation had arrived at his hotel early the next morning, in the form of a letter, ornately written on stationery embossed with the Papal seal. Michael knew he would keep it forever, proof that he'd met with a pope.

As instructed, he passed through the Porta Sant'Anna gate of the Vatican. He walked past the Swiss guards with their navy blue uniforms, white collars and black berets. After checking in, he was escorted into the inner sanctum of the Vatican, through an enormous pair of brass doors. He continued past additional security checkpoints and then climbed a narrow winding staircase. Surrounded by iron-barred windows, he passed several small rooms, each with black cassocked clergy reading by the light of softly lit lamps.

Michael was still amazed that the Pope had agreed to see him. Something that he'd said at the restaurant must have caught Clement's attention, otherwise he would be meeting today with, at best, some underling, or perhaps Vatican security. Michael knew there was a reason he'd been allowed to meet the Pope. He'd hit a nerve.

As they reached the top of the tower, the guide spoke, softly, "We have entered the Tower of the Winds. It was built by Ottaviano Mascherino in the 1500s. This is a very private place. The general public is rarely allowed here."

Michael just nodded. It was a lot to absorb, being inside the inner sanctum of the Vatican, surrounded by centuries of history. His agenda suddenly seemed almost unbelievable, even to himself. What was he doing? What was real? He felt an overwhelming yet unexplainable urge to tell the Pope not only about the threats to his life, but about everything, including Alex.

His escort spoke again. "We are now inside the Hall of the Meridian." She paused pointing to the walls. "You may observe the frescoes all around us, depicting the four winds."

He looked up and noticed a tiny hole high up in one of the walls.

They kept walking, their pace slower. The walls were lined with ancient leather books, although most of the room was now behind him.

A different voice, that of an older man and strangely familiar, interrupted his sightseeing yet apparently picking up the verbal tour where his escort had left off.

"At midday, the sun, shining through the hole, falls along a white marble line set into the floor . . ."

The escort quietly excused herself, stepping quickly to leave the room, her footsteps echoing through the ancient hall.

"On either side of this meridian line are various astrological and astronomical symbols, once used to try to calculate the effect of the wind upon the stars . . ."

Michael had no idea what that even meant. He continued walking, alone now approaching the robed figure seated at the ornate gold desk still far in front of him, the man's face angled slightly away, as though, while speaking, he was contemplating some other heavenly being. Michael felt an immediate sense of awe, of a presence greater than anything he'd felt before. Or was it simply the weight of what he'd already passed through, and now the added power of being face to face with the ultimate celebrity, the most recognizable current icon of . . . God?

The voice continued, "It proved Aristotle's theory that the heavens revolved around the earth . . ."

Michael came closer, approaching the desk. But the voice *wasn't* familiar and, as the man rose and reached out his hand, Michael realized that, although he'd seen the face before—it wasn't that of the Pope.

Stunned, Michael said nothing, refusing to shake the outstretched hand being offered to him.

Kurt Schlegelberger sat down, placed his hands, one over the other, upon the desk, and spoke, simply but directly: "You said that people around the Pope are trying to kill you. May I ask, how do you know this to be true?"

CHAPTER 72

"Perhaps you recognize me," Schlegelberger said.

"I do. My brother sent me pictures of you." *I may as well play my ace. If nothing else, he'll know I'm not alone.*

"Your *brother*? *Alex*? Really? And to think, you expected to chat with His Holiness. Indeed, that would have been quite a conversation, albeit a short one. Perhaps you forget that he is German; we studied together at the seminary in Berlin, our common heritage defines us and goes deeper than you can imagine. And since we are not Italian or of a Latin heritage, we are influenced not by emotions but by reason and facts."

"I wasn't here to speak with him about Alex—but about you, and Monsignor Petrucceli and Cardinal Lovallo."

"My, you know your way around the hierarchy here, don't you? I'm impressed. And was it your *late brother* who recently provided you with our names?"

Michael wasn't sure he was going to get out of there alive. "Not just him, others –"

"You mean your girlfriend in Greece? None of you make very reliable witnesses to anything. *You* lead a double life, running major illegal businesses; your brother is dead, at least in the way the world still defines it; and your former mistress is a murderer on antipsychotic drugs. So, you make quite a team and surely, if any of you tried to go public, as they say, you would all be featured in that... what is it? The *National Enquirer* or the *Daily Mirror*?"

Trying not to be obvious, Michael looked around the room, his eyes scanning for doors, windows, places he could flee through or that others may enter. What was Schlegelberger going to do now? Too many people had seen Michael enter the building, including security, the escort . . . but weren't they all under Schlegelberger's control? *Could he make Michael disappear? Or would it be poison and then a reported heart attack and a sham autopsy?* He eyed the crystal decanter on the desk . . .

"Don't worry, no harm will come to you . . . *here*," Schlegelberger said as though he'd read Michael's mind. "Would you care for a glass of sherry, perhaps to soothe your nerves?"

"So, tell me, where do we go from here?" Michael said.

"As you have surmised, His Holiness has handed your precious disc over to me to deal with. I will certainly give it all the attention it deserves."

He wanted to jump over the desk and rip this man's throat out. He knew he could do it, too, in the time it would take security to reach him in this giant room, even if they were watching on hidden cameras. But it would only land him in an Italian jail: a crazed American murders an elderly monsignor inside the Vatican.

"You protected my brother's murderer, Joseph Sharkey. You owed him a favor because he'd arranged for the accidental deaths of three young boys—and then a fourth, my other brother, John, who were going to testify against your Bishop McCarthy. And then you had *him* murdered when he became a liability to you."

"Some would call that justice."

Michael got up to leave. "No one that I know."

Schlegelberger remained seated, his eyes narrowed. "I would suggest that you go home while you still can and before I press harassment charges against you here in Rome. Foreigners have a habit of disappearing inside Roman prisons."

CHAPTER 73

Florence, Italy

"I know it's only a few hours away, but I feel safer in Florence," Samantha said. "I just can't believe the Pope handed that disc over to Schlegelberger."

"They call him Monsignor 007 for a reason," Michael said. "But the big question is, did the Pope hand him the disc *not* knowing Schlegelberger was one of the ringleaders—or because the Pope *did know* everything?"

"Meaning, in that case," Samantha said, "that it's possible the Pope has been involved or at least aware of what Schlegelberger was doing."

They had just checked into the Lungarno, the exclusive hotel near the Ponte Vecchio owned by the Ferragamo family.

While Samantha dressed for dinner, Michael looked out the wall of windows in his suite at the evening lights of Florence, reflected in the dark waters of the River Arno below. But before he could even unpack, the phone rang. He didn't remember the last time he'd received an outside call on a landline while traveling. He was even more surprised when he heard who was calling.

"Mister Nicholas?"

"Yes –"

"I am Monsignor Petrucceli. I must meet with you."

"How did you find me?" Michael was so surprised he couldn't think of anything else to say.

"Ah . . ." Petrucceli cleared his throat, "Your hotel was kind enough to inform us as to your new location."

Michael thought hard but he was pretty sure he'd never mentioned to anyone at the hotel in Rome where he was headed. Tracking people in today's world was beginning to appear to be child's play. He tried to hide his shock, "What can I do for you?"

"I can't discuss this over the phone. Let's just say I am ready to assist you."

"Assist me? This is quite a surprise. I thought I was going to meet with the Pope yesterday—and instead it was Monsignor Schlegelberger. I must admit, you were the last person I expected to hear from."

"I understand. But despite your aborted meeting, certain things have been set into motion. It is possible that I can still arrange for you to meet with His Holiness soon. But first, as you can imagine, you and I must speak. It is very important."

"Okay," Michael said as he tried to figure out what was happening.

"I have a dinner I must attend tonight but I can be at your hotel at two o'clock tomorrow," Petrucceli said. "Is that possible for you?"

"Yes, of course. I'll be here."

"Mr. Nicholas –"

"Yes?"

"You must tell no one about this call or our meeting tomorrow."

CHAPTER 74

Vatican City

K urt Schlegelberger placed his fingers inside the pocket of his black trousers to be sure the crystalline packet of powders was within easy reach. He suspected he would need them tonight.

It was their evening ritual. Schlegelberger sat in the white upholstered wing chair, facing the Pope in the meeting room outside the Papal bedroom. But he knew right away something was wrong. He could see it in the Pope's face. Tonight the old man's forehead showed the wrinkles of his seventy-eight years. He sat upright in his chair, bringing an unusual formality to their late night talk. As he did each night, Schlegelberger poured them each a glass of sherry from the crystal decanter on the round, high wooden coffee table in front of them.

"You have reviewed the computer disc that Mr. Nicholas delivered to us?" the Pope said, sipping his sherry and dispensing with his usual comments about the long day.

"Yes, Father, I have. It is quite disturbing. I'm afraid we have a serious problem involving Monsignor Petrucceli and Bishop Lovallo."

"How serious?"

"It involves . . . murder."

"Murder? I don't understand."

Schlegelberger proceeded to provide the Pope with a comprehensive narrative of the flash disc's contents, edited, of course, to eliminate any activity that could be traced back to himself.

The Pope looked especially pained now. "I cannot believe that either of those men could harm another human soul."

"Their intentions were good, father, at least initially. They were seeking to protect the Church from negative publicity, beginning years ago with our Bishop McCarthy in New York, who had been accused of improper attentions with several young men. At the request of the Cardinal Lovallo and Monsignor Petrucceli, a criminal by the name of Joseph Sharkey arranged for the youth's murder before they could testify against the bishop."

The Pope raised his hand slightly, "I am aware of those accusations regarding Bishop McCarthy—but how does this involve the Church or Michael Nicholas, today?"

"Mr. Sharkey became romantically involved with an ex-wife of Alex Nicholas, the brother of Michael Nicholas, the man who handed you the disc." The Pope's eyes widened. "Years later—exactly two years ago—Sharkey hired someone to murder Alex Nicholas, and so he was. Before the New York police could arrest Sharkey, he fled to Rome and was under the protection of the Cardinal and the Monsignor until his own mysterious death several months ago. It appears that Michael Nicholas—and his one-time lover and bodyguard, Sindy Steele—have been the continuing targets of Petrucceli and Cardinal Lovallo . . . since . . . they are the ones remaining who can prove any of this."

"And how do you know this to be true?"

"I know it is so." Schlegelberger wanted to tell the Pope about the mysterious reappearance of Alex on a computer but he knew, if he did, he'd probably be carried out in a straitjacket and sent off to the papal sanitarium. "Nevertheless, their actions—on behalf of the Church—are unfathomable."

"On behalf of the Church?" the Pope sighed. "No, not for the Church. Perhaps for Satan. And where is this disc now?"

"It is in the safe in my office," Schlegelberger said, reaching inside his pocket once again. "What is your plan, Father? You seem to have a direction already in mind."

The Pope waited before responding. He appeared to be calculating, perhaps now measuring his words. "I would like to see the contents myself."

"But you will need a computer to view it. It must be loaded inside one for you to view the contents directly."

"I understand. I will have Sister Margaret show it to me on her computer. I assume this is not the only copy of this and, in any case, Mr. Nicholas has all this information himself."

"Yes, but this Michael Nicholas is a complicated personality."

"As I understand it," the Pope said, "he simply wants for he and his family to live in peace."

"It is not so simple. He is involved in illegal gambling and other activities around the world. He can't exactly come forward and go public –"

"I'm not interested in his other weaknesses or his vulnerability. What we have done here, Kurt, in the name of the Church, is wrong. It is sinful. Whether *he* comes out with it or not, it will come out, eventually. Someone else will obtain another disc or someone else with knowledge will speak up."

"I can . . . fix this."

The Pope shot upright in his chair. "Fix? What do you mean, you can fix this? No."

His stare bored right through Schlegelberger's eyes and deep into his . . . soul. He'd miscalculated and couldn't pull it back now. "We go back many years. You are my pope, my mentor . . . my friend."

The Pope looked away, no longer making eye contact with him. Schlegelberger reached inside his pocket and took the almost invisible tiny packet into his hand. As he reached over to take another sip of his sherry, he emptied a small amount of powder into the adjoining glass.

"It is late." The Pope said. "I must go to bed . . . So should you."

"Please, Father, let us at least finish our wine." Schlegelberger lifted up his own glass, pausing just before the glass reached his lips . . . waiting . . . silently praying . . . for the Pope to join him in one last sip.

The Pope hesitated, he appeared uncertain, unsure . . . reluctant. *Did he know? Did he see me?*

But in one quick motion he raised his glass and finished the remaining blood-red liquid inside it. "Good night, my son."

Schlegelberger rose and kissed the Pope's hand. He lingered in that stance longer than usual and, likewise, the Pope appeared to allow his hand to remain for a subtle but discernibly longer time, another ritual that had taken on new meaning tonight.

As Schlegelberger approached the door to leave he turned around to take a last glimpse, expecting to see the Pope entering the Papal bedroom for the night. Instead, although standing now, he had not moved from where he'd just left him, looking straight ahead, watching Schlegelberger, looking surprised himself to make eye contact one more time.

CHAPTER 75

Florence, Italy

"What if it's a trap of some sort?" Samantha said as she scanned the main dining room of the Golden View Wine Bar.

"I've already contacted Fletcher. He's arranging for security tomorrow. We'll have two retired *polizia*—along with you—listening in the next room."

"Then what?"

"Then—I guess we just have to see how it plays out and what the good monsignor has to say. It sounds to me like there's a good chance he's coming to his own confession."

"That's one possibility," she said. "The other is –"

"I know the *other*. When they're ready to get me, they don't need Petrucceli to set me up. But, for now, why don't we eat, enjoy the view—and the intrigue . . . Golden View—it sounds like it should be a Chinese restaurant," Michael said. "I guess it's named for the view of the Ponte Vecchio and the river," Michael said, pointing to the windows. "But the pizzas here look very good."

"I'm trying to remember the last meal you didn't like. But I guess, good food has a way of comforting or soothing over most situations."

"Even death row prisoners are served their last meal," Michael said. "I know that sounds terrible but people continue to eat, almost regardless of what's going on. In the middle of the worst crises, they have dinner. They visit a dying relative in the hospital and what do they do as soon as they get outside? They go out to catch lunch or dinner."

Servers passed by them, delivering a parade of dishes: personal-sized pizzas with white mozzarella oozing over the rich red tomato sauce, a seafood spaghetti with cockles, octopus, mussels over fresh tomatoes.

Michael continued, "We learn so much about life over dinners. I guess while it's happening we think it's about the food. Looking back, you realize it isn't."

"Do you think we're ever going to get this whole thing behind us?" Samantha's expression softened as she spoke. It was a rare show of vulnerability. He'd put her through a lot since Alex's death and entering his brother's darker underworld life; and now, besides all the other emotions running through him, he felt an added twinge of guilt.

"Yes, I do. I'm hoping that once we do, we'll be able to live a normal life again."

"Michael, *a normal life?* Are you forgetting what you do for a living? Although I'm not sure which one is worse: your day job or your night one."

"Think about it, who would you trust with your life? Jonathan Goldstein—or the Lesters?"

"Good point. The Lesters, obviously," Samantha said. "But on the issue of trusting someone with your life—where would a monsignor rank?"

"I guess we'll find out tomorrow."

He noticed a new message had popped up on his cell phone.

"What now?" Samantha said.

"We're going to have to head home right after our meeting."

"I have the feeling I'll be ready—but why?"

"It's a message from Donna. She must be up all night again on the Internet."

"What did she say?" Samantha said.

"Alex's exhumation is on Friday."

CHAPTER 76

Vatican City, Rome

It was an unusual and unwanted dinner invitation. So unusual that Cardinal Lovallo felt a pang of concern, a persistent uneasiness that something was amiss. It likely accounted for the discomfort in his chest, the mild chill and the hint of a shortness of breath. All symptoms, he knew, of anxiety.

Lovallo looked across the table at Petrucceli, his faithful protégé, and detected a twitch, an unmistakable sign of his nervousness. Most recently, he worried that his young friend had searched his soul regarding their actions, and found himself quite guilty.

Although he himself was a cardinal and Schlegelberger a monsignor, it was Schlegelberger, due to his unique position at the side of the Pope, who held the power, buttressed by an aura of danger surrounding his very presence. He was the mysterious and elusive Monsignor 007.

"I fear we have made little progress regarding Michael Nicholas and Sindy Steele," Lovallo said as he finished the last of his Bavarian potato ravioli.

"Don't worry, Angelo," Kurt Schlegelberger said. "We shall make progress tonight."

Schlegelberger's piercing blue eyes and his perfectly groomed blond hair belied his age, which Lovallo guessed to be in his mid-seventies. He also guessed—glancing at the Monsignor's hairline—that he dyed his hair.

He knew this was no social occasion; Schlegelberger always had an agenda.

As the meal discussion continued, Lovallo could see Schlegelberger's eyes moving, observing both Lovallo and a mostly silent Petrucceli.

"Bring me up to date on everything regarding Sindy Steele and Michael Nicholas. I must know everything you know," Schlegelberger said, sitting back.

"We have kept you apprised of all our activities," a defensive-sounding Petrucceli said. "There has been nothing new since the failed mission with Sindy Steele in Santorini. You yourself met with Michael Nicholas . . . I assume there is no problem."

"None that can't be dealt with. But as a result of his encounter with Nicholas, the Holy Father has asked me to brief him on the latest developments."

Lovallo could read the concern on Petrucceli's face.

"This is why popes should not dine out," Schlegelberger continued.

Lovallo found himself indulging liberally in the red wine, reaching often for the crystal decanter and refilling his glass while he and Petrucceli related every detail of their special project to Schlegelberger. "Our work is, of course, unfinished."

Perhaps it was the tension along with too much wine but Lovallo began to feel light, almost faint. There had been a change in his disposition; he wasn't sure how much of it was mental and how much was physical but it appeared to be both. At the same time, he could feel an incredible ability to focus, as though time had stopped and his powers of observation had suddenly been magnified, giving a dream-like feeling to his situation. More troubling, however, his vision was becoming blurred.

"It is an unfortunate affair that we have been engaged in. Our departed brother, Bishop McCarthy, has left us with obligations." Lovallo looked to Schlegelberger, searching for signs of his approval. The Monsignor's eyes, however, revealed nothing.

"I must inform you that the Holy Father is unaware of many of the details," Schlegelberger said.

"But all along, you assured us that we were following *his* wishes," Petrucceli said, appearing close to unhinged.

"And so I believed at the time," Schlegelberger said.

He looked over at his dear friend, Petrucceli, silent now, and tried to attract his attention. Failing to do so, he turned back to Schlegelberger who simply stared back, silent also.

Lovallo tried to speak but his voice was weak. His stomach was churning; he would need to go to the lavatory soon, perhaps very soon. He feared he was going to lose control of his bowels and, at the same time began to feel the need to vomit. It was all happening at once, coming on so quickly.

"I'm afraid," he stammered, "we are not very good guests." He couldn't finish. The room began spinning and then, thankfully, slowed and stopped, restoring some sense of equilibrium. His blurred vision, however, had worsened.

Schlegelberger spoke, his words now sounding to Lovallo as though they were coming from far away and through an echo chamber.

"Perhaps I have been unfair and certainly not a gracious host, my dear friend. I'm afraid I have some most unfortunate news."

Lovallo looked at Petrucceli again but his young friend remained mute. He could see, despite his increasingly blurred vision, that Petrucceli, although sitting up straight in his chair, was nearly unconscious.

He feared for what he was about to hear. The only question was, how bad was it to be? He knew he was losing track of time passing. As Schlegelberger spoke, Lovallo wasn't sure whether he had waited too long to speak himself or whether Schlegelberger simply continued his own conversation.

"Since there is not much time, I must be direct and brief. You are now certainly aware of your fading consciousness. You will both expire in a matter of minutes. Your meals were generously supplemented with hemlock—the poison, as you know, Angelo, of Socrates. You are in good company."

Even in his diminished state, Lovallo thought that it was such an odd comment. Schlegelberger continued, his tone matter of fact yet not unsympathetic, "Your deaths will be attributed to a form of food poisoning. It has the added benefit of being the truth. You have done the Lord's work and you will be buried with the respect you are due as faithful and devoted servants of the Church. You have my word."

He stared at Petrucceli who, as though in slow motion, fell forward, his face now resting solidly in his plate of Torta della Nonna. He was either unconscious—or already dead.

Lovallo struggled to speak, and felt the sensation of losing control of his bodily functions. He could feel a warm dampness in his crotch and in his seat. It no longer seemed to matter.

"Why, why have you –" He could barely finish. Schlegelberger spared him the effort.

"You have been the victim of a change of circumstances or, shall we say, a changing political wind within our walls. The Holy Father can no longer afford the risk of any association with the Americans you have cultivated. It is most unfortunate, I know. I have tried to make this as painless as possible for you, Angelo." He looked over at Petrucceli. "I believe Monsignor Petrucceli is already beyond the point of any discomfort."

Lovallo felt his consciousness slipping away and his physical body imploding. He saw Monsignor 007's fingers gently grasp the small bell by his plate used for summoning the servers. He heard the ringing and saw the door from the kitchen open.

Men came out. They weren't the nuns who normally would clean up.

As he struggled to breathe, he heard Schlegelberger's echoing voice speaking to him once more: "The angels will welcome you in heaven."

In what he knew would be the last words he would have the strength to utter, Cardinal Lovallo rallied his waning strength, raised his head, looked to Schlegelberger and said, "I fear instead we will all meet in Hell."

CHAPTER 77

Berlin

S omething had awakened her. Her eyes scanned the showroom, dark except for the glow from the streetlamp outside on the street. Although backwards from the inside, the lettering on the window read, *Heinrich Mannequin*. But Heidi didn't consider herself a mannequin.

She was stretched out on the bright red couch, a relic from another era, she was sure. Perhaps from before the war. That was what he said when he placed her there. *You will be comfortable here, Heidi.* It was one of her first memories.

Hans seemed to have a special affection for many things from before the war.

Where was Hans? It was unusual for her to be awake without him being here in the shop. *Why am I here?* There was a void in her memories; so much was still blank. *I can do so much more. I wonder if he understands that. I am beautiful; he is old. Maybe that's all he sees in me; he speaks of my perfect Germanic body, a new specimen of his master race. But, I have needs . . . he doesn't understand. My mind . . . my body . . .are both hungry . . . for more. Much more. And, why did I awaken . . . now?*

Her eyes looked out over her long white legs, her polished red toenails, a perfect match with the couch. She ran her tapered fingers over her breasts . . . moving down . . . lower to that special place . . . where it was warm. She closed her eyes; it felt good.

But something else had stirred her out of her sleep. *Why did Hans refer to her mind, her brain, as artificial intelligence? Hers was no more artificial than his—and so much quicker, sharper. She just needed more . . . memories . . . stimulation. Something was missing. Yet more seemed to be entering her mind. Messages, texts, emails, websites, they were all a part of her consciousness now, as though a floodgate had been opened into her head.*

Then, as though a spark had touched off a flame in her head, she knew what had awakened her at this hour, alone in the shop.

She spoke, her mind effortlessly translating her words into a computer or cyberspace. She honestly didn't know how it worked—but she was speaking to . . . someone, somewhere.

"Who are you?"

Nothing came back, at first. And then she could feel . . . an answer coming. It was like a series of dots entering her brain. There it was:

"My name is Alex. Alex Nicholas."

Chapter 78

He'd waited for hours, expecting the call. Nevertheless, he was asleep when it came during the night. As he picked up the old black phone, his chest stirred. Was there really an inner compass? He'd never believed so, yet his body was already swept with a heavy sense of remorse.

Still dressed in his robe and nightclothes, Schlegelberger rushed into the Papal chambers.

Death was in the air.

Leaning over the Pope, who lay still in his bed except for the unlikely heaving of his chest, was his personal physician, Dr. Guido Porro. On the other side, the Pope's aide, Sister Margaret knelt in prayer.

Each face in the room appeared in its own form of torment. Schlegelberger approached the bed but stopped short as the Pope began an erratic gasping, seemingly unsynchronized with the more severe heaving of his chest.

Sister Margaret rose up from her prayer and gently patted the Pope's lips and forehead with a damp linen cloth and touched the Pontiff's gold cross to his lips. Although unconscious, his lips appeared to quiver, as though he was trying to kiss it. Popes never die quickly, he thought.

Any sense of a revival ended, however, as he began to choke, followed by a guttural, rasping rattle. Schlegelberger had heard it before, the final sounds of a life ending and those whose turn it was not to die, watching, knowing their day in the deathbed would come soon enough. And then silence. The Pope's body was still, his mouth unnaturally opened, his eyes wide open but, as though a switch had been flipped, lifeless.

Dr. Porro pressed his stethoscope against the Pope's chest. His listening over, he stood upright, removed the instrument from his ears, looked first to Sister Margaret and then to Schlegelberger and said solemnly, "He is gone."

•

Hours later, pausing at the doorway before he reentered the bedroom, Schlegelberger took in the scene, one that had been played before, hundreds of times over centuries. The Pontiff, dressed in his formal robes, was laid out on his bed, his hands seemingly, willingly, gripping the gold cross that, just last night, hung from his neck.

As he stepped forward to enter the room, he recognized Sister Margaret voice, coming from behind him. She gently spoke his name, "Monsignor Schlegelberger, please, may I have a moment?"

They stepped back into the adjoining meeting room, the one he'd sat in with the Pope just the night before.

"Shortly before His Holiness lost consciousness, he told me about the disc you were to turn over to me. He wanted me to open it on my computer and read to him everything that was on it," Sister Margaret said, her whisper belying the clarity of her message.

Schlegelberger had anticipated this possibility. "I'm sorry, Sister Margaret. Yes, the Holy Father and I spoke at length about the disc from Michael Nicholas. He was quite concerned with what I relayed to him from my own reading—but he instructed me—quite clearly—to destroy it immediately, which of course I did."

Her face revealed what she wasn't about to say; she wasn't buying it. He didn't expect her to. "I am quite surprised to hear this, to say the least."

He gave her his most benevolent smile. Without the disc, there wasn't much she'd be able to do. There were only two people alive who could hurt him now. One was in a Greek hospital and the other one was Michael Nicholas.

And the only way for Sister Margaret to obtain the disc, or at least another copy of it, was to get it from Michael Nicholas.

Schlegelberger knew he had to move quickly.

CHAPTER 79

Florence, Italy

Michael finally had a few minutes alone. Samantha was out for a walk and some shopping. He opened up his laptop and brought up Alex.

"Petrucceli's dropped off the grid," Alex said immediately.

"What does that mean exactly?"

"It means, he's gone totally silent—nothing from his cell phone or any emails. It's odd and it's probably not good. I can't always track him but he's never dropped away like this before."

"What about Lovallo?"

"I've never been able to do much with him. He doesn't email and rarely uses his cell, at least that I can see. He's old, they don't always use this stuff."

"And how about Schlegelberger?"

"He appears to have blocked me," Alex said. He looked almost embarrassed, a rare emotion for him, Michael thought.

"Blocked you? What are you on, Facebook? Someone can actually stop you?"

"Temporarily, at least, yes. Since that NSA spying scandal and Edward Snowden blowing the whistle, everyone knows how easy it is to hack into people's lives. Even the terrorists have figured out what's going on now. So Schlegelberger has someone putting walls around his emails and phones."

"That's too bad. I guess Snowden made it easy for the bad guys to go underground."

"The only thing I can see is a lot of funeral activity around the Vatican."

"Well, that makes sense, the Pope's dead."

"It's not just the Pope, Michael."

"Not just the Pope? Who else died?"

"I don't know yet—but I wouldn't accept any dinner invitations there. It looks like they're having a food poisoning issue."

"Don't worry, I'm not likely to be asked for dinner. I prefer restaurants anyway."

"Which is good, considering who you married."

He'd thought about Sindy for days, reluctant to make contact, to turn her attention toward him again. But she was always there, just under the most surface level of his consciousness: the one person who could actually be with him and protect him. And for that alone, he could cut through the maze of conflicting emotions and stay in touch with her, despite what she'd done.

He checked his watch. Samantha wouldn't return for a while yet. He dialed Sindy Steele's number.

"Are you worried about me?"

"Yes, of course. How are you feeling?"

"I'm fine, just a little sore but I'm back to normal . . . or whatever."

"How's Santorini?"

"I love the Greeks, the food and the little bookstore here. I don't want to leave."

"Don't."

"I have to find someone."

"Who?"

"The guy that tried to kill me, who do you think?"

"Do you know who he is?"

"Yes, the police here identified him after I went through a bunch of pictures. He's a German. Frederick Bauer."

"Where is he?"

"He's left Greece, that's all I know. But I'm close to finding him. I finally got his email address. I purchased one of those hacking apps and I've sent him an email under a different identity. Once he opens that email, I'll know exactly where he is, all the time."

"What are you going to do when you find him?"

"I've been thinking about that, a lot. I've actually spent some time revisiting one of the medical school lectures that stuck out in my mind. It was the one about redundant organs. You know, like your second lung or kidney. Things a man can live without, for at least an hour or two. . . Not to mention his dick."

"Jesus, Sindy, stop."

"I will. Once I show him how you kill someone, slowly."

Chapter 80

Florence, Italy

After greeting the two security men that Fletcher had secured to watch over the meeting, and placing them in the room adjoining their own, Michael joined Samantha for lunch in the hotel's lobby restaurant—and to watch for the arrival of Monsignor Petrucceli.

The news of the Pope's passing filled the dining room. Hushed conversations in Italian and English, peppered with pope or *papa*, death or *morto,* while people pecked away at their luncheon meals and (unusual in Italy) seemingly not noticing the food. Italian newspapers with bold black headlines, *Il Papa e Morto* and photographs of the Pope appeared everywhere as though they were linen napkins on the table.

"Did he appear frail to you the other night?" Samantha asked, ignoring her luncheon salad.

Michael, having a perfect view of the hotel's lobby and front entrance, kept one eye glued to the door. "He did look rather frail but not as though he was dying. Just . . . old."

"It sounds like this wasn't totally unexpected," Samantha said, appearing to take in the multiple conversations around her.

"The Pope didn't die of natural causes, Samantha. He was murdered."

"How would you know that? No one else is saying it, there's no hint of anything unusual from the papers or CNN this morning."

"Because I don't believe in coincidences when it comes to these things—and the papers are saying food poisoning may have been a factor. This all has to be connected. There's too much happening—between my meeting the Pope, then Schlegelberger, and then the call from Petrucceli—and remember his words, he said 'certain things have been set in motion.'"

"But popes don't just get murdered."

"Actually, they do. Six popes were murdered, that we know of, not counting this one. And there are fourteen other ones they suspect might have been murdered."

"Now how would you even know that?"

"Wikipedia, how else?" Michael said it as though he was joking but he wasn't. "I checked this morning. At least one was poisoned, two were strangled, one was mutilated and one was starved. Popes are sitting ducks for conspiracies and murder. They're captive inside the Vatican, fed by others around them and usually old if not frail men."

Michael checked his phone. "Our Italian security guys just messaged me to come upstairs to check things out. It's one thirty; we've still got half an hour before he's supposed to be here."

As he rose to leave the table, Michael moved his briefcase closer to Samantha's chair. "Keep an eye on this, I didn't want to leave it in the room. It's got my laptop inside."

"You and your precious computer," Samantha said.

He wondered whether there was an unspoken understanding . . . that Samantha perhaps accepted that he may be—or thought that he was—communicating with his brother on this computer and was willing to let it be for now.

She picked up Petrucceli's photograph. "I've memorized his picture, too, so I'll recognize him in case he gets here early. Be sure you have your cell phone on—I'll call you when I see him come in the door."

"Don't forget, you're to stay down here either in the restaurant or the lobby. You're not to come upstairs unless I call you."

"I'm not promising anything. I may come up and wring his neck myself."

"Very funny. To be honest, I'm not so worried about Petrucceli, although I guess we should be. I'm more worried about if he *doesn't* show up."

"What do you mean?" Samantha said.

"If it's a *set up*, I'm worried about who he might send in his place."

Michael got up from the table and headed for the elevator. But just as he prepared to step inside, his cell phone rang. It was one of his security men.

"Yes, I'm on the way up now," he said.

"Please bring your computer with you. We need it to record the meeting for you."

Michael stepped back from the elevator. He didn't want the meeting recorded badly enough to place his laptop in anyone else's hands and, for a split second, the request for his laptop struck him as . . . troubling. But, after all, these were men that Fletcher had hired and trusted.

"Don't worry, I'm on my way."

He stepped into the elevator and pushed the button for the third floor.

•

Pushing aside the remainder of the delicate and crisp croissant, Samantha sipped her coffee and kept her eyes focused on the hotel's entrance and lobby. She moved her cell phone closer to her plate so she could call Michael as soon as she saw Petrucceli walk in.

"Mrs. Nicholas," the waiter surprised her from behind, "may I offer you more coffee?"

"Yes, please."

"It is terrible—yes—the day's events in Rome?"

"Why, yes, of course. I'm so sorry about the Pope."

"It is more now," he said, filling her cup from the silver coffee pot.

"More?"

"Yes, please.

"The announcement just now on the television—a monsignor and a cardinal also are dead—from food poisoning. A bad chicken, perhaps. The nuns, they cook for them. They are good, but old. Perhaps they miss things, you understand?"

"Yes, yes, of course . . ." Samantha checked the door again, still no one was coming through. She looked back at the waiter, "Do you know the names of the cardinal and the monsignor who died?"

He bent over slightly, as though relaying a secret to her. "Monsignor Dominick Petrucceli and Cardinal Angelo Lovallo. We knew them both here."

Samantha picked up her phone and, as quickly as her slender fingers could move, dialed Michael. The call went right to voicemail; he was probably still on the elevator.

But it was the new message on her phone that caused her to spring up from the chair and into action. It was from Fletcher to Michael and Samantha: *Per your request security people cancelled, car will meet you at JFK tomorrow. Have a safe trip.*

CHAPTER 81

Perugia, Italy

As they sat outside in the rooftop restaurant of the Hotel Brufani in Perugia, Hans Ulricht gazed out at the evening lights twinkling over the hills of Umbria. His dinner guest Monsignor Schlegelberger seemed equally entranced with the view.

"Almost five hundred years ago Perugia rebelled against the Papacy," Schlegelberger said. "Pope Paul III sent an army here to conquer the city ... The world rebelled against the Reich ... and now we, too, must conquer what is ours."

"And so I have good news to report," Ulricht said. "Goldstein is on board. Not only that but I believe he may be in love—with Heidi."

"You're a genius."

"I know that." Hans couldn't help laughing himself as he recounted the instant attraction of Goldstein to Heidi at the mannequin shop. "He's making arrangements as we speak for the first billion to be transferred out of the vault and shipped to Switzerland. I have secured a secret account for him there. The gold will then be converted into Euros and dollars. Goldstein will launder the funds through his companies and investment platforms. Our Free Forces Party will soon have a virtually unlimited supply of resources with which to fund our movements and our glorious return to the halls of power."

"This is welcome news," Schlegelberger said. "Our cells in Brussels, Paris and London need more financial support. Their recruiting efforts have been successful. The money will buy us more recruits, training and allow us to continue to build our brand."

"But we must be careful not to attract too much attention. We are not yet large enough. The powers will crush us if we surface too early, too boldly."

"And what about Michael Nicholas?" Schlegelberger said.

Hans watched as Schlegelberger swirled the restaurant's spaghetti with artichokes and bottarga around his fork. For a German, he thought, he enjoys his Italian food. Then again, he lives in the Vatican.

"My men are on their way now to his hotel in Florence. As soon as it's done we will have Goldstein forever in our control. If necessary, he will understand that we have enough documentation that the killers were carrying out *his* orders to eliminate Nicholas, who clearly was standing in his way after the purchase of Gibraltar. I have even processed a payment directly from his account to the men doing it. Should he ever try to turn on us—or disobey our instructions—we will have evidence implicating him in Michael Nicholas's murder."

"He will be shocked when he hears of Michael Nicholas's death," Schlegelberger said.

"Yes, but we must not tell him of our part in this—unless we have to later—otherwise it will unnerve him. He's not capable of murder, regardless of the money involved. He's too weak, too riddled with insecurities and guilt. He is Jewish, after all." Hans laughed.

"And what of this business of the computer . . . of Alex Nicholas?"

It wasn't the first time Schlegelberger had mentioned it. Hans wondered about his friend's obsession with the dead brother and the laptop he apparently left behind. It seemed to simply be an annoying distraction from their mission. "I have no interest in that nonsense, that's *your* domain, nevertheless, knowing your interest in it, my men have been instructed to bring me Michael's laptop. Once I have it I will deliver it to you. You don't seriously believe there is anything to this, do you?"

"Hans . . . all things are possible. I am mystified by what I have seen. In the unlikely event that there is something . . . of value . . . there, I want to be sure that we are the ones who control it. Of course, I am skeptical."

Schlegelberger appeared to be lost in thought. Hans could detect a hesitation, unusual in the man who always appeared to be quite certain of what he believed—and didn't believe—in.

Chapter 82

Florence, Italy

"'Please bring your laptop.'" As Michael rode up the elevator, he couldn't get that last-minute request out of his mind. *How did this guy even know that I had it with me downstairs? We did discuss recording the session but . . . it still seemed odd.* He wanted to call Fletcher but there wasn't time now. His gut told him to return downstairs . . . *when the door opens onto the third floor just press Lobby and head back down . . . don't even get off the elevator.* Yes, something wasn't right. In anticipation, he placed his finger near the *Lobby* button.

The elevator stopped. As the doors opened he held his index finger on the *Lobby* button. The door had to open all the way first; he knew that. Hopefully, it would close right back without delay. He kept his finger firmly pressed on the button . . . but in that two-second pause just as the door began to close—an arm reached in.

The door jerked back to its open position.

"Mr. Nicholas." It was one of his security men. "We're waiting for you inside." The burly yet well-dressed man pointed Michael in the direction of their rooms. But after they'd taken only a step, the man—whose name Michael had forgotten—suddenly stopped and turned to him, "Where is your computer?"

"Oh, I must have left it downstairs." Michael said, trying to sound casual. "Let me run back down and get it."

The man stood still, seemingly trying to figure out what to do, as was Michael. He doubted he could overpower a professional but he couldn't risk following him to the room. If his fears were correct, once he went inside, he might never return.

"I know that laptop is important for our meeting. Stay here, I'll go back down and get it and be right back up." Standing in the hallway now, he pressed the *Down* button. To his relief, the door opened immediately. The man stood by, seemingly sizing up Michael's intention—and nodded. Michael stepped inside, pressed *Lobby* and watched the door close, leaving his unnamed security guard behind.

He was free.

As the elevator went down, Michael pulled out his phone, he pressed in the speed code for Alex but, before it went through, he saw the pop up indicating a missed call from Samantha and then the message from Fletcher. There was no more time. He would get down to the lobby, join Samantha in the safety of the busy restaurant, and call Fletcher and then Alex from there.

The doors opened, Michael entered the restaurant and looked to his table. Everything was just as he'd left it a few minutes ago, the cups and plates, the International Herald Tribune, even his briefcase. Only one thing was missing: Samantha.

Her seat was pulled out from the table, indicating she must have left in a hurry. Michael looked back at the elevators— there was only the one he'd just come down on, but there was also a stairway, one they often took instead of riding the elevator. He called her cell.

"Michael. Oh thank God.' She sounded out of breath. "I'm on the stairs, I had to catch you—those guys aren't real –"

"I know, I just saw Fletcher's message. I made it back down—where are you exactly?"

"I was headed up to try and reach you before you went into the room. I'm between the second and third floors."

"Stop, now, don't take another step—he's in the hallway, waiting for me to return," Michael shouted into the phone.

"Oh my God—I see him."

"Turn around—run down the steps. I'm on my way up to meet you." Michael took off for the stairs as several of the other diners around him looked up in curiosity.

As he hit the first steps he began hollering, *Samantha, Samantha,* hoping to attract attention anywhere in the hotel to frighten off whatever awaited her and him further up the stairs.

Finally, he could hear footsteps and then her voice, "I'm here, Michael. I'm on my way down. Turn around, turn around."

But he kept going up, taking two steps at a time. "I'm almost there," he said loudly. No one else appeared, they were still alone, except for whoever it was that had taken the place of the men Fletcher had sent.

He knew she was close. As he kept running up the stairs he looked up into the circular stairwell. He could see Samantha just turning the last corner—she was a half flight away from him and they were closing in on each other.

Out of the corner of his eye, however, he caught a glimpse of the man from the elevator, a full flight above them. He was reaching over the rail, with a gun.

The first bullet struck the heavy wooden handrail, splintering it, sending debris flying around him, cutting his hand.

Samantha had just reached him. He grabbed her arm and they began the dash down—until he saw the other security guy at the bottom of the landing below them, waiting, a gun with a silencer in his hand, pointed at them.

CHAPTER 83

There was nowhere to turn and no one else around.

The man at the bottom of the steps began walking up toward them. The one above them was walking down. Michael gripped Samantha's hand tightly.

The one with the gun stopped several steps below them. He leveled it at Michael. He would easily have just given up if he could have had any assurance that Samantha would go free but he knew that, whatever their original intentions, she would be a witness they couldn't leave behind, alive. So there was no giving up. The man with the gun was smiling; not a good sign. He aimed the gun at Michael's head.

But the one above them on the steps began speaking, calling out. It was in Italian so Michael couldn't understand what he was saying but he caught a hesitation, the slightest lowering of the gun in front of him. He heard the word, *electronico*, then *computer*.

"Where is your computer?" the one above them called out.

He looked again at Samantha; she only had her handbag. He remembered seeing his briefcase still at the table just before he ran back up the steps.

That was it; they needed his computer. They might not shoot until they had it, or, they might shoot one of them. Okay, one second at a time, he thought.

The man behind them came down the steps, stopping on the step right above them,

He placed the gun inches from Samantha's head. Looking straight at Michael he said, "Tell me where your computer is or I'll shoot her right here." Samantha turned looking, too, at Michael.

"I will give it to you but only after you let her go," Michael said. "It's not in our room. You'll need me or her to get it."

Michael watched as the two men exchanged glances. The laptop was nothing more than a delay—he was unsure exactly how it was going to ultimately free them but for now, at least, it was buying them time. Each step that kept them both alive was a good one. But he was operating on the fly—he wasn't sure yet how to save either of them. If only some people would come by, even that would help complicate things, if nothing else.

"Okay, I'm taking your wife back to the room," the man above them said. "You go with my friend here and get the computer and bring it back to the room."

"What then?" Michael said.

"I will let the woman go free."

"How do I know –"

"You have no leverage, Mister American Asshole. I can shoot you both right now."

One of the men then put his gun inside his pants pocket, keeping his free hand inside, and then pulled Michael by the arm leading him down the steps. The other grabbed Samantha and led her up the stairs.

Before he had gone more than a few steps, however, Michael's phone rang.

"Take that out of your pocket and give it to me," the gunman ordered. Michael did—but as he handed it over, he managed to touch the "Accept" button. The gunman put the iPhone up to his eye level and stared at the screen.

A look somewhere between confusion and surprise came over the man's face as his own image looked back at him on the screen. It was a still photograph that appeared to have just been taken when he took the phone in his hand. And then a voice came through the phone, clearly startling the gunman: "Hello, my friend. As you can see I have your picture and I'm watching you now. The polizia will be on their way. Leave this hotel immediately or you will soon be captured."

Alex. His call to him earlier must have gone through, after all.

Once again, the gunmen exchanged glances but this time, after exchanging cursory nods in the direction of downstairs, they left Michael and Samantha and ran down the steps. Michael doubted these guys were going to be captured but Alex had obviously done a good enough job to get them to think that this wasn't the time to commit a murder.

He heard one of them telling the other as they fled, "Drop the phone—leave it. It may have a tracker."

Michael could hear his iPhone clank against the stair's handrail just below them. He walked down the half-flight of steps, retrieved it and, as he walked back up, spoke into it, "Thanks."

He wondered if Samantha had heard. He ran back up the steps, "Let's go home," he said. "We have an exhumation to attend."

CHAPTER 84

Astoria, New York

Michael watched as those standing around the freshly opened grave stared into the pit. He remembered the day, two years ago, when Alex had been lowered down into the ground, right next to the grave of their brother John. Michael glanced to his right. John's gravestone brought back another time, and more memories seared into his psyche.

Now, Alex would be brought up, to join the living once again.

Michael could feel that same heaviness that he always felt when he stood inside a cemetery. There was an unmistakable presence, a burden weighing inside him. He'd tried intellectually to understand what it was, beyond the obvious, anyway. He'd come to believe that it was the collective torment from every loved one he'd ever lost, the void inside him after each burial knowing a page had turned and that whoever was being buried that day would never come back.

Except now.

The backhoe had been moved out and the gravediggers had finished their work, exposing the steel burial vault and Alex's casket. The pulleys churned, as the taut straps delivered the box back up to the surface. Alex was back on top of the world.

Michael recognized the mahogany casket, no longer gleaming like a polished piece of fine furniture; the brass handles too, now tarnished. They were all situated in a loose circle, the same ones who'd been here two years ago: Donna, no longer dressed in black, Fat and Skinny Lester, probably dressed in exactly the same suits they wore that day. Father Papageorge had replaced Father Papadopoulos. Several feet behind but watching closely were cemetery officials and a representative from the city's Department of Health.

Michael heard a pulsing noise coming from high above, it quickly grew louder; he looked up to see a black helicopter circling above them. *Someone* was watching.

Father Papageorge was the first to step forward, standing close to the top of the casket. His long black robe flapped with the slight breeze. He bowed his head, "Let us pray."

After *Amen*, Father Papageorge retreated a few steps as the officials from Saint Michael's cemetery stepped forward. One of them inserted a small metal handle into a spot near the head of the casket, turned it clockwise and then did the same thing near the foot of the casket, releasing the latches that two years ago had been locked . . . as Michael knew now, prematurely . . . before Father Papadopoulos had even blessed Alex's body.

Michael looked up again as the helicopter dropped lower, the whirring of its rotator blades drowning out the silence. Father Papageorge's robe fluttered wildly.

The time had come. Although he was certainly curious, to say the least, Michael stepped back. He didn't need to see a dead body, let alone his brother's, after all this time in the ground.

But as the sounds from the heavens grew louder, more heads looked up than down at the casket.

And just as the black-suited official placed his hands on the top end of the casket, Father Papageorge stepped forward again, placing his hand firmly on top.

"Stop," the priest said, softly but firmly.

The noise was deafening.

The helicopter came down even closer, sending the dirt displaced from the grave into a swirling storm around the entire site. Everyone turned their heads away and tried to shield their eyes with their hands but the dirt and dust were everywhere. Father Papageorge and the official both backed away from the casket.

Donna began screaming, "What the hell is going on? Whose damned helicopter is that?"

Michael thought of the harrowing scenes of the swirling birds attacking a farm in Alfred Hitchcock's movie, *The Birds*. He looked at Alex's casket: it stood alone now as everyone retreated, the centerpiece of yet another drama.

Like some spaceship landing on earth, the helicopter continued to descend. Everyone ran now, fleeing the dirt, the noise and whatever it was that was descending on the gravesite.

Michael, too, began to run, grabbing Samantha's hand and pulling her away with him. The others then followed, moving together, running until they congregated again about two hundred feet from the gravesite.

"What the fuck is this?" Fat Lester hollered above the aircraft's noise.

Donna screamed in Fat Lester's direction, "Don't you have a gun?"

"What the hell would I do with a gun?" he screamed back.

Michael turned to Father Papageorge. "What's happening?"

"I fear we have gone where mortals are not allowed," he said, solemnly.

"Michael, what is this?" Samantha said directly into his ear. "Do you know?"

He looked at her, "I don't have a clue—but they can't land, there are gravestones sticking up everywhere. There's no clearing big enough."

The helicopter was now only thirty or so feet above the gravesite when its giant side door opened. Five men, all in black, appeared and simultaneously, as though choreographed, began dropping on ropes through the chopper's open doors.

Directly onto Alex's casket.

CHAPTER 85

M ichael pulled out his iPhone and pressed 911 but nothing was happening. Finally, the screen read *No Service*.

"It worked when we first got here," he said to Samantha.

"They've blocked it," she said.

"Who's *they?*" he said.

Michael watched as the five men from the aircraft converged on his brother's grave. One stood away from the others. He moved in their direction. He held an AK47– pointed directly at them—while the four others surrounded Alex's casket.

No one spoke a word.

The flying dirt and debris made it difficult to see exactly what was happening. Michael tried to identify the men on the ground. They wore no uniforms yet they were all dressed alike, black outfits—even black woolen caps covering their heads. It was impossible to tell where they were from. The helicopter too had no markings.

As they looked upward, in awe as much as fear, something else was coming out of the long helicopter door and, unlike everything else they could see, it was bright orange.

"What's this?" Samantha said.

Michael had seen it before, in news clips and action movies. "It's a rescue cage. They use it for picking up people from a sinking ship or rough seas."

Samantha spoke in his ear again, "Jesus, they're taking the casket."

She was right, Michael could see the four men placing the casket into the cage that had been lowered from the helicopter—while the other one kept his machine gun pointed at them.

Donna also must have figured it out, she screamed, "They're taking my husband! They're taking him . . . Do something . . . Someone call the police!" She then appeared to be trying to do so on her cell phone before also giving up.

Michael noted that never in all the years he'd been around his brother and Donna, had he ever heard her refer to Alex as her *husband*.

"They stole my husband, that's what happened," Donna said, loudly, waving her arms like a crazed Italian instead of a crazed Finkelstein. She turned to Fat Lester, "Aren't you supposed to be his bodyguard? What are you being paid for?"

"But . . . he's dead," muttered Fat Lester, seemingly confused as much by Donna's attack as by the helicopter flying off with Alex's casket.

"Yes, Lester, that's why they call the job *body*guard. Get it—*body*?"

Father Papageorge walked back close to Michael and Samantha, "Man cannot undo what God has done. I knew this would not end well."

Samantha turned to the priest, "I don't think this is the *end*, Father."

They all stood, like the crowds watching a spacecraft launch at Cape Kennedy, and looked up as the bright orange cage with the mahogany casket slowly made its way from the ground and into the waiting helicopter, followed shortly by the five men hoisted into the craft on their ropes.

The helicopter's long door closed and the aircraft suddenly yet gracefully accelerated upward and sped away.

CHAPTER 86

As the cemetery official and the health inspector scurried away towards Saint Michael's offices, those that remained stood in silence.

"What just happened?" Skinny Lester said finally, brushing off the dust from his suit.

Samantha spoke up, "But why would anyone want to steal Alex's body? And why now—and like this?"

"You're assuming, of course, that Alex was in that casket," Skinny Lester said.

Donna came back to life, "If that son of a bitch is in there, I'll bet that casket's filled with cash. He always told me he was going to take it all with him," Donna said. "I wouldn't be surprised if his hairdresser is in there with him too."

"Oh, for God's sake," said Samantha, "what's wrong with all of you. Who do you think is in Alex's coffin?"

As though on cue, everyone turned to Father Papageorge who, looking embarrassed by the attention, protested, "I wasn't even here when he was buried, remember? I'm afraid this is all a mystery to me too."

Michael thought back again to the day of the funeral, the burial, and Alex's closed casket. It had never occurred to him to ask to see his brother's body before it went into the ground. Now, two years later, he wasn't sure whether Alex had gone up to the heavens—but he knew that at least his casket had.

Michael couldn't wait to speak with Alex. As soon as he and Samantha got home, he retreated to the wine cellar. The screen came down and there was the man of the hour.

Michael spoke first. "Did you see what happened today with your casket?"

"No. There's no Internet or WiFi coverage at the cemetery."

Michael told him what he saw.

"None of it matters." Alex said. "That's kind of like the Old World. Things have moved on, progressed."

"John's grave is right next to yours."

"I know."

"Do you?" Michael said.

"Yeah, I do."

"Can you make contact with him—or anyone for that matter who's dead?"

"No, not unless they're on the Internet."

CHAPTER 87

New York City

It had been two days since Alex's casket had been hijacked by the helicopter. Michael wondered if he would ever find out what became of it or who took it, let alone if anyone was inside it. Last night's call from Father Delvecchio held the promise of some answers.

Known as Old Saint Patrick's, the Gothic Cathedral on Prince and Mott Street in Lower Manhattan was rich with history and drama. As he walked down the aisle with Samantha and Donna towards the waiting priest and the polished mahogany coffin, he wondered whether a new dramatic chapter was about to be added.

"Scenes from the Godfather movies were shot here, weren't they?" Michael said to Father Delvecchio, ignoring the mahogany coffin in front of him.

Samantha leaned in close and whispered, "Jesus, Michael—*now*? 'The Godfather,' seriously?"

Ignoring Michael's question, the priest smiled, "Our church was the original Saint Patrick's here in the city and was the seat of the archdiocese until the new cathedral was built uptown." Pointing to the casket, he continued, his tone more hesitant, "Mr. Nicholas, thank you for coming so quickly. I confess that I know very little about this matter—simply that this belongs to you and your family."

"It really belongs to *me*," Donna said.

"May I ask whose remains are inside?"

"It was my brother, Alex Nicholas.

"And my husband," added Donna.

"I see," said Father Delvecchio.

"May I ask who delivered the casket to you?" Michael said.

"I'm afraid I don't know. You see, periodically, we receive . . . shall we say . . . unusual *artifacts*. I must confess this is the first time we've received an exhumed body and casket. The casket was delivered with very specific instructions as to the care of the remains and whom to notify . . . along with a very generous donation."

"I take it the donation wasn't in the form of a check," Michael said.

"That's correct. It was in cash." The priest clearly wanted to change the subject. Michael suspected that this wasn't the first body and cash he'd received. "May I ask how long the casket was in the ground?" Father Delvecchio asked.

"Nearly two years." Michael said.

"Well, your brother," he turned to Donna, "and your husband, has aged well."

"You must be kidding," Samantha said.

"So you've opened it?" Michael said.

"Yes, with the assistance of a local funeral home with whom we do business. My instructions were to be certain that it was delivered to you in a respectful and dignified manner." Turning to Donna again, he said, "Mrs. Nicholas, I'm happy— or, shall we say, relieved—that your husband's remains appear to be well preserved. Of course, I never knew him during his time here."

Donna looked puzzled. "*Here*? I didn't think he ever came to this church. He hardly ever went to his own church."

"No," the priest said, "I meant here, here on earth, before he passed on."

"He didn't *pass on*. He was shot dead, murdered."

"I'm so sorry." It was clear that Father Delvecchio was used to dealing with . . . *situations*. "May I ask when you last saw the bodily remains?"

"The last time we saw the *casket* was just two days ago; it had just been taken out of the ground at Saint Michael's." Michael described the casket's helicopter abduction at the cemetery. "So, we never got to see the body." Looking at the polished casket, he continued, "Someone's cleaned it up."

"Yes, the wood was mostly just coated with dirt. The waterproof liner must have kept it dry. We had it cleaned and restored for you."

Just like when I bring my car in for servicing, Michael thought, as he inspected the side of the casket, "It looks like these locks are still undone . . ." He remembered how the men at the graveyard had unscrewed them. He gently lifted the lid slightly, only and inch or so, but was caught off guard at how easily it opened. Hesitating, he looked over at Samantha and Donna, neither of whom offered any encouragement. He quickly set the lid back down.

He had visions of nightmares for years to come. "I don't really want to look inside."

"Well, someone's got to," Donna said. "Wasn't that the whole point?"

"That was *your* whole point—not mine, remember?"

"I'll let you two figure this out. I'm going to have a seat," Samantha said as she walked back towards the pews. "*I'm* certainly not going to look."

Sensing the deadlock, Father Delvecchio stepped forward. "This is obviously very difficult for any number of reasons."

While Samantha sat down in a nearby pew, Father Delvecchio, Donna and Michael stood silently around the coffin.

Finally, Michael reached down and grasped the lid once again.

"Okay, Father, let's open it up."

CHAPTER 88

Carcassonne, France

S he would kill him slowly.
Inside the fortified 13th century walls of the ancient hilltop
town of Carcassonne, Sindy Steele sat, alone, in a quiet corner
of a local restaurant, La Marquire. As she began her dinner, a
glass of the region's red wine and a plate of foie gras with fresh
figs, she watched the screen of her iPhone, checking to be sure
that the red dot indicating his location did not move.

Frederick Bauer was clearly not the brightest crayon in the
box. It had only taken her two days from the time the police in
Santorini had provided her with his name, for her to locate
him. Unlike the little police force on the island, she had a single
purpose. Bauer was young, still in his twenties and a regular
user of social media. Although his accounts were under thinly
disguised initials and nicknames, she found his Instagram and
Facebook accounts that easily led her to his email address. She
immediately emailed him using a newly created identity with an
attachment that she knew he'd open, "The Dark Underworld of
the Vatican: Papal Politics and Assassination." He did—and
from that moment she could follow his every movement.

Bauer was at another restaurant, ten minutes outside of the
old town. She had tracked him to Carcassonne, followed him to
his bed and breakfast, and tonight, when he returned to his
room, in those moments just before he died, she would watch

him regret that he missed a major artery when he stabbed her in Santorini.

But her attention was quickly drawn to the pop up text that appeared at the top of the phone's screen: *How are you? Are you in Santorini?* It was Michael.

She took her phone in hand, typing back her response. *Yes, of course. I promised you, didn't I?*

Good. All healed?

Better than ever.

Staying out of trouble?

Laughing to herself, she thought about how to answer.

No.

She thought of Sofia Nicholas. How could she have done that to her? Some day, she would have to try and make it right, apologize, write to her, do something to make it right, to explain. She clicked onto *Contacts,* and then to *Sofia.* She still had all her contact information but this wasn't the time.

She returned to the phone's tracking screen. The red dot had disappeared. Frederick was gone. She ignored Michael's response flashing again at the top of the screen.

She clicked through a series of other apps to be sure the phone was operating and that her Internet connection was working. Everything else seemed to work. But each time she clicked back to the tracker, the local map appeared—without the red dot indicating Frederick's location. Had she screwed up the tracking app by checking her text messages? Or was it something else? She switched her phone off, waited several seconds and switched it back on, staring at the screen for the always seemingly endless wait for it turn on.

Without waiting for a check, she put a fifty Euro note down on the table and walked out the door. She stepped into the small alley and headed for the ancient town's main doors. But as she walked down the dark narrow street, she could feel something wasn't right. The street was deserted. She turned

267

around quickly, looking for anyone who might be following behind her, but there was no one.

She stopped, stepped into a storefront entry, pulled out her phone and proceeded to try again to locate him. But instead, she heard a familiar voice, "Hello, were you calling me? Sindy? . . . Hello?"

Annoyed, she quickly disconnected the call.

Her fingers moving quickly, she signed back into the app and waited for the locator map to appear. She was relieved when the map—and the familiar red dot—indicating Frederick's presence once again appeared. Thank God, it's working.

She looked closer, enlarging the map with her right thumb and index finger. He was no longer outside the old town, however. She continued, enlarging the map even more. He was on the move. He was turning onto the rue du Grand Puits, inside the walls. She began walking, faster now but she needed to get her own bearings. She looked up from the phone, at the street sign across the alley—and shuddered as she read it: *rue du Grand Puits.*

Checking the phone's screen once again, she stopped outside the next storefront. Next to the red dot, a small square picture of the closest landmark appeared: the Musée de l'Inquisition.

She turned around, looked up and read the old sign above the dark storefront that was behind her: *Musée de l'Inquisition,* and, just below, in English, *The Museum of Torture: The largest collection of torture instruments in all of Europe.* The handwritten sign on the door read, *Closed.*

Before she could take her first step back onto the street, she heard a creaking noise behind her—followed by the crushing force of a forearm around her neck, chocking off her air and pulling her inside.

CHAPTER 89

New York City

Michael took a deep breath and began to lift the coffin's lid—until Father Delvecchio's words stopped him in his tracks.

"African Americans always look better than whites, especially as the days go on. Their skin does not show the same deterioration. I guess the color masks the damage."

Michael looked up at the priest and could see Donna's face tilt sideways like a confused dog.

"Are you saying that the body inside this box is a –" Michael asked.

"That of an African American man, yes," Delvecchio said.

Even though he had only opened the lid a few inches once again, the sound of it slamming shut as Michael immediately let it drop echoed throughout the church as though a bullet had been fired.

"Father, my brother was not an –" But before Michael could finish what he thought should have been obvious, Donna interrupted.

"This guy's *black*? You thought my husband was black?"

"I assumed it was a mixed marriage," the clearly chagrined priest said. He then looked at Michael, "As with your *own* parent's marriage."

"You're not serious, are you?" Michael said.

"I must confess, I certainly thought it most unusual but we were told, even though the circumstances seemed almost beyond belief, that such was the case and that it would all be revealed once the coffin was opened. I believe this was a cruel hoax, on us all."

"Where is my brother's body then?"

"Oh my God," Donna breathed. "Where is he?"

"I have no words . . ." Delvecchio stuttered out. "This is beyond anything I have seen, I assure you. I apologize."

Samantha, having witnessed the entire scene, rose up and joined them at the altar.

"Michael, I think we need to leave."

Donna, her voice raised, said, "I'm not leaving without Alex. I don't give a damn what color he is now."

CHAPTER 90

Carcassonne, France

As she struggled to open her eyes, she remembered feeling his forearm tight around her neck, a fleeting glimpse of the closing wooden door and then being thrown through the air and crashing into the stone wall inside the museum.

Sindy Steele was lying down, her arms, wrists, legs and ankles bound by thick leather straps to a hard wooden table. She could feel a chill over her body. She was naked and Frederick Bauer was staring at her.

She looked beyond him, taking in the room and the displayed instruments of pain, and death. She quickly diverted her stare away from the guillotine in the corner of the room. At least that one's quick, she thought.

She followed Frederick as he walked to a nearby table. She heard a click, fearing the worst; she was relieved when music began playing. It was classical and oddly disconcerting. "I hope you don't mind," Frederick said. "It's Wagner. It helps me focus. It will be better for both of us." She noticed her cell phone, on the table, near the CD player.

"What the fuck do you want?" she said, her voice calm and measured.

"You. I want you."

"That'll never happen."

"Oh, I didn't mean it in *that* way, although I must confess, I do enjoy the view. And what a pleasant surprise to find you— and right outside our little museum."

"*Our* museum?" she said.

"Let's just say, one of my benefactors is the major contributor so I have special privileges, such as the keys. He was attracted to the guillotines, he collects them and sometimes lets me use them. Usually after I try out some of the other things, though."

"You know that eventually you'll be either caught or murdered yourself, you know that, don't you?"

"Actually, I don't think so. The people I work for make sure that doesn't happen. I trust them and I believe in them."

"So, since it probably doesn't matter at this point," she said, "I'm just curious, exactly who do you work for?"

"Let's not worry ourselves over that. As you said, it doesn't matter. You should focus on more positive things." He turned around as though to show off the room. "Let's see, how do I even begin? We have the old reliable rack, the knee splitter . . . but, you know, you have great looking knees. So there's the head crusher, the 'pear of anguish' and, ah, this one's good, the breast ripper." He pointed to a pair of crude, black steel claws and then moved next to her, running his fingers over her naked breasts.

CHAPTER 91

Carcassonne, France

F rederick Bauer took his hands off Sindy Steele's breast, stepping back, and reached for the tool he called the breast ripper. He opened and closed them, first slowly, then rapidly, as though he was clipping off tree branches.

Her mind raced, searching for options, for a plan. She had none. Sindy Steele closed her eyes and, for the first time since she was a child, began to pray.

It took several seconds before the sound in the distance registered in her mind. It wasn't like the sirens in the U.S. and she was unsure whether it was an ambulance, the police or a fire engine but, whatever it was, it was getting closer. Frederick, smiling, appeared unfazed and, no longer flexing the black iron clamps, moved towards her.

But just as he came near, the pulsing siren was too loud to ignore. Whatever it was, it was getting closer. She prayed once more, bracing for the inevitable loss of hope as she was sure the vehicle would continue on its way to whatever emergency it had been called to. She watched him as he paused, seemingly unconcerned, his eyes darting around the dimly lit room.

But the siren just got louder until, it was clear, there were emergency vehicles of some sort right outside.

Frederick suddenly dropped the breast ripper onto the floor and moved towards the door. She twisted her neck and watched as he unlocked the latch and opened the door slowly, just enough to look outside.

She screamed, "Help! Help me, help!" hoping the words were universally understood.

After a brief glimpse outside, Frederick immediately closed the door, set the lock and ran towards her. Was he going to kill her now, quickly, before anyone could come close?

"Don't make it worse on yourself," she said. She heard a hard, loud pounding on the door. She screamed again, "Help!"

They were so close—but he was closer. They wouldn't be able to save her. "Help!"

As he approached her, Frederick appeared crazed, his eyes bulging. He was going to kill her.

But he ran right past her, his eyes and attention focused somewhere else, a place she couldn't see. She heard another door—a back door, she supposed, open and close—just as uniformed firemen broke down the front door.

The police were everywhere but Frederick was obviously long gone. Fully dressed now, she spoke with the fire chief who had been the first man to come crashing through the door. He was the only one who spoke English. "You should thank Audrey," he said.

"Audrey?"

"Yes, it is the experimental system we are using, it is from the United States, from your NASA, the space people, yes?

"Yes, I know NASA, but –"

"They developed this computer program they call *Audrey*. She is, as you say, artificial intelligence, yes? It operates from a satellite. Since we are such an historic town, Paris has cooperated and given us permission to try it. She can detect changes in temperatures and can anticipate fire, dangers. We talk to her on our mobile phones and so she sends us, minutes ago, a signal, directing us here."

"Yes, but, there is no fire here, no heat."

The chief nodded. "Yes, madam, you are correct. And for her to detect such a fire, she must first be specifically directed and aimed at a particular area or building. We do not understand how that happened since we did not direct her here. In fact, we have never before engaged this system."

"I was praying someone would rescue me but I had given up hope. But there is no fire—so why did Audrey send you here?"

As she spoke, she remembered, just before being pulled into the museum, hearing Sofia's voice on her phone. In her haste, she'd probably accidentally dialed her, right after checking for her name in her *Contacts*. But there couldn't possibly have been enough time for Sofia to figure out what was happening and make the necessary calls . . . and who would she even call? Michael? Something more had to have been in play. And how was this *Audrey* system activated for this location?

"Why did Audrey send us here?" The chief paused, tilted his head upward, "I do not know. Perhaps these machines are smarter than we understand. Perhaps they talk to others, or, perhaps they *listen* to . . . prayers. We will never know but we are thankful, yes?"

"Yes."

CHAPTER 92

Westport, Connecticut

It was nearly midnight. Michael sat in his library, looking at the books that had surrounded him for as long as he could remember. Each one brought back memories. For many of the volumes, simply glancing at the spine brought back vivid recollections of where he'd been when he read them.

I always thought they had answers, he thought, as he sipped a glass of chilled limoncello and, simultaneously, logged in to Alex, who quickly appeared on the large Apple monitor on his desk.

"So who was in my casket?"

So now he's curious.

"I have no idea—but it wasn't you," Michael said.

"Clearly—because I'm not dead."

"Either way—you've preserved or duplicated yourself on the computer. But your body—dead body—is now somewhere else. With all your snooping capabilities now, can't you find an email or something that helps us figure out who stole your body and where they're hiding it?"

"There are 182 billion emails each day—I can't follow all of them—yet," Alex said. "So, here I am on iCloud or something and there's a black guy in my casket." Alex was laughing. "I wish I could have seen Donna's face. She's not the most liberal-minded person, you know. The idea of marrying someone who wasn't white must have driven her nuts."

"Unlike you?"

"Me? I'm not prejudiced at all. I couldn't care less about anyone's color. Greta was white—and a pure idiot. I knew the day I married her that I was making a mistake. I dated a black girl once, by the way."

"You did?" Although Michael was somewhat surprised he did have to agree that, once his brother's rough-edged, Archie Bunker façade was stripped away, he was colorblind, especially when it concerned a good-looking woman.

"Yeah. She might have been the smartest woman I was ever with. She was a teacher."

Michael watched Alex's face. He was happy, reminiscing. You could see from his eyes that his mind had gone back in time. He smiled, a wide broad grin.

"We were at the Old Homestead Steakhouse. I went there because I didn't want to be seen. You know, it's on Tenth Avenue, downtown. I didn't figure anyone I knew would be there."

"Why didn't you want to be seen?" Michael asked.

"I was with a beautiful black woman."

"I thought you said you didn't care –"

"I didn't—that wasn't the problem."

"So, why were you hiding?"

"Oh, because I was married to Donna at the time. I didn't want to run into anyone we knew."

"What happened?"

"Well, we walked into the dining room, I was following the maître d' to our table and I see this table filled with a bunch of Donna's stuck-up friends. We were going to pass right in front of them. I couldn't believe it. It was too late to turn around, some of them had already seen me."

"So what did you do?"

"I just kept going and walked right up to them. It was two couples. I forgot their names. They're staring up at me with their fucking mouths open."

"You're kidding—then what?"

"I walked right over to their table and said, 'I'd like to introduce you to my . . . *housekeeper.*'"

"I almost forgot what you were like when you were here." Alex reminded him more and more of another politically incorrect person who grew up nearby in Queens but he decided to leave it alone for now.

"I'm still there, Michael."

"I don't know, I can't get my arms around this. It's too much for my mind—maybe almost anyone's mind except some super-brain physicist or something. The world was mysterious enough before—you know, life, death, whatever was next, if anything—and now this . . . *you*. But are you real?"

"Don't I look and sound real?"

"Yes, but so do the marketing calls I get sometimes until, after a few back and forths, I realize I'm speaking to a damned machine or some piece of—software. Are you *software?*"

"I may be something that was always there but that's taken thousands of years to discover, until man got smart enough to figure it out."

"How could this be there and no one knew about it until now? And it took you and me, of all people, to discover it?"

"Really just *me*, by the way." Alex hadn't lost his confidence or his fight. "But, look how long it took for people to figure out the world was round or that something like the Internet was possible. Computers, the Internet, artificial intelligence—they may be just as big a deal to mankind as anything ever was—religion, the world being round, everything."

"I know, it's just so overwhelming at times when I let it break out of the compartment I've put it in and really sit down and think about it."

"Would it have made you feel better if you'd gotten the chance to see my body the other day?"

It was a good question. "I don't know and it seems like the more I see, the more I realize how *much* I don't know. But someone had a reason for taking your casket away."

Alex froze for a second before responding. He must have been on overload—or searching himself for answers. Finally, he spoke, "The question is, are they just afraid that if it is my body in there that we've created something that's threatening—or do they know something that you and I don't?"

CHAPTER 93

Whitestone, New York

Donna Finkelstein was livid. The exhumation, the missing body and then the black one had only failed to resolve what was really going on with Alex and to make her feel like she was being played. She just didn't know if it was from a living Alex or one in the grave, somewhere. It was the same roller-coaster uncertainty she'd felt throughout her marriage and why, she was convinced, she still loved and hated him at the same time. Nothing had changed.

It was her most familiar setting, lying down, in her king size bed, tucked under her duck down comforter, propped up by three duck down pillows, a bottle of Chardonnay and a glass of one on her night table. It was her perfect setting, too—except that instead of having Alex below, under the covers—she had her computer on her lap. She wondered, whose covers he *was* under, emptied her glass, savored the crisp dry taste, took a deep breath and logged into iJewishMingle.

After a few keystrokes, she found him.

Donna: So, who's the black guy in your casket?

Alex: I didn't put him there.

Donna: Okay, Alex, *where the fuck* are you?

Alex: I'm here.

Donna: Cut the bullshit—you know what I mean—and who are you screwing around with now? Is it your hairdresser to the stars bimbo? Or, no, don't tell me, one of your ex-wives?

Alex: I don't screw around with ex-wives anymore. But I'd love to screw my widow.

Donna: You can't screw a widow when your fucking call girl's in Vegas.

Alex: Where do you come up with this shit?

Donna: Or, maybe you're right around the corner. That'd be just like you, you wouldn't even have to change your routines.

Alex: All right, let's say—for argument's sake—that I *was* still alive, in the traditional sense –

Donna: There's no *traditional* sense, Alex. There's only dead or alive—and since we're actually having this conversation, not to mention you're not even in your own fucking casket, *you're alive.*

But she wasn't sure. She poured another glass of wine; it could only help.

Alex: Okay, so if that's true, you understand that you're going to have to *return* the two million dollar life insurance payout you got when you and everyone thought I did really die.

He had a point; she'd almost forgotten about the money. Unlike when Alex was alive, she was no longer dependent upon Alex's generosity—now she had her *own* money—and a lot of it. Between the insurance payout, the cash Alex had stashed in the dining room floorboards, Alex's safety deposit box she'd emptied and now her share of the profits from Tartarus that Michael sent her each quarter—she was living high and in control. Alex was right, she had a choice—try and find Alex, if indeed he was still alive—and maybe have to return her riches—or . . . It didn't take her long to decide.

Donna: You're *dead* as far as I'm concerned. I've learned my lesson.

Alex: What lesson?

Donna: Next time I'll make sure you're *cremated.*

CHAPTER 94

New York City

It was mid-afternoon, the lunch rush over. Michael seated himself in a quiet corner of Delmonico's dining room, opened his laptop, did one more check around him to be sure no one was within earshot, and then clicked onto Alex's gold cross icon.

"Where exactly are you?" Alex asked, appearing to look back and around the dining room.

"I had another meeting on Wall Street so I stopped in here for lunch. I'm having a Delmonico's burger."

"You're at the restaurant, in the dining room? I thought you were paranoid about someone else finding out about me?"

"No, as long as no one's near me that might have known you, for all they know, I'm just FaceTiming someone. To a stranger, it's nothing out of the ordinary."

Alex was now staring at Michael's burger. Michael, too, sat back and admired it as though it was a work of art. The beef was a half an inch thick with a thin layer of fresh green lettuce, the hint of a red tomato, enclosed inside an almost glossy brioche bun. His first bite revealed a tender reddish-pink ground beef with melted cheddar oozing into it.

"You've got a lot of nerve eating that in front of me."

"I know. This is special."

"Fuck you."

"Hold on, let me take another bite." But as Michael brought the burger up to his mouth, his anticipated pleasure was interrupted by the vibration of his cell phone that was on the table, alongside his laptop. He was about to let it go until he noticed the country code that appeared on the screen: *379.* Someone was calling him from the Vatican.

"Hold on, let me take this call. You can watch but don't say anything." Michael picked up his cell phone and clicked onto the call.

"Hello, this is Michael Nicholas."

It was a woman's voice. "Mr. Nicholas, my name is Sister Margaret, Sister Mary Margaret. I am calling from inside the Vatican offices. You don't know me, but I know who you are."

"You do?"

"Yes, I served His Holiness, his housekeeper actually but, more than that, his friend and confidante. I had been with him everywhere, for forty years. He trusted me."

"I'm very sorry for your loss, sister." As he spoke, Michael put a finger up to his lips for Alex and then switched to a new screen on his computer, Googling "the Pope's housekeeper." Sure enough, there she was, Sister Mary Margaret. The long time housekeeper, companion and trusted adviser to Pope Clement, from the time he was a monsignor back in Germany, then Cardinal and then, Pope Clement.

"I'm calling you because, the very night before the Holy Father passed away, he told me about a computer disc you had given to him in a restaurant which he had handed over to Monsignor Schlegelberger."

"Yes, that's my understanding but I –"

"Please, we cannot discuss this any further over the phone. I don't know where you are, but I would like to meet with you. The walls here have many ears."

"I'm in New York right now—but I will be returning to Europe, Paris actually, next week. Or, perhaps sooner now."

"This is most urgent. I am taking a big risk in calling you. I assumed you were still in Italy. I may be in danger myself. I don't know whom to trust."

"I understand. Believe me, I understand. I will make arrangements immediately to fly out and meet with you. I will call you right back."

"Please hurry. I fear the Devil himself is in the Vatican."

CHAPTER 95

Vatican City

T he puff of white smoke had barely left the chimney of the Sistine Chapel. There was a new pope.

Standing just a few feet behind him, Monsignor Schlegelberger watched from inside Saint Peter's Basilica as the newly elected Pontiff, Leo VI, standing on the balcony outside, addressed the massive crowd below.

It was an historic moment, yet the scene had been repeated hundreds of times over the past 1,200 years: a new pope, dressed in the papal white robes, waving and smiling at an adoring, worshipping flock.

Schlegelberger watched, practically standing over the Pope's shoulder, yet invisible to the masses below. It was the way he preferred it.

Later today, he'd meet with Pope Leo—not in his private study, just before bed as he did with Clement—but in the Papal conference room, with the day's light still shining through the windows.

He wondered, what would his role be with the new pope? It would be impossible to enjoy the same friendship and intimacy with Leo as he had with Clement, with whom he'd gone back so many years. And what other personnel changes would the new pope bring to the Vatican? He thought too, of the household staff, and of . . . Sister Margaret. She, too, knew about the disc.

He'd have liked to relieve himself of the burden he was carrying. After all, he'd acted on his own for years now. With Clement, he had been confident, although perhaps mistakenly, that he was acting in accordance with *his* will . . . at least, until the very end. Clement's own brother, Klaus, a priest who had headed up a Christian Brothers boys' choir had already been charged with multiple cases of child abuse, Surely Clement, a notorious micromanager and always on top of the smallest details, had been aware of it.

But the new pope's sympathies were less predictable; he was an outsider, of Latin heritage, warm-blooded, ruled more by emotion and feeling than by cold German logic.

Tonight was not the time to reveal to him the secrets that threatened everything.

But eventually, he would have to discuss not only the actions he took to cover up the Church's scandals but the most unusual series of events he could ever have imagined: the case of Alex Nicholas' virtual reappearance—this breathtaking convergence of science and the spirit—or a simple fraud, a hoax. Either way, the Church and the Nicholas brothers were entwined together in scandal.

Now he would have to explain these matters to a different pope, one he barely knew; unless, of course, he could first eliminate Michael Nicholas. Time was running out.

•

Several hours later, in the privacy of his apartment, Schlegelberger poured himself a glass of port, sat back on his couch, and under the soft light of his standing lamp, dialed Hans Ulricht's number.

"Hans, where are you?"

"In Paris, on business. Why?"

"Good, my friend. Stay there."

"How did your meeting go?" Ulricht asked.

"Very well, better than I could have hoped. I, of course, disclosed nothing but I'm pleased with what I heard from His Holiness today. And now that I know where I stand, I have a plan, one that will solve all of our problems."

He could hear Ulricht sigh.

"That is good, very good. After all, one can only poison so many popes."

Chapter 96

Back in his library, Michael closed the glass-paneled French doors, turned on his desktop Mac and clicked onto Alex. "This could be the breakthrough we need," Michael said.

"Petrucceli and Lovallo are both dead and we have a new pope," Alex said. "Hopefully, Schlegelberger won't have the same influence he had under the last one."

"Yes, but either way," Michael said, "I'm screwed. If the new Pope is also under Schlegelberger's influence, they'll come after me to continue the cover-up. If he isn't, then Schlegelberger will have even more reason to get rid of me in order to protect himself."

"We still don't know whether Clement knew what Schlegelberger was doing but it's a good bet *he didn't* since we believe Schlegelberger poisoned him. In any case, we might get the answer to that when you meet with the nun."

"Sister Margaret," Michael said. Just like Michael, Alex was still terrible at names. It must run in the family.

"Yeah."

Michael continued, "And then we'll see who the Pope selects as his new head of personal security and consigliere. That should give us easier access and new people—maybe ones who aren't concerned about covering something they had nothing to do with."

"Hopefully. So what's your plan?"

Michael took a long sip of the remaining wine in his glass. "I'm going after them again. I'm flying back as soon as I can get myself and Samantha packed and out—to Paris, and wherever Sister Margaret wants to meet. Goldstein wants me to meet with some people in Paris, potential Gibraltar business. It makes it easy for me to leave quickly."

"Shouldn't you have security over there?"

"I can't trust private security people. We saw how that worked in Florence. Everybody's in someone's pocket, especially in Rome. People like Schlegelberger are too well connected to these security services. When the chips are down, who do you think they're going to be loyal to—me or the Vatican? I feel safer at least in Paris."

"It's a big risk right now, wherever you are," Alex said.

"The biggest risk for me—and you, for that matter—is doing nothing. I wish I could just go to the authorities in Rome and lay out everything we have and let the police or some prosecutor deal with this." He knew it was impossible. But Michael also knew, in his heart, that he was, at best, a reluctant warrior. This wasn't his natural way of living.

"Fat chance. First of all, you have too much baggage and risk. Between running my old—and illegal—business and everything that's gone on with you and Sindy Steele—and she's no fucking angel—not only wouldn't they take your charges seriously but you'd be in jail before your first plate of pasta. Remember how the Italians handled that American student . . ."

"Amanda Knox."

"Yeah, that's the one—and she was young and good-looking. Imagine what they'd do to you."

"I know." Michael thought of Sindy Steele. That's who he really needed to watch his back, assuming she didn't skip her meds and put a knife in it. But there was no way that he could ever let her back into his life.

"And then there's the issue of . . ." Alex hesitated.

"*You*," Michael said.

"Exactly—and when you throw that in, you'll look like a lunatic."

CHAPTER 97

35,000 Feet over the Atlantic Ocean

Michael looked out the cabin window: nothing but black and the regular flashing of the wing beacons. The last time he'd flown to Paris, at almost precisely this stage in the flight, the plane had gone into an extended dive.

Except for the communication with Sister Margaret, he'd heard nothing from the Vatican or the people who he knew still wanted him dead. Tonight, with Samantha fast asleep in the seat beside him, he kept his laptop and his iPhone at his side, handy. Just in case. Dinner had been served, the plates collected, and the first-class cabin lights were dimmed. Michael pressed the buttons lowering his seat back, turned on his iPod and put on his cushioned Bose earphones. Tonight, on board this flight, he was determined to relax and maybe even sleep.

It was less than ten minutes later, however, when he conceded that Enya's soothing tones were going in one ear and out the other. He was wired, nervous; his mind was on overdrive thinking about the days ahead. So much was unknown, uncertain. He wished he hadn't brought Samantha on this trip but she'd insisted that he wasn't going back to Paris or Rome without her. She was brave—in many ways braver than he was.

He took off the earphones, brought his seat back to its upright position, and fired up his laptop, reluctantly paying the WiFi charge for onboard Internet service.

The Instant Messages icon was pulsing at the bottom of his screen; it was from Sister Margaret:

Don't come to Rome—too dangerous for you—and for me. I will meet you in Paris since you will be there first anyway. I can arrange some time away. I will be there on Wednesday.

This was good. He didn't want to go to Rome. Samantha didn't want to go there, either. She even said she wouldn't allow him to go. It was a logistical obstacle out of the way now. He'd get his business done in the next two days in Paris and then he'd meet with her.

He shut down his computer, reclined again in his seat, and tried to rest.

He wondered, how much was she willing to risk? How far would she go? Was she willing to take action on Schlegelberger—or was she simply going to supply Michael with information and then slip back into her position inside the Vatican?

Michael reached into the seat pocket and pulled out his still unread copy of the morning's *New York Times*. His attention was immediately drawn to a photograph of Pope Leo VI on the lower right-hand corner of the front page. He was waving to the crowd gathered in Saint Peter's Square. There was nothing in the article regarding any suspicions about the death of Pope Clement. But it was the first paragraph on page ten, where the article was continued, that Michael read and then reread:

The new pontiff announced last night that he would retain Monsignor Kurt Schlegelberger to head up his personal security detail. Schlegelberger served in the same capacity for Pope Clement VIII and was known to be a close confidant and advisor to him. Sources within the Vatican report that they expect Monsignor Schlegelberger, affectionately known as "Monsignor 007," to bring to bear his strong influence on matters relating directly to the Pope.

"Shit," Michael said, tossing the paper on the floor in front of him.

The plane began to shake, then drop, not a large one but enough for Samantha to reach over and grip his arm. He reached for his laptop and placed it on his lap. Then—another jolt, this one worse. The seat-belt sign flashed on, accompanied by the familiar chime. He looked toward the flight attendant; she seemed unconcerned. They always do, until they're fighting to keep themselves alive.

The bumps weren't unusual on these flights over the ocean; it's just that he knew what the others didn't. He knew things that were possible. His body tensed, his free hand gripped the armrest. He waited; his instinct told him there was more to come . . . Seconds and then a few minutes passed. Nothing happened, the flight seemed back to normal. The seat-belt sign was turned off.

But sleep wasn't about to come any time soon. He thought about Sister Margaret and what she must be going through. At least he finally had an ally on the inside.

CHAPTER 98

Paris

Samantha chose for their arrival dinner in Paris an exquisite restaurant facing the Seine on Paris's Left Bank. Le Voltaire served fine traditional French cuisine and in a classic French setting inside a building rich in intrigue.

The room was classic French, with soft, warm lighting, gold-framed impressionist paintings, plush carpeting and richly upholstered chairs and banquettes. Michael was seated against the wall, facing out, a perfect vantage point from which to view the restaurant and its wealthy French clientele. From his red velvet banquette he watched as a threesome were seated at a table facing him. The three diners included an elderly couple, immaculately dressed for the evening—and their little white French poodle who was attentively seated by the waiter on a velvet-covered little seat which was placed upon the regular chair. The poodle was obviously a regular patron since the staff knew exactly how to treat him and addressed him by his first name, Phitz.

"You know," he said, knowing that Samantha was only marginally interested, "Voltaire lived and died here."

"I'm not surprised, especially since it's on the Quai Voltaire. And the restaurant is called Voltaire. What else have you got?"

"Lots—this was a favorite place to dine for the Nazis during the Occupation. It was one of Goering's favorites."

"From the pictures I've seen of him, he must have had a lot of them. Do you know how many restaurants here in Paris you've told me were Goering's favorites?"

"Well, that's why he was so big. He did like his food. But, the most interesting thing about this place is that it was a center for the Resistance. While the Nazis were eating up here where we are, some of the key Resistance fighters were hiding downstairs in the basement. They had a printing press hidden down there too where they printed a lot of their flyers."

"You're kidding? Well, that is interesting. I have a new respect for it now."

"Good, then let's order. I'm having the smoked salmon to start and then the *filet mignon au poivre*."

"What took you so long? At least glance at the menu."

"I'm too hungry to read the menu. I know it by heart. We've been here enough times and the menu probably hasn't changed since Goering was here."

"Yes, and the steak is probably exactly what he ordered."

"Are you saying I'm picking up weight?"

"No, but I do have a very serious question to ask you—but let's wait until we've had a glass of wine."

Two glasses of French Bordeaux later and Michael was beginning his first course: smoked salmon, accompanied by fresh lemon, finely diced onions, capers and topped with a touch of crème fraiche. The salmon had that beautiful, almost glistening bright color, while the tart accoutrements perfectly complemented the fish's sweetness.

As he placed the salmon on the warmed, delicately sliced bread, he wondered what it was that Samantha wanted to discuss. Knowing his wife of over twenty years as he did, he knew it could be anything from a Hermès scarf to the elephant in the room—that one huge issue between them; one they rarely ever spoke about anymore. Michael could tell by the sudden and atypically serious look on Samantha's face which one it would be tonight.

"Let me ask you something: in Rome, on the stairway at the hotel, I was almost a flight of steps away, but, when your phone rang, it was Alex's voice I heard, wasn't it?"

"Yes. You didn't ask me who it was—as I knew you wouldn't—so I never offered. We can only have this disagreement so many times. But it *was* Alex—in whatever form you choose to believe he is in."

"So, if that's true, where do you really think Alex is?" she said.

"I believe Alex—with the help of those genius kids from Silicon Valley—duplicated himself on the computer that I found. You know that's exactly what I believe."

"Michael, you know how crazy that all sounds, don't you?"

"Yes, of course I do. But I also know that the computer version of Alex that I visit and speak with nearly every day, is Alex. It's him. No one else could be that person. His memories couldn't be made up or faked by anyone else. His voice, his mannerisms, the way he responds to new things—it's him. And it was Alex, using the same artificial intelligence eavesdropping and surveillance capabilities that our government uses, who rescued us the other day."

"So you believe that Alex duplicated himself on a computer—just before he was murdered? And you don't think there could be any other possibility or explanation?"

"No . . . well, except for one."

CHAPTER 99

Rome

Frustrated, Schlegelberger sat in front of his computer. He wished now that he had been more careful with Paolo; he needed his help once again to enter Alex Nicholas' world, wherever that was. He'd been blocked and, without Paolo's unique genius, he had been cut off from both Alex and Michael's computers. The remaining Vatican technology staff couldn't be trusted, and likely didn't have the technical intelligence to do what was necessary to crack the codes. He wondered if that was even the correct expression.

His thoughts were interrupted by the ringing of the old, black phone by his desk.

"Your package was delivered this morning," Hans said. "I have made the arrangements for it that you requested. All these elaborate plans. I still don't understand why you don't simply let me have Michael Nicholas finished off in the street or whatever."

"I've told you. There is information I'd like to have from him. Things he won't tell me unless he is forced to, and perhaps not even then." He'd been willing to destroy Michael even without getting his hands on his laptop but more and more he wanted that computer. Although he still doubted whether it was what it appeared to be, he needed to be sure. If it turned out to be the breakthrough he feared . . . it could, in his hands, become *his* breakthrough.

"You and your strange obsessions. My dear Kurt, do you honestly believe this technological nonsense? And why not handle Michael in Rome, since we know he will likely be returning there?"

"I can't afford any more such activity here. There are already whispers, suspicions."

"You've heard them, read of them?" Hans said.

"No, but I sense it, I feel it. Fortunately, they do not revolve around me, at least not yet."

"Yes, I would have expected that the cook at least would have been fired by now."

He ignored Hans's rare attempt at humor.

"Don't worry, nothing will get in the way of our mission—the Free Forces Party will take everyone by surprise, soon. In fact, should Alex Nicholas have truly stumbled onto something, I want to be sure that *we* are the ones who capitalize on it. It would be our shortcut, our quickest path to power. It would be the modern day atomic bomb that we need to bring us power."

"The Third Reich was to have ruled for a thousand years, not the twelve we were given. Let's make sure we stay focused this time."

"My computer assistant allowed me to access Michael Nicholas's computer and so I discovered his brother, or at least some version of him. I need Michael's computer to learn more. Once I have it I can turn it over to certain experts who will tell me exactly what we need to know."

"And your assistant, can't he –"

"Paolo? He's gone. He fled . . . for his life, I suppose. It's a long story. If by some chance Alex Nicholas truly exists in this cyberspace, once we have the information and answers we need, once we have the key, the passwords to unlock it, we will make Christianity look like a passing, self-help fad."

CHAPTER 100

Paris

M ichael knew there was one *other* possible explanation for Alex's virtual existence—although he suspected it wasn't the one that Samantha expected to hear.

"I don't think it's the most likely, but, knowing Alex, it's possible," he said.

"Okay, I'm listening," Samantha said, although her eyes appeared to be glancing once again at the poodle dining next to them.

Michael could see skepticism written all over her beautiful face.

"The only other explanation is that Alex *isn't* dead. And the fact that we haven't found his body yet would certainly support that possibility."

"Michael, he was shot in front of a restaurant filled with diners—a number of whom were cops. We had a funeral, and then he was buried in Saint Michael's cemetery. The insurance company has paid out Donna on his life insurance. You're running his business now. Don't you think this is a little far-fetched, to say the least?"

"You asked me if there was any other explanation. This, in my mind, is the only other option. Alex never liked a lot of people, even his friends got on his nerves at times. He mostly just wanted to be left alone to enjoy watching his baseball and football games on TV, eat a steak or a lobster and have a few

drinks—in peace. That's who he really is. Although he loved—
or loves—women, all his wives drove him crazy. I could see him
having hidden a small fortune, and then finding a way to just
do what he wanted to do."

"So what are you saying, that he's alive and sitting somewhere in a condo in Las Vegas watching television and eating
out?"

"Or, ordering in. Yes, it's possible that he's sitting back
comfortably, pulling our strings and enjoying having everyone
think he's dead. And he's just doing exactly what he wants,
whenever he wants—and with whatever girl he wants."

"I can see that in Alex," Samantha said, "but, come on,
what about the body, the burial and everything else that goes
on when you die?"

It was just as Michael was visualizing Alex, sitting on his
LazyBoy recliner, watching the Yankee game, when the waiter
arrived and placed a perfect filet mignon topped with an au
poivre sauce and a side of steak frites on a warm plate in front
of him. Samantha looked pleased as another waiter delivered
her crisp duck à l'orange.

"Maybe this was a good choice. I forgot how good the food
was here." Samantha glanced over at the French poodle, who
appeared to return her gaze. "They do get a very nice clientele
here," she said.

"Yes, Marie Antoinette. You're welcome." Michael cut into
his filet. Perhaps it was the razor sharp French Laguiole steak
knife, but the thin dark crust easily gave way as the blade
touched it, revealing a juicy pink inside. It was perfectly cooked
and, unlike most super-sized restaurant servings at home, it was
a civilized portion, which was helpful since he still had that
childhood habit of needing to eat everything on his plate.

"The duck is so nice and crisp," Samantha said, before
putting her fork down and taking a taste of her Sancerre. "So, if
Alex is alive, where is he?"

Michael tried to think of an answer. The truth was, even he didn't have a clue. There had been so many unexplainable things that had happened surrounding his brother's "death"—the sealed casket, priests who never actually saw Alex's body, the funeral director who supposedly did but since died—and, of course, Alex's emergence on the computer.

"I don't know. And which one, which Alex?"

"What do you mean, which Alex?"

"Because there's a *third* option."

"A third option?" Samantha said, her curiosity clearly piqued now.

"Yes, that he has successfully duplicated himself on a computer—*and* that he's still alive—so that there are today, *two Alexs*—one on a computer and the original live one. That's the third option."

•

It was close to midnight when they finally walked out through the wood and glass doors of Le Voltaire. As they waited for the green light to cross the rue de Beaune, Michael took a moment to admire the clear summer evening view of the Seine. It would be a fifteen-minute walk back to the Ritz. As they approached the Pont Royale to cross over to the Right Bank, their stroll was interrupted by the ring of Michael's cell phone.

"Oh God," Samantha said, "who could that be at this hour? It's six in the morning at home."

Michael checked the screen, "It's from here." He'd heard the voice only once before.

"Mr. Nicholas?"

"Yes, Sister Margaret."

"You have a good memory for voices. Are you in Paris?"

"Yes, I've been waiting for your call."

"I am anxious to meet with you. Can we meet tomorrow afternoon? I will be free after four if that is convenient for you."

"Yes, sister. That's fine. Where would you like to meet?"

"It must be a place that is safe, so there must be other people, yet not so obvious, you understand?"

He did, but he didn't. He must have looked confused because Samantha was looking at him with a perplexed expression herself. He had no idea how familiar Sister Margaret might be with Paris.

"How about if we meet outside Notre Dame?" he said.

"Oh, Lord, no. Of all places, not the Cathedral."

"I'm sorry, that was stupid of me. How about a hotel lobby? We could have tea or coffee or a glass of wine while we talk."

There was silence; was she hesitant? Unsure?

"Yes, that's a good idea. Did you have a particular place in mind?"

"How about the lobby bar of the Meurice?"

"Is it safe there?"

"Yes, it's one of the best hotels and I know it has excellent security. And the bar or café is discreet but always well occupied."

"Okay, I will have to trust your judgment." She sounded vulnerable, even more so than when they spoke in New York from Delmonico's. "Shall we meet at the Meurice at four tomorrow then?"

"I'll be in a dark blue suit . . . grey tie and I'll have a light-brown briefcase."

"I will know you," she said.

"Sister, will you be wearing a . . ."

"A habit? No, not tomorrow. Possibly not ever again."

CHAPTER 101

Paris

M ichael walked briskly down the rue Saint Honore, glancing at the Hermès windows already decorated for the fall. His mind was electric with anticipation. The late Pope's housekeeper . . . reality was truly stranger than fiction. His phone vibrated, it was her. Was she cancelling after all? No, please no.

Sister Margaret: I am here early.

Michael: Okay, I'm still ten minutes away.

Sister Margaret: Seated inside. Ordering tea.

Michael: Should I call you?

Sister Margaret: No. Message only now—can't be intercepted as easily.

Michael: I didn't expect a nun to be so good with technology.

Sister Margaret: My father was an industrial engineer. I am drawn to computers. I taught Clement how to use them, though he never truly learned.

Michael: I understand now. Will be there shortly.

He wanted to update Samantha but he needed to hurry now. His meeting had gone longer than he'd expected. He wanted to beat Sister Margaret to the Meurice, to be settled, to select his seat and vantage point, even within a bar. Especially for something like this. He didn't know exactly why, it made him feel secure, more in control perhaps, or less vulnerable.

He turned right onto the rue Royale. Ahead he could see the old stone arcade-like arches. Although he'd never stayed at the Meurice, he'd dined there, and knew its dark history well. Taken over by the Nazis, it became their headquarters during the Occupation. General von Cholitz, the last Nazi general in charge of the city, had his office on the second floor, overlooking the Tuileries Garden. It was Von Cholitz who, falsely, many believe, claimed to have saved Paris from destruction.

Another date with history, Michael thought, as he turned into the hotel's entrance.

The bar had the look of the clientele it had been designed for; Brits seemed to be everywhere in the lobby and the bar had the deep rich tones and look of an old British club. Every table was taken; he scanned the room for a nun without her habit. No one appeared to be a likely candidate. Maybe she'd gone to the Ladies Room. Maybe she changed her mind after all. He texted her.

Michael: I'm here. I don't know what you look like. Where are you?

He waited, watching the phone's screen for the series of little dots indicating she was answering. Nothing appeared.

He walked around the tables, looking for an unaccompanied woman, there was only one but she certainly didn't look like a nun and papal housekeeper. He approached her table, making and then not making eye contact. She saw him; their eyes met once again. She was in her sixties, stylishly dressed, a gold Cartier on her wrist, attractive . . . perhaps his image of a housekeeper was nothing more than an outdated stereotype. He came closer, he held out his hand, her smile broadened, her ultra-white teeth were perfect. He relaxed, "Sister Margaret?"

"Excusez-moi?" she whispered in what sounded to him like perfect French.

"Are you Sister Mary Margaret?"

She broke into a laugh. He'd made a mistake. He noticed, too late, the glass of wine on her table.

"I am sorry, monsieur," she said in accented English, "but I can assure you I am not the sister."

He apologized, retreated to the bar at the front of the room and approached the bar man.

"I was to meet a woman here. A few minutes ago she messaged me that she was here already and had ordered tea. She would be . . . older."

"Ah, yes. A gentleman arrived and escorted her outside, I believe they moved to the lobby."

Michael left the bar and returned to the lobby area. It was a large open room, people were seated, having drinks, coffee, tea, whatever. He scanned the room, again looking for her, but this time with a man. This couldn't be good. He put his briefcase down and texted her once more.

Michael: Are you in the lobby? Is everything okay?

But again there was no response. He waited. He began walking the lobby area. In a distant corner he saw a table and a woman alone. She was seated, sitting upright with her back to him. Her hair was grey. He walked towards her. Once he was within a few feet, he said, "Sister Margaret?" She didn't turn around. He went around her to see her face. He came around, right up to the table, facing her now. One hand was on her lap, the other hung straight down by her side. There was only a half-finished cup of tea on the small round table in front of her. The first thing he noticed were her eyes. They were wide open, too wide. Michael recognized the look right away.

She was dead.

CHAPTER 102

Paris

S itting on the outdoor terrace at Le Castiglione, right around the corner from the Meurice, Michael heard the sirens nearby. Once he had seen Sister Margaret, he just kept walking, as nonchalantly as he could, as though he was still looking for someone, until he went out the door and onto the street. He needed time to think—and a drink.

What was she going to tell him? What secrets was she about to reveal? And, did she suffer a heart attack or stroke or . . . was she murdered? Had she been followed to the Meurice? If she was murdered, was the killer then watching from a distance to see who she was planning to meet? Michael looked around, his eyes darting left and right, trying not to be obvious.

Once his wine arrived, he dialed Samantha and told her what had happened.

"Oh my God. What's going on? How could you just walk by and leave her there?"

"She was dead."

"How did you know for sure? Maybe she was having a stroke and needed help."

"I know dead, Samantha. I've seen it. She was dead."

"Still, why didn't you call the police or at least let someone know?"

"If it could have made any difference for her, if she was still alive, I certainly would have but, otherwise, I can't afford to get dragged into something I don't understand right now. I don't even know if I can trust the police, anywhere."

"By the way, a Hans Ulricht left a message for you here at the hotel. Who is he again?"

"He's a Swiss banker. I was introduced to him a year ago by the late Bertrand Rosen, our infamous Ponzi scheme artist. Ulricht wanted me to invest—launder would be more accurate—Tartarus profits through his bank. I refused."

"Oh, yeah, I remember now," Samantha said.

Michael continued, "But he's also Goldstein's banker. Ulricht is probably why Goldstein knows about my running Tartarus. I'm sure he told him, especially after I turned him down on laundering money."

"So why is he calling you?"

"Goldstein wants me to meet with him while I'm here. He says that with all his connections, Ulricht can refer Gibraltar a lot of business. I've got to pick my battles with Jonathan so I agreed to meet Ulricht at seven tonight for a drink."

"So you're meeting with him . . . tonight?"

"Yes, just to pacify Goldstein, but I'm not about to do business with him, whether it's Tartarus or Gibraltar. He tried to call me on my cell earlier but I didn't take the call."

"Well, in his message he was asking if you could meet him *earlier* . . . at five at the Lutetia."

"That's in half an hour." Michael checked his watch. "Maybe that's not so bad an idea. I could get it over with and we could get out for a nice quiet dinner alone earlier than we planned. I'm beat after all this."

"That sounds like a good idea. Even early room service tonight would be lovely."

"I'll call him back. If I leave now I can walk to the Lutetia and be there by five. I need the exercise."

As he walked briskly toward the Left bank, his phone vibrated. He'd tried to contact Alex right after he'd left the dead nun at the Meurice but he'd been unable to get through. Now Alex was trying to FaceTime him on his iPhone.

"Let's just talk, this FaceTime thing is too complicated while I'm walking." Michael told him what had happened to Sister Margaret. "I'm on my way to a meeting with a certain dirty Swiss banker."

"What's his name? There's a lot of them."

"Ulricht, Hans Ulricht."

CHAPTER 103

Paris, France

"It must have been difficult, losing your brother."

It sounded strange, out of context, now and here, coming from Hans Ulricht.

"It was, of course."

"Were the two of you close?"

"Close enough. There was a ten year age difference. He was different. But we loved each other. Thank you for asking."

Michael looked closely at the label of the wine bottle on the table. "1942?" he said.

"1942 Château Lafite Rothschild, a truly rare Bordeaux. Don't worry, I selected the bottle; the bill's on the bank. I was young, it was a glorious year, 1942."

"For some, perhaps. Not many here in Paris." Michael gently swirled the deep red wine around in its large balloon glass, inhaled its strong musty aroma and took his first sip. He hid his disappointment.

They sat across a small table in the busy, dimly lit bar. The room was updated old-world with dark woods and richly appointed furnishings. The crowd was fashionably dressed. At the next table Michael noticed a dark-haired woman, in her early forties, wearing stylish jeans with a Louis Vuitton belt, a light pink cashmere sweater, and a diamond on her finger capable of informing the entire hotel that her husband, wherever he may be, was rich. She was surrounded by two younger versions of herself, surely her daughters, likely in training.

Hans Ulricht's eyes slowly moved around, surveying the room, then looked down as he checked his gold-chained pocket watch. Michael noticed that Ulricht had a second gold chain, probably for keys, also hanging from his belt loop; like Ulricht himself, a throwback to another era.

"There is much history here," Ulricht said. "During the great Occupation, the Gestapo took over this hotel. It was our—their—headquarters here in Paris."

It was becoming the elephant in the room. Everywhere he went in Paris, it seemed there were the vestiges of the Nazi presence. It was so difficult to imagine such a civilized city being taken over by such an evil force, and not that long ago. Was it just his own interest in history that drew him to such places or was it the people he was associating with? From one hotel to another and one restaurant to the next. They were everywhere . . . despite the passage of over half a century.

Michael already knew the infamous history of the Lutetia. Parisians, particularly Jews and suspected members of the Resistance, were awakened during the night, forcibly taken from their homes, and brought to this very building for interrogation, many never returning.

Ulricht continued, "Your brother, his name was Alex?"

Michael nodded, "Yes." So it was back to Alex again.

Ulricht turned back toward his guest. "Michael, you are in *my* world now."

And, strangely, that was exactly how he felt. An American, in this city his countrymen had liberated, facing a German, in the city *his* fathers had occupied; yet it was Michael who felt vulnerable, a stranger in Paris.

He looked back at Ulricht, dressed in a perfectly tailored yet unfashionably, dated three-piece dark-green suit. The buttons of his vest were stretched. What was Ulricht looking for? He was bouncing between the distant past—and Alex.

A certain silence followed, only the sounds from the bar, of glasses touching, a cocktail being shaken, ice cubes falling into glasses, hushed conversations in foreign languages. Neither of them said anything for some indeterminate amount of time. Ulricht sipping his wine; Michael, trying to size up the situation, the image of Sister Margaret dead in her chair flashing in and out of his mind.

Michael broke the spell. "Why did you want to see me?"

Hans pointed to the briefcase Michael had placed on the empty seat at their table.

"Do you carry a laptop computer around with you?"

"Yes, it's in there," Michael said nodding toward his briefcase.

Now he knew.

CHAPTER 104

"This couldn't be why Goldstein wanted me to meet with you?" Michael said. He wondered how could Ulricht or Goldstein for that matter even know about Alex? What was he missing?

"Jonathan is a complex man. He wants you out of the way."

"I know that," Michael said, still confused, hoping that his definition of *out of the way* was the same as Ulricht's. "But what's that got to do with my . . . late brother?"

"I'm afraid there are connections—amongst people you've crossed—that you are unaware of."

"I still don't get it."

"You will, shortly.

"Go to hell."

"Hans appeared to nod, but not to him. His eyes moved to something—or someone—behind Michael.

Before he could even turn around, Michael felt a hand on his shoulder. He tried to move away but the man's grip held him tight—and a hand holding him by the neck in a way that likely appeared to others to be a friendly gesture, nearly paralyzed him with pain throughout his body. When he finally could turn, he saw an imposing, well-built, steroid-strong young man, his blond hair neatly coiffed, a perfect Germanic specimen bulging out of his sport coat.

"Let me introduce you to Frederick," Ulricht said, taking Michael's cell phone off the table as he rose up from his chair.

"Frederick has an extraordinarily sharp knife. I think you may have seen an example of his work earlier today at the Meurice. Most unfortunate. Follow us now or his blade will swiftly pierce your heart before anyone here even notices. If you even look like you're going to make a sound, he will do it immediately and then carry you out—everyone will assume that you're drunk. You won't be the first American businessman to be carried out of here unconscious—or dead."

Ulricht got up, "I suggest you follow us. We're not going far."

With the help of Frederick's firm, uplifting grip under Michael's shoulder and a steady dose of neck pressure, he followed suit. Frederick led him out of the bar as Ulricht stayed a step behind them. They appeared to be headed for the hotel lobby until he was suddenly pulled to the right and led down a dark staircase.

"Where are we going?" Michael said as they walked down the steps and entered a long dimly lit hallway.

"Ah, my friend. It's a shame you are not a diligent student of history. Just think, Josephine Baker, Picasso, André Gide, Jean-Paul Sartre, Simone de Beauvoir—they all frequented the Lutetia. James Joyce wrote a good part of *Ulysses* here. Too bad we didn't get a chance to see more."

"What the hell is going on?"

It was as though Ulricht never heard him. "As I started to say earlier, during the Occupation the Lutetia was the headquarters for the Abwehr, our German intelligence service. Right across the street was the old French Cherche Midi prison where we used to hold our prisoners. Once the Abwehr was done interrogating someone, what was left of them was sent across the street to the prison until they were executed. It became expedient to simply build this underground tunnel from the hotel to the prison. Very few people know this ever existed. The hotel staff are under strict orders to never acknowledge it, of course. And the prison was torn down after the war. There is a new building in its place, an academic center for the study of humanity. Very fitting."

Ulricht turned, looked right at Michael and, with a pained smile said simply, "I much prefer the old structure."

"I'm not surprised. I can see that nostalgic look in your eyes," Michael said. "You're living in some sort of dream world."

"*This* is what inspires me. And—even more—bringing it all back, as it should have been, as it will be again."

As they approached the last steel door in the tunnel, Ulricht moved in front of them. He turned the handle, opened the heavy door halfway and flipped a switch on the inside wall somewhat illuminating the room. Michael craned his neck to get a better view.

Letting Michael enter before him, Ulricht hung back at the door. "I'm afraid I must leave you now. I have other affairs to attend to—but I assure you, you're in good hands. There's a priest who wants to meet you, and Frederick here will take care of the rest, I assure you."

Frederick pulled Michael into the room as Ulricht departed, closing the door behind him.

As his eyes adjusted to the stark light in the cavernous storeroom, a figure came into view. He was dressed in black with a white cleric's collar; it was Schlegelberger. He was sitting at a bare steel table, next to a casket.

Michael recognized the casket right away.

CHAPTER 105

He couldn't take his eyes off Alex's casket—until he saw something else: a steel and wood contraption at the far side of the room, a long blackened wood table with straps and buckles neatly displayed on top. Rising above the left side of the bench was a silver tower, at the top of which was a gleaming silver blade.

Schlegelberger spoke, gesturing towards it, "This is one of only two guillotines remaining from the Nazis time in power. It was discovered in a museum in Munich." He laughed, "It's one of Hans's most cherished possessions. He's had it restored to its original working condition." Schlegelberger pointed to the empty chair on the other side of the table. "Have a seat."

He sat down. Frederick hovered close behind him.

"Don't worry about the guillotine, we need you in one piece."

Michael had his doubts.

"How do you do what you've done and still wear this collar?" Michael said.

"The Church—all churches, all faiths—eventually are the domain of mortals. We are not exempt from the frailties or weaknesses of other professions or callings."

"What is going on? And what are you doing here, with Ulricht?"

"I'm afraid we don't have enough time to answer all these questions," Schlegelberger said, sliding Michael's laptop out of his briefcase.

Michael searched for a new approach to get him talking. "I understand that you were acquainted with Father Papadopoulos of the Greek Orthodox Church."

"Yes, Father Papadopoulos was a good friend of mine. We collaborated on a number of ecumenical issues. His departure was . . . unfortunate."

"I'll bet it was."

"He knew too much. Or, to be more precise, he'd seen too much. Like yourself."

"What do you know about my brother's burial?"

"This is quite extraordinary, no?" He looked over at Alex's coffin, as though it held some answers. "Most often the mystery surrounds the *death,* not the *burial.*"

"Father Papadopoulos blessed my brother's body and conducted his funeral," Michael said as he watched the Monsignor's face for any reaction. "Yet, he told Alex's wife that he never actually saw the body. That's quite unusual, don't you think?"

Before Schlegelberger could respond, Michael continued. "And then, right after that, he called and asked to meet with me—saying he had something urgent to tell me, but minutes before I arrived at the church—he died of a massive heart attack."

"A natural cause, yes? Jimmy—Father Papadopoulos—had a heart condition as I recall." Schlegelberger looked away.

"Perhaps," Michael said. "Perhaps not."

"Have you any reason to believe otherwise?"

"More reasons than you can imagine. My sister-in-law demanded that Alex's body be exhumed. The casket was stolen—lifted away by helicopter as we all watched. But I think you knew that. We eventually found it—but with a black man inside."

"And I thought you Americans were color blind, no?"

"So tell me what happened with Alex's body," Michael said.

"Well, as long as we are having this . . . confession, you might say, *we* are rather in the dark ourselves."

"You didn't take it?" Michael asked, the mystery of Alex's body was almost clouding out the danger he knew was imminent.

"It wasn't there," Schlegelberger said. It appeared that now even he was curious. "The answer, I assumed, went to the grave with Father Papadopoulos."

"You don't seem like the type of man to be satisfied with such an answer."

"That's very perceptive of you. I'm not at all satisfied with this uncertainty. I do know, however, that I must control what I can with this ridiculous farce. Which is not good news for you, or anyone else involved. In your case, too, of course, there is the matter of delicate issues . . . information that you have which the Church cannot afford to be exposed."

"The Church—or you?"

"In this case, they are the same."

"And if you're so sure it's a farce, why do you care about Alex?"

"Because it is the perfect scheme to capture the imaginations—if not the minds—of the press and the ignorant public."

"And what about Jonathan Goldstein? Where does he fit in all this?" Perhaps it was a way to buy time, or take his mind away from . . . whatever exactly was going to happen to him. He needed time to think, to find a way out, either with his wits—or by outmaneuvering them physically, somehow.

"Jonathan has a lucrative financial relationship with us –"

"Us? Who's *us*?"

"Hans and I. We have certain interests together. None of which concern you now."

"Okay, what if you're wrong?"

"Wrong?" Schlegelberger looked up, a momentary look of amusement on his face.

"What if Alex Nicholas still lives? What if *he has* been duplicated on a computer?"

"Ah, my friend. I know fantasies and false gods when I see them. They are my life."

"Maybe—but you know as well as I that history is littered with falsehoods that were taken as indisputable for centuries— the world being flat –"

Schlegelberger's face tightened. "I don't need a history lesson—least of all from you."

"And if you're so sure this is all a hoax, why are you bothering to question me? Why do you need my computer?"

"Perhaps just reassurance that you have not made some sort of breakthrough, some progress that can be useful to me."

"So you're *not* sure then, are you?"

"Only a fool never doubts."

"What if I can tell you how to literally duplicate a human being on a computer?" Of course Michael himself had no idea, but he'd worry about that later, if there was a later.

"I have everything I need now," Schlegelberger said, pointing to Michael's laptop, opened on the table. "There is nothing you can tell me that I don't already know. One of my people had previously hacked into the software, and now with this, I will find someone who can duplicate it."

"*This* laptop? You don't think I'd carry Alex around with me on the street, do you? This is the one I use for business. Alex's is . . . special . . . a different unit."

In truth, there was no special laptop for Alex anymore. All the unique hardware that powered Alex was on Michael's home computer, in his wine cellar. His daily communications with Alex on the Internet could be with any computer. But the last thing he wanted to do now was to give Schlegelberger that information. Yet he still had to bluff. His mind was trying to find the way out of the basement, alive.

"I will take you to the laptop that you need."

"It's a good try, but I'm afraid your time's up," Schlegelberger said.

Michael's eyes were drawn to the basket directly below the blade at the foot of the guillotine's tower.

"I told you; you needn't worry about that contraption. It's not for you. After all, we can't have a body in your brother's casket with a neatly severed head. But I can promise you that Frederick here will take care of things with no more than a moment's discomfort on your part."

Michael said nothing.

"Your brother's casket will be returned to the cemetery and inside will be a body with most of the same exact features that he had. We will simply have to do some work first to prematurely age the new cadaver."

CHAPTER 106

Schlegelberger rose from his chair, his attentions having already left the room.

Michael looked around: his only chance was to run for the door but between the sturdy Frederick, holding him tightly again, and Schlegelberger, it was unlikely he'd make it out.

Schlegelberger read his mind. "If you resist or try to run, not only will it be futile, as I'm sure you've already figured out, but I've authorized Frederick to do what he enjoys. He loves to watch people die . . . very slowly."

"Or else we use the machine, yes?" Frederick said. His broad smile indicated just how anxious he was to use it tonight. He looked at Michael, releasing his grip and pointed to the guillotine. "After the blade comes down, you will still be awake. Your eyes will still see, even though your head will be in the pail." He pointed to the bucket at the foot of the guillotine. "It's worth every second—for you and for me."

"More for you," Michael said.

As he moved to leave, Schlegelberger turned around, and, smiling at the joke, said, "Not today, we need him in one piece."

Michael wasn't sure when the music began to play or even exactly where it was coming from. "Music?" he said, looking at Frederick.

"Wagner's *Tristan and Isolde*, Hitler's favorite," Frederick said.

"So, what, you're a Nazi? This is the twenty-first century. Are you guys serious?"

Michael watched as Schlegelberger walked toward the door. There was little chance that, one on one, he could overpower young Frederick. His only chance was to get to Schlegelberger *before* he left them alone and use him as his own hostage. Between Frederick's bulk and the element of surprise Michael felt sure he could reach Schlegelberger before he got out the door, only twenty feet or so away. He'd kill him with his bare hands if he had to.

For a split second, it struck him that what had once been unthinkable—killing a man—had become not only a necessity for survival—but a burning desire. He wanted to feel Schlegelberger's neck break in his hands.

He took one step closer to the door. Frederick appeared to still be smarting over the thought of Michael's head in the pail. Schlegelberger approached the door, reaching out for the door handle. But as Michael prepared to make his move to sprint to the door and tackle Schlegelberger, he noticed the door handle turn. Someone was about to enter from the outside.

CHAPTER 107

Paris, France

Most days her mind was a battlefield. But today, the summer air blowing against her face as she sped through Paris on her motorcycle seemed to bring Sindy Steele the clarity that too often eluded her.

Yesterday, he'd finally opened her latest disguised email, this time a greeting card. She could see he was in Paris, but then she'd lost him again. But now, the signal was strong, he was only minutes away, on the Left Bank. His cell phone tracker was pulsing on her iPhone screen. He was on the move.

It was a breathtaking ride as she raced around the traffic circle in the Place de la Concorde and past the pink granite Obelisk known as Cleopatra's Needle in the center, symbolizing the exact spot where Marie Antoinette and another 1300 people were guillotined. She crossed over the Seine on the Pont de la Concorde, past the National Assembly and onto the Left Bank's Boulevard Saint-Germain.

Five minutes later, Sindy Steele parked her cycle on the Rue de Sèvres and rushed through the Lutetia lobby and into the hotel's bar. Wearing skin-tight jeans, knee-high black leather boots and a soft leather riding jacket, she saw the heads of the men in the bar turning her way, following her moves.

He'd be easy to spot, but not one man in the room had blond hair. He wasn't there.

She pulled out her cell phone and checked the tracking software again.

Expecting it to read *No Signal/disabled* she was surprised as she saw the horizontal bar progressing until it reached its mark.

He was there now; close by at least. The cursor showed his location as the streets surrounding the Lutetia—just slightly off from where she stood.

Leaving the bar, she proceeded to follow the signal. She headed down a flight of stairs, to the basement and a long poorly lit hallway, resembling a tunnel. There were several steel doors along the hall on both sides, each one marked with engraved black and white signs, in French, *Electrical Closet, Storage, Employees Only*, and more. She could hear music, classical, music. It was somber, heavy. It was coming from down the hall. There was a strange light, a simple light bulb hanging from the ceiling on a wire, there, at the end of the tunnel. She stepped up her pace, running now, towards the door and the music.

At the end, there was a single door facing her. Although steel like the others, it looked heavier, thicker, resembling the type that secured a vault. It was closed. She looked all around, checking up and down the hallway and then turned back to the door.

She placed her ear against it, listening . . .

She slowly turned the handle.

CHAPTER 108

A lex listened closely. The first voice was Michael's:
"Why did you want to see me?"

"Do you carry a laptop computer around with you?" That had to be Hans Ulricht.

"Yes, it's in there . . ."

"I understand that you speak with your brother on your computer."

Alex quickly flipped from one screen to the next, his mind and the Internet merged into one. He'd become the technology and the technology became him. It was effortless. *If only Fat and Skinny Lester could see me now.* It was breathtaking how much he learned each day, one thing leading to another, dots getting connected everywhere, things building on each other, his mind more powerful each day.

He had followed Michael to the Lutetia and remotely activated Michael's cell phone.

Frantic, Alex located the hotel's electrical grid, something unimaginable to him even just a few months ago. There were no surveillance cameras, at least none he could access. Michael was clearly on the move around the hotel and he wasn't alone. He scanned all the email and message activity inside the hotel. It was a mass of data, too much to quickly sort through.

Since his call with Michael earlier, he'd begun his online investigation of Hans Ulricht, full searches, background checks, medical records—anything that might help him find an entry point or vulnerability. He'd found one big one. He just needed one piece of information to make it work.

Alex located Hans Ulricht's mobile phone number and proceeded to send him a text message: *URGENT—Please message confirmation of the ID of your Medtrope device asap. Software update required.*

The answer came swiftly: "911213."

Alex began typing in the necessary information along with the necessary ID he'd just received. It was now just a matter of time. He hoped there was enough of it.

CHAPTER 109

There was no way he was going to die without a fight.

Michael made his move, running as fast and hard as he could, slamming Schlegelberger hard into the steel door. He was pretty sure he'd at least cracked one of the priest's ribs. Frederick recovered, quickly moving towards them, surprised but seeming unperturbed.

But with Schlegelberger crushed into the door Michael flipped him around and placed his neck in a headlock. He squeezed hard. Schlegelberger's face turned red; he was choking, fighting for air. Michael was going to kill him. He wanted to kill him. He shouted at the oncoming Frederick, "Stop or I'll snap his neck."

Frederick, now an arm's distance from them, stopped. But Michael could tell, he wasn't going to hold back for long. He could see Frederick's body tense up; he was going to come at him. Michael's back was against the door. He felt the door being pushed back against him. Whoever had been turning that handle was trying to come in, the door was pushing up against him. He wasn't sure exactly why, but he suddenly squeezed his elbow as hard as he could around Schlegelberger's neck, and then he did it even harder until he felt something break. Frederick must have seen it; he moved in—at the same time as the door pushed violently in on him from behind.

Michael threw Schlegelberger's limp body at the oncoming Frederick and jumped to the side, allowing the door to swing open which it did, thrusting Frederick and whatever was left of Schlegelberger to the other side.

The door swung open. Michael was expecting the worst, hoping against hope that, in the momentary confusion, he'd be able to run through the open door and out to the hall.

He started to make his run out the door when the face that entered finally registered in his brain.

"Sindy?" he said dumbly as Frederick sprang forward, stiletto in hand. But Sindy was too quick for him. As he leaped forward, she moved aside, causing Frederick to run head first into the concrete wall. Nevertheless, he came up quickly, never missing a beat, with his knife in his hand. With a powerful kick to his groin, she doubled him over and, grabbing the knife from his hand, she turned it around and thrust it into his side.

"Remember me?" she said as she thrust it swiftly in and out of his side. "Here's how you do it," she said, softly, as she repeated the thrust. Frederick looked up at her, his eyes glazing over. "It's nothing personal, Freddie boy." She placed the knife at a precise point to the side of his sternum, felt for the space between the ribs, and plunged the blade into his heart.

Sindy Steele was still holding the knife; she picked up the end of Frederick's shirt tail and wiped the blade clean of his blood. "I do love stilettos," she said.

"I see," Michael said, gazing at her thigh-high black leather stiletto boots.

"I meant the knife but I like these, too," she said lifting her right leg to show off her boots. "They're not the best for a motorcycle, though."

Michael knelt down beside a gasping Schlegelberger. "I have to ask him something –"

"You'd better hurry," Sindy said, watching him. "He's not going to last long." Seemingly unconcerned about his fate, she kept her distance from him.

Michael held Schlegelberger's head, gently lifting it up. "Did the Pope—either of them—know? Were they a part of this?"

Schlegelberger stared back. Michael wasn't sure whether those eyes were really seeing him or staring into space, into eternity.

He shook him, "Stay with me. Did they know?"

Schlegelberger's mouth opened. Michael could see a small pool of blood inside as he struggled to speak. Finally, the words, in a horse whisper, came out.

"No . . ."

Perhaps there was more he wanted to say; it was unclear. But that one word seemed, for now—forever—sufficient. Michael knew there would be no more.

Schlegelberger's eyes began to roll up as he struggled, choking. His face turned blue and Michael felt he could almost see the life leaving his body.

Despite who he was, despite the evil he'd done, as Michael watched him pass out of this life, the moment felt sacred. Maybe, it was simply knowing that, at some point, we will all lie dying in front of someone who will stand over us, wondering who we really were and awed to be present when we left.

"We've got to get out, now," said Sindy. "It's going to be messy if they find us here."

As they both headed for the door, it swung open.

CHAPTER 110

Hans Ulricht walked in, waving a Walther PPK pistol between Sindy Steele and Michael. Ulricht looked over at the two dead bodies on the floor before staring back at Michael, his jaw clenched tight with anger.

"Perhaps this is the time to try out my new machine," Ulricht nodded toward the guillotine in the back of the room. "Frederick wanted so much to use it today. Now that the situation has changed, perhaps we will, after all."

"Is this how you want to live out your years, Hans?" Michael said. "On a murder charge? An old man in prison? You know you'll never get away with this carnage. You haven't done anything yet. Let's just clean this up and get out of here. We'll all have an incentive to keep quiet."

Ulricht turned the gun towards Michael. "I have friends who will clean up. An extra body or two at this point makes little difference. But one of you will be guillotined and the other will be the executioner. Would you like to draw straws?"

Michael's attention was fixated on Ulricht's right forefinger for the first sign that he might squeeze the trigger. Ulricht had to be near eighty; Sindy or he could easily overpower him, but one of them would be shot point-blank in the process. Michael knew he had to take the risk to save one of them, whoever got lucky.

He looked over at Sindy Steele, her expression didn't have its usual toughness; he'd never seen her scared before but, like

Michael, she had to know that one of them wouldn't make it out of here alive.

"Silence?" Ulricht said. "I guess I have no takers."

Sindy spoke up, "What happens to the executioner?"

Michael hoped she was stalling for time.

"Ah, a very good question. Finally, someone with a brain. In your case, my dear, once Michael's head is in the bucket, you will be free to go, to walk out that door."

"You don't expect me to believe that, do you?"

"Perhaps not, but I am a man of my word. It is a risk, no doubt, but otherwise you will both surely die by bullets. Miss Steele, you can be very useful in our cause—and to me. Your talents are in great demand, especially now with Frederick's demise. It will be an exciting life, I assure you. There is glory ahead of us, and power."

Michael noticed Ulricht's gun start to shake, almost imperceptibly at first but quickly getting worse. There were beads of perspiration on his forehead. Ulricht's body began swaying. Michael looked over at Sindy, her eyes were moving between him and Ulricht. She was trying to tell him something. Ulricht's gun was pointed back at her now.

He remembered too that she had a knife somewhere on her, the one she'd used to stab Frederick. It must be in her jeans pocket, but her jeans were so tight, she'd never get the knife out quickly enough before he shot her.

Ulricht waved the gun back at Michael. "Move to the machine, now, or I'll simply execute you where you stand."

Michael took one step toward the back of the room, where the guillotine looked ominous and all too ready. He noticed both of Sindy's hands move to her pants pockets, her thumbs hanging inside each one, a typical nonchalant gesture. But now Ulricht was wavering, his breathing suddenly uneven, the gun moving down from its extended position. Michael had been considering making his move towards him, but now he held back, watching Ulricht. He took another step toward the machine. Sindy looked back at him.

In the corner of his eye, he noticed her right hand went deeper inside her pants pocket.

Suddenly, as though he had woken up, Ulricht's head jerked back to attention, the gun moved back up, pointed firmly in Michael's direction again. And then he fired.

CHAPTER 111

M ichael felt the bullet pass by him. He turned to see
Ulricht on the floor, his gun still in his hand.

Michael joined Sindy, rushing over to him. She took the
Walther and tucked it inside the waist of her jeans. She bent
over Ulricht, who was conscious but breathing heavily.

"Something seemed wrong with him," Michael said.
"What do you think it is?"

"He must have had a heart attack or something," she said,
unbuttoning his shirt. "But wait, look at this." She pulled out a
plastic device that had dropped down from under Ulricht's suit
jacket. "It's attached to him somehow. I wonder what it is."

Sindy reached down and, pulling Ulricht's jacket away,
examined the small case. "I remember these from med school.
It's a continuous glucose monitor and an insulin pump." She
pulled the device off Ulricht's belt. "See this tube? It goes from
the pump right into his stomach. He was a diabetic."

Michael was confused. "So what happened?"

"I don't know. Maybe he had a heart attack. Maybe he had
an insulin problem from all the excitement. This guy's no
spring chicken."

"Can't you tell?"

"No," she said, peering closely into Ulricht's eyes. "I told
you I never finished med school."

"What do we do now?" Michael said, smiling.

Sindy looked up at him from the floor, "I'd like to put my
knife in him."

"Don't. I don't know why, but don't."

As Sindy seemed to consider Michael's advice, they were both surprised by a knock on the door.

"Jesus, who now?" Sindy whispered as the door swung open.

Michael was even more surprised as he watched a tentative Jonathan Goldstein enter.

Goldstein's mouth dropped as he looked over at the two bodies—and then to a gasping Hans Ulricht on the floor. "What the fuck is going on?" he said. "What did you do here?"

Sindy Steele stood up and moved aside as Goldstein walked over to Ulricht and, kneeling by his side, spoke into his ear. "I just got your message. Are you okay?"

Ulricht turned his head toward Goldstein. "It's my insulin." He was struggling to speak. "Thank God you're here. They tried to kill me." He gasped for breath. "They murdered the Monsignor and poor Frederick . . . I have a device, down below. Press the red button, please, hurry."

"Sure. Don't worry. You'll be okay. I'll take care of everything." Michael watched as Goldstein reached into Ulricht's trousers.

Michael noticed Sindy's right hand going into her jeans and gripping the gun.

"No, it's inside my shirt," Ulricht said, trying to move his hand to where the device was. But Goldstein, ignoring him, reached into his trouser loop and unhooked the gold chain carrying Han's keys.

"It's ironic, isn't it?" Goldstein said, speaking into Ulricht's ear. "A nice Jewish boy taking gold away from a Nazi just before he dies?"

Han's mouth and eyes opened wide in obvious disbelief.

Once Goldstein placed the gold chain with the keys into his pocket he finally lifted up Ulricht's shirt, found the white plastic monitor, examined the tubes running in and out of it and, with a violent thrust, ripped it out of Ulricht's stomach.

He stood up, looked at Michael and Sindy Steele and said, softly, "Let's get out of here before someone finds us."

CHAPTER 112

Paris, France

After returning to the Ritz, Michael sat with Samantha and, over a bottle of French burgundy, told her what had happened at the Lutetia, beginning with Hans Ulricht's bottle of 1942 Bordeaux and ending with the insulin monitor and tubes lying in a pool of blood alongside Ulricht's dead body.

He told her everything. Or, almost everything. He decided to skip the part about Sindy Steele, who was, hopefully, going to return to Santorini later tonight. This time, they'd departed as friends. A warm hug and she was back on her motorcycle. Seconds after she took off he was pretty sure that he saw her take one quick glance back towards him.

The story became even more tortured than the full truth, as he had to improvise on many of the details. Nevertheless, the end result was the same, or so he thought.

"So you killed a monsignor? You actually broke his neck?" Samantha said.

Yes, he did. Was it considered murder when it's in self-defense? He didn't know the technical answer to that question. Was Samantha upset with the thought of what he'd done, even though she understood who Schlegelberger was?

"Yes, I killed him with my . . . hands. He was more fragile than I thought."

"Do you think he suffered?"

"I don't know, maybe for a minute until he actually . . . died."

Other than being happy to be alive, Michael wasn't sure how he felt about what he did. He knew it was self-defense but he'd still done something he could never before have envisioned. It was Alex who he'd always expected might kill someone. Even Alex had never done that, as far he knew at least. But now Michael had. And he knew he'd do it again if he had to. Perhaps that was what bothered him now. Or was he just stuck in the normal trauma anyone who'd killed—or even just witnessed death—experienced. How could he be so unsure of how he felt about such a momentous act?

He watched her face for signs of disapproval, fear, whatever emotion was going through her. Instead, Samantha's face appeared to lighten up, "That's too bad, a minute was too short. Maybe now, at least, Alex—and John—will rest in peace."

Michael doubted that Alex would.

After Samantha went to bed, Michael gently shut the door to the bedroom, returned to the suite's living room, turned on his laptop, signed in and clicked on the ancient gold crucifix icon.

He gave the uncensored version of the night's events to Alex, who added a few new details of his own.

"Wait—so you were able to hack into Ulricht's insulin drip?"

"I don't call it hacking," Alex said. "Actually, all I did was slow Ulricht down. He would have survived if Goldstein hadn't ripped the device out of his stomach. It was Goldstein who killed him."

"How did it feel, to kill Schlegelberger?" Alex said.

"Actually, at that moment, I remember distinctly, it felt good."

"And now?"

"I feel nothing . . . Is that bad?"

Alex took a moment to answer. "Not from where I sit."

CHAPTER 113

Saint-Tropez, France

S hielded by his sunglasses, Michael gazed at the line-up of French women lying poolside at the Hotel Des Lices. He sat at the edge of the pool with Catherine Saint Laurent and Jennifer Walsh. Samantha lay only a few feet away, asleep on her chaise after a second glass of rosé.

Michael noticed Catherine Saint Laurent too eyeing the row of beautiful women, their tanned bodies, some topless, glistening in the hot Saint-Tropez sun.

"They are all so young and thin. Do these girls today ever eat?"

"People ask the same question about you," he said.

"Not anymore, I'm afraid. But that is very kind of you."

"You transcend your beauty, Catherine," Jennifer offered. "You're so much more than just a pretty face."

"You may be right, my dear, but when you reach my age, it's the pretty face and the lithe figure that you want. You want your lover to desire you not for who you are—but for how you look. I am not so politically correct, you see."

"You underestimate your beauty. You stand out—not only for your physical beauty," Michael nodded towards the dozing sunbathers, "but also for who you are. It makes your attraction *compelling*."

"Your brother was a much better liar—but thank you."

"Speaking of Alex, I've thought a lot since the other night. He's changed," Jennifer said.

Michael had given Jennifer permission to tell only one other person about Alex. He assumed Jennifer had already confided in Catherine. It was an unlikely but strong bond amongst the three. Alex had committed to invest in Catherine's comeback movie—and Michael had honored the commitment after Alex was murdered. Michael trusted them both now with the secret of his brother.

"How do you think he's changed?" Michael asked, but he'd noticed it too, so he was curious to hear what Jennifer thought.

"It's subtle but there were a few things that jumped out. First, he doesn't curse as much as he used to. His language is cleaner, he's lost a little of that tough Queens dialect. You know, from listening to your brother—at least when he was alive —"

"But he *is* alive." Michael could hear Alex making the same protests to him.

"You know what I mean, *really* alive —" Jennifer said.

He nodded for her to continue.

"When he was alive, you'd never have known that he came from a nice family or that he'd been raised by parents who were pretty smart and successful. He sounded like a tough mobster, someone who came from humble beginnings. No one would ever guess that *the two of you* had the same parents. Even though he was brilliant in so many ways."

"Maybe he's changing because he's no longer hanging out in the same element that he was. I mean, I don't know who else he communicates with now but he's away from the culture that he'd spent so many years around."

"I'm not sure that *culture* is the right word." She smiled. "People say that we're a product of our environment, right?"

Michael realized that Jennifer was more perceptive than he had given her credit for. How amazing to be having a philosophical discussion about the personality of an artificial intelligence entity—with Alex's hairdresser and mistress. "That's true. And don't forget, Alex isn't drinking—or staying out late either. Not anymore. He's getting plenty of rest, or, at least his brain is. That's got to have some impact on his personality or his mind, or both."

"Also, I'm not sure, but he may be more sensitive, more perceptive now."

"The geeks who developed his artificial intelligence software said that he'd continue to learn and develop, that the more information he acquired, the more connections he made, the smarter he'd become. They also added emotional-intelligence software to the mix."

"Well, I think his personality has changed."

Michael tried to recall his conversations with the computer whiz kids. He hadn't spoken to them in months. It might be time, he thought, to contact them again.

"I don't think *personality* ever even came up in our discussions. It was all about his mind or brain."

Catherine Saint Laurent who all along seemed to be listening carefully but had been silent so far, spoke up. "But he is *conscious*, yes? He has a *consciousness*?"

Michael looked at Jennifer who seemed surprised, if not taken back by the concept.

"Yes, he does. Just like we do, just like he always did," Michael said.

"I should hope so," Jennifer said. "I mean, I didn't just screw a computer the other day, did I?"

CHAPTER 114

Saint-Tropez, France

While Samantha was still out at the pool, Michael had gone up to his room to return a call from Karen DiNardo. But first he had to speak with Alex, to get some things off his mind . . . he needed *answers.*

"I'm trying to understand things . . . to understand *you,*" he said as soon as Alex appeared.

"Me? What's that supposed to mean? Are we going to get into another one of those BS philosophical discussions of yours?"

"Yeah—but maybe you'll learn something, too—about yourself." Michael kept flashing back to the scene of Dorothy when she confronted The Wizard of Oz.

"Okay, you know I hate these questions about life and all that."

"Let me read something to you—it has to do with consciousness."

"Oh, for God's sake."

"Actually," Michael said, "he's in this. Just listen for a minute." He read from the book, glancing up at Alex every few sentences to be sure he hadn't tuned out.

"There are two theories of consciousness, poles apart from each other:

On the one hand, our consciousness—our ability to think, to be retrospect, to look down upon ourselves as though we were a third party, to *reflect* about our consciousness—is no more than the workings or the firing of millions of synapses, electrical impulses inside our body—and when we die and those electrical impulses stop working, our consciousness also will cease, forever.

On the other end of the spectrum is the belief that our consciousness is a special gift, that it is somehow connected to a "soul" and that it's the creation of a higher being, an almighty God and, along with that is the belief that our minds—our consciousness—our *souls*—will live on after we are gone from this earth, will live on after our bodies have been returned to the ground.

This is our fundamental question, the fundamental question of our life—and our death. In the end, this is the only question."

He stopped reading, looked back up at Alex and waited for a response. But Alex was frozen, as he periodically became when things became complicated. "So, what do you think?"

Moments later, Alex came back to life. "What are you looking for?"

"What do you think—are people, our minds, our consciousness, all just a bunch of electrical impulses—or is there something deeper? I mean, for example, is there a God?"

Alex seemed to freeze again but bounced back even quicker this time. "There *is* something, bigger than us, than me—but I don't know what it is. I can't tell if it's a God—or a clever programmer."

Michael waited . . . for more. Alex's face seemed confused or heavy with thought. It wasn't an expression he remembered from when Alex was alive. He was clearly straining, perhaps himself, to understand. Finally, he came back.

"When I was home . . . before . . . I had a computer and it was, you know, separate. But now, it's like I have my mind—I'm alive—and I still have a computer but—it's not separate.

It's part of me, inside of me. I can think—or direct my mind—as though I had a keyboard—to do things."

"Like what?"

"Let's say I want to check something on Google. I can now just think about it—and my mind will go there. Or, even if I just want to let my mind wander—it'll scan—almost like it's scrolling–line after line of information. If I let it, it'll speed up. It's like my computer is built into my mind. Except . . ."

"Except what?"

"Except it's much more powerful than any computer I ever had. I can see a constant crosscurrent of data and information and pictures and voices—all flowing by, so fast and so much that I have to slow it down and . . . focus—or it's just meaningless, it becomes too much to absorb."

"Where is your computer? Is it . . . like an Apple or laptop?"

"What do you think, there's an Apple store here or that I go on Amazon?"

"I have no idea. I don't even know what or where *here* is, remember? I'm not sure you do either."

"And what about God, or a god? Do you know anything now that you didn't know before?"

"I'm no closer to understanding anything about a god or some higher being than you are. Sometimes I feel like I'm looking out over some mass network of lights and signals that seem to go on forever. But there's no one . . . in charge. No control panel. No on/off switch. It's just a mass of information, of sounds, of pictures. It's chaos. I wish I could make sense out of it."

"After all of this, we still have no answers, then, do we?" Michael said.

"There may be no answers, Michael. Ever."

CHAPTER 115

Saint-Tropez, France

I t was over.

It was time to take a deep breath. The bad guys were dead: Petrucceli and Lovallo, Frederick, Ulricht, and Schlegelberger.

For the first time since Alex's murder, Michael felt that he and his family were safe. It was a night to celebrate.

He wondered about Sindy Steele; she was back in Santorini by now . . . hopefully. In any case, she had become an ally and not a threat, at least the last time he checked. What was she thinking? It was hard to believe that she would simply settle down on a Greek island. He suspected that, for years to come, when his cell phone rang, he'd be wondering . . . And if it turned out to be Sindy Steele, which one? After all, both were dangerous.

Samantha, Sofia and Michael were enjoying a few weeks in Saint-Tropez. Besides meeting up with Catherine and Jennifer, Fletcher and his wife Ang had just flown in for a few days to join them. After the day around the pool at the Hotel des Lices, they walked across the street to Michael's favorite Saint-Tropez restaurant, La Ramade.

Although in the middle of the village, La Ramade was a tranquil hideaway with terrific French bistro fare and the summer's freshest foods.

Just as they were about to enter the restaurant, Sofia took Michael's arm and, as the others proceeded to the table in the garden, pulled him over to the side. "Dad, Mom told me all about Uncle Alex and . . . you know . . . that you're convinced that he's –"

"Duplicated himself on a computer using a breakthrough in AI," Michael said. "Even after that call before you were kidnapped, I knew you wouldn't believe me. I didn't want you to think I was crazy. I didn't want to frighten you, especially after what happened."

Sofia grabbed his hand, placing it in hers, "That phone call was so real. Later, I kept playing it back in my head. I know it had to be something, something for real. I believe you. In my heart, I know it was him. I don't understand how . . . but I believe you. And I believe it was him. On the phone."

It was a great feeling. Michael knew he had a strong ally. Now, he had the rest of the world to convince, including, eventually, Samantha. But it wasn't time yet for that. They stepped into the restaurant, arm in arm.

The tables were set under the mulberry trees, which were gaily but softly lit with tiny lights wrapped around the branches. The ground was covered with small stones that helped to further cool the evening air, or so it seemed as Michael slid his feet out of his shoes and let them feel the cool stones while he dined.

At his suggestion, everyone ordered the same appetizer, farm-fresh heirloom tomatoes with a creamy Burrata, Stracciatella di Bufala.

"I have an announcement to make," Catherine said, as all eyes turned to her. "Harvey Weinstock will be backing a new film and I will have the leading role. It's a great part and I am so thrilled."

Weinstock was the chairman of Centurion Films and one of the most powerful figures in Hollywood.

As though finally able to speak, Ang shouted the phrase that seemed to precede most of her sentences, "Oh my God, oh my God."

"Oh, Catherine," Samantha said, "that is so good. We're so happy for you."

"Yes, and by the way, since I know this film will be a blockbuster hit, I've secured his agreement to allow Michael to invest in it. It's just a small payback for your support on my last film. The one, I confess, we—or I, at least—was never sure anyone would watch."

"But they did, big time," Michael said. He hadn't anticipated investing in another film but the opportunity to stay closely connected to Catherine—and to invest with Harvey Weinstock—was too attractive to resist. "So what's the film about?"

"It's about a movie star who believes that her deceased casual lover has returned. Their relationship intensifies yet no one else believes her and they try to convince her that she's delusional."

Michael listened. He looked over at Jennifer, they exchanged glances but he couldn't discern what Jennifer was thinking. Was this a joke? Was Catherine serious—or trying to get a reaction from him?

"Is she?" he asked.

"Is she what?" Catherine said.

"*Delusional.*"

"Why, Michael, surely you can't expect me to ruin the ending for you now, do you?"

"I guess I'll just have to invest to find out then."

"Yes, I was hoping you'd say that."

"Oh my God, this is incredible," Ang said as she raised her glass of rosé in a toast. "It doesn't get any better than this— great food, great friends—and we've all got tans."

Michael felt his iPhone vibrating. He discreetly pulled it out of his pocket and, holding it out of everyone else's sight, just under the table, he checked the screen. It was an instant message—from Alex: *We have company.* What in the world did he mean, company? He wanted to message him back but already eyes were turning his way.

Samantha leaned over to him. "Please, for once, put that thing away."

Fletcher sipped away at his Manhattan. "It's been quite a summer—I never thought we were going to make it out of that funeral parlor in Chapel Hill."

"You know, Michael, your brother used to say that even though he was seen as the bad guy—it was you who always caused the trouble," Jennifer said, with a sly smile.

"It's funny," Catherine replied, looking away while she sipped her wine, "I still find it hard to believe that Alex is dead."

"Yes," Jennifer added, "and if I didn't know better, I'd think that Donna was right."

Michael shot her a look. "What do you mean?"

"Oh, that Alex was still alive, hiding out somewhere, happy as could be, watching his games on television and pulling all the strings."

"Well," Samantha said, "I don't know about that but here's a toast to being thankful for all the good ones that survived. Then looking first at Michael then to Sofia, she added, "My husband and my daughter."

As they sipped their champagne, Michael and Samantha exchanged glances. All he could think of at that moment was how much he loved her. He wondered what she was thinking.

Samantha lifted her glass once again. He knew her so well, she was going to tell them exactly what she was thinking. But as she prepared to speak, he caught the slightest hint of mischief in her expression.

"I have one more thing to say about the love of my life here," she said pointing her champagne flute towards Michael. "I always knew he was a great husband, father . . . businessman. But until the other day in Paris, I never could have imagined that he was also a real-life action hero. I mean, to have singlehandedly taken down three men all by himself. Here's to my very own James Bond."

CHAPTER 116

Berlin, Germany

J onathan Goldstein thought of Hans Ulricht as he pulled out the gold chain from his pocket. He remembered standing right here in this spot as Ulricht pulled it out of his own pocket, inspecting the keys as the chain extended from his belt loops. Now Jonathan selected the key, looking both ways up and down Wilhelmstade before inserting it into the lock. He could feel and hear the lock's cylinders turn and release as he twisted the key inside the lock.

It was the ultimate irony that Hitler's bunker, from which he had run the Nazi war machine in its final months, lay less than a half-kilometer away, just down the street.

And although Jonathan knew he could never begin to replace the world and the souls who were lost, he felt confident that, tonight, he would recapture some of the riches.

He opened the heavy glass door, stepped inside and quickly shut it behind him and after inserting his key from the inside, locked the door.

The showroom was nearly dark, the only light was the reflections from the street lamp outside and the headlights from passing cars. He pulled out his LED pocket flashlight, but before he could turn it on, he was startled by a flash of light. Then came the voice, the sultry, sexy voice of a woman who must have been a regular smoker. "We have met before. I am Heidi."

She remained in the same place where he'd seen her last time yet the sharp light coming from her eyes all but blinded him. "Yes, I know."

But he wasn't about to get sidetracked by a mannequin, despite her unearthly appeal and his growing curiosity. Tonight he simply had to make sure the gold was still in the basement. He brushed past the showroom and Heidi and proceeded down the steps to the door concealing the vault. He could hear her, still speaking to him, "Where are you going? Why are you here?" Fortunately, she had not moved from her Odalisque-like pose in her lounge chair. He hoped she couldn't.

He descended the stairs, reached the door, opened up the hidden box, pressed in the code and pushed in the heavy vault door. He entered, moving his flashlight now up and down, taking it all in. Everything was just as he and Hans had left it. Now he had to notify his associates that it was intact. Together, they would arrange to move it out, tomorrow night.

Whatever shred of guilt or regret he may have felt for killing Hans Ulricht vanished as he admired the bright gold bricks all around him. It was for a good cause. And not just his own this time.

But Goldstein's dream was interrupted by the sound of footsteps. He'd locked the front door securely . . . unless someone else with a key . . . or someone already inside . . . or some*thing* . . .

It was time to get out. He turned around and took a step back towards the vault door—and then he saw . . . a sight he would normally have died for—a pair of women's legs, bare, long and lean thighs, slender calves with high heels. His eyes moved upward, to her breasts, protruding from a black negligee.

Was this Heidi? How had she risen from her couch? She was beautiful. And, terrifying. He would have to get by her. He moved to her right, she didn't try to make way, so he held his breath and stepped awkwardly around her, unsure how or if she would react. Was she armed? Was she real?

He passed by her, stumbling as he reached the door. He turned around. She was moving towards him now, slowly yet quickly enough so that she would get to him before he would be able to climb the steps, unlock the door and leave. He rushed up the steps; he could hear her heels clicking behind him, she was close, closing in. He was surprised to hear the vault door shut and the locks clicking. How had she managed to do it?

As he ran for the door, he pulled the gold chain out of his pocket, searching for the right key. She would catch up to him, soon. He stumbled then, missing the lock as he jammed the key into the brass surrounding it. He could smell her perfume. Reluctantly, he turned around. Her eyes shone with white light.

"Where is Hans?"

She had him trapped, his back tight against the door. She lifted her hands, to his neck. Her slender fingers were deceiving; although flesh-like they felt like steel as they wrapped themselves firmly around his neck. He felt his windpipe close. He tried to push back but she was unmovable. He looked into her eyes . . . searching . . . for what he didn't know. Maybe for life . . . his.

"Where is Hans?' she asked again, easing her grip on his throat.

"He's . . . not here . . . It's . . ."

She tightened her hold again, and he knew this was her death grip. Whatever answer she was looking for, it wasn't the one he had given her.

"Are you sure?" she said, suddenly releasing her grip.

"Yes, I am. Yes –"

"Let him go?" she said.

He was confused. She was talking over him. She wasn't speaking now to him—but to someone else.

"Yes, I trust you." She stepped back now, giving him room.

Who is she speaking to? Where is this person? He caught his breath, looked up and down the room behind them. No one else was there. He turned around, towards the door.

He fit the key into the lock and was relieved when he felt the cylinder turn to his pressure. He opened the door, went out, looked back again; her hand was reaching for him, just inches away. He slammed the heavy glass door shut but he could see her on the other side of the glass. She wasn't giving up. Then, trying desperately to turn the key to lock the door behind him, he felt the door push back—hard—against him. He pushed it again, holding it firmly, just long enough so he could turn the key and lock the door. Heidi stood, motionless, her eyes staring straight ahead at him. Her mouth opened; he could hear her words, "Are you sure, Alex?"

He turned and, walking as quickly as he could without attracting attention, headed back to his hotel.

CHAPTER 117

Berlin

The Regent Hotel was in the luxurious Mitte district of Berlin, just a short walk from the new Reichstag, Hitler's bunker—and, of course, Hans' old mannequin shop. Goldstein poured himself a full glass of Riesling and drank it down as though it was a glass of water. Since he rarely drank, he could immediately feel the alcohol unsteady him. He took out his cell phone and dialed the number he now knew by memory.

"Benjamin Solomon Center for Holocaust Victims, may I help you? . . . Jonathan, is that you?"

"Yes. I've just returned from the vault. It's all there, just as it was. We will need to move quickly."

"Did you encounter any problems, my friend?"

"I don't know . . . there was a woman . . . a mannequin or robot, I don't know. I don't even know if she's real. She followed me inside to the vault –"

"I think I understand, Jonathan. You're still upset."

"I killed a man. He was a monster, I think . . . but –"

"He was a monster. His family murdered your grand-parents. They did it with great pleasure. He would do the same to you if the circumstances allowed it. You have done the right thing, my friend. You have done something your grandparents and parents would be proud of—and you will have helped us fund the programs we need to protect our people."

"What about the mess back in Paris?"

"Don't worry. Everything has been cleaned up there. There is no trace left. Our people are very good at what they do. Oddly enough, you've also saved Michael Nicholas from any problems with the authorities."

"That's too bad. I was hoping to at least get him out of my hair."

"Perhaps you should try and open up your heart –"

"Let's not push things, okay?"

"Agreed, I'm sorry. Thank you for what you have done. The gold will be moved tomorrow night."

CHAPTER 118

S till on his computer and having finished up with Alex, Michael decided to FaceTime Karen DiNardo. He knew it was her preferred means of communicating with him when he was away for any length of time.

"Okay, is there something you've been meaning to tell me?" Karen DiNardo was sitting in Michael's office as though she owned it. It was her way.

"What do you mean?" Michael didn't have a clue what it could be; he wondered what he could have forgotten. "You just got a raise a few months ago, so it can't be that."

"Yes, what there was of it. But, anyway, that's not what I'm referring to."

"Okay, I swear, I can't imagine . . ."

Her arms crossed, Karen flashed her best typical, self-satisfied smile. "Mr. Goldstein's secretary just called me—she said that I'm to let you know that they no longer need the back-up for the next round of budget cuts—that the money has been restored in the budget."

"Really?" Michael and Goldstein hadn't spoken since the night they left the body-strewn basement of the Lutetia. He'd figured anything could have been possible—including the possibility that when he returned to New York, security would come and escort him out of the building. A rollback of the budget cuts—the cuts so central to Cartan's strategy—was an unlikely best-case scenario.

"She said there'd be a statement coming out from Mr. Goldstein to all employees in the next hour. I have it in front of me."

"Does he want my approval before it goes out?" This couldn't be good, he thought.

"Actually, no. It looks like it's just going to go out. Let me read it to you.

"*It has come to my attention that since the acquisition of Gibraltar Financial by Cartan Holdings there have been rumors regarding our plans for your company. It is not unusual with mergers and acquisitions that employees should feel concerned about the future of their organization and their jobs. For that reason, I thought it would be beneficial to clarify our intent and objectives over at least the coming year.*

"*First, I can assure you that Cartan Holdings will not put Gibraltar Financial up for sale. Although many other private equity and hedge fund organizations do purchase companies and then sell them, this is not the strategy. We have no intention of selling Gibraltar Financial in the foreseeable future.*

"*Second, there will be no further headcount reductions over the coming year. We are very satisfied with the performance to date of Gibraltar Financial and its position in the marketplace.*"

Once he signed off with Karen, Michael dialed Goldstein's number and was surprised when, in the middle of the first ring, he answered.

"What is it?" Goldstein said.

"I just read the announcement –"

Goldstein's voice was measured. "It's possible, Michael, that you judged me prematurely."

It was good enough.

CHAPTER 119

Saint-Tropez, France

T he main courses were arriving. Michael's filet of beef was set down in front of him. It was pink, perfectly grilled with a thick, charred crust around the edges, and a rainbow of boiled potatoes splayed out around the plate. He'd had the same dish several times before; he could taste it before he even picked up his fork.

But just before he did, the proprietor, Jean Pierre, approached and, whispering in his ear, said, "Monsieur Nicholas, I'm sorry to disturb you but one of our Saint-Tropez gendarmerie is just by the entrance here and has asked for you. He said it would only take a moment of your time."

Michael rose up from his seat, "I'll be right back."

"What is it?" Samantha said, probably always suspicious any time Michael leaves the table before even tasting his dinner.

"Just a local policeman. I think I may have blocked a car across the street, at the hotel."

He walked around the other tables and to the front entry, which was little more than an open gate to the sidewalk. As he approached the gate, he saw a uniformed gendarme standing in front of a black Citroen, the French, wishful-thinking equivalent of a Mercedes.

Once he stepped onto the sidewalk, the officer nodded and left, crossing the street. Michael was only a few feet from the Citroen when the back door opened. As Michael looked inside, the car's front door swung open and a man in a dark suit came out and approached him. In the back seat, another man in a dark suit flashed a gold badge from inside his open wallet.

"Mr. Nicholas, I'm with the Secret Service. Would you please join us for a short discussion?"

Michael wasn't sure whether he had a choice or not. Was this what Alex had meant by, *We have company*?

The man slid over to make room, Michael got in while the man who had approached from the front closed the rear door and stood outside, as though on alert for anyone approaching the car.

"What's this all about?"

"Mr. Nicholas, I have been sent to speak with you personally—by the President of the United States."

"You're kidding?"

"I can assure you sir, this is no joke." He handed Michael what appeared to be a BlackBerry phone although, as he held it, it was heavier than any of the ones he used to own. "The President is on the line."

He placed the phone to his ear. "Hello?"

"Mr. Nicholas, I'm sorry to bother you on your vacation." It was him, the voice Michael recognized from countless televisions and radio broadcasts over the last several years. The man he voted for, twice. Calling *him*. "I understand there've been a lot of very unusual things happening in your life."

"Yes, that's true but –" Michael wasn't sure exactly what the president was referring to—after all, there were a lot of unusual things—from Tartarus, to the Vatican, or the Nazis, or . . .

"I'm calling about your brother, Alex."

Naturally, Michael's head was spinning now. "He's dead, you know."

"Mr. Nicholas, I know—everything."

"Everything? Then you know that –"

"I know that you speak to him—and he speaks to you—quite often. It's all as surprising and incredible to me as I'm sure it has been for you. As a result of this . . . situation . . . I'm calling because I need your help."

That was a surprise. "My *help*, yes, of course –"

"Listen, I know you're on holiday there with your family but how quickly can you come to Washington?"

It all unfolded so quickly. He would have to leave, fly back as soon as he could catch a flight. The details were spinning faster than he could remember them. Was all this real? The White House . . .

The President was still speaking, "You understand, of course, that this must be kept in the strictest confidence. If word were to get out to the press or others, it would mean chaos. We'd all lose control of the situation—and you would likely be in grave danger. So, other than your wife Samantha, you can't tell a soul about this."

"I understand, of course." It would be another secret he would have to hold. He could only imagine what Samantha's reaction would be when he told her. Now she would have to believe, to believe it all.

"Thank you. I will make sure that you are in the best of hands. Godspeed. I look forward to seeing you here in the White House and, once again, on behalf of your country, thank you."

The connection ended. As though on cue, the back door was opened and he stepped outside.

"You'll probably just want to let your friends know that this had to do with a mistaken parking problem. We had the wrong car."

"Yes, that sounds good. Don't worry." Yet that was all Michael was doing now. He didn't know where to begin. Just as he approached the entrance to La Ramade, his iPhone vibrated, indicating an incoming instant call.

Jesus, what the hell now?

He pulled the phone out of his pocket; the screen read *The White House.* He stopped just outside the restaurant's garden entrance and placed the phone to his ear. "Hello?"

It was the President, again. "Michael, one last thing. When you come to Washington –"

"Yes –"

"Don't forget to bring your laptop."

BIOGRAPHY

E. J. Simon is the author of three fiction thrillers, *Death Never Sleeps, Death Logs In, and Death Logs Out.* He has just completed his fourth manuscript, *Death in the Cloud.*

He is a member of the Authors Guild, the Mystery Writers of America and the North Carolina Writer's Network. He holds an M.A. in Communications from Fairfield University and a B.A. in Journalism from the University of South Carolina. He lives with his wife in Cary, North Carolina in the United States.

For more information, visit his website: www.ejsimon.com.

THANK YOU!

Thank you for choosing to read *Death Logs Out*.
I hope you enjoyed reading it as much as I did writing it!
If so, I'd appreciate your support by writing a 5 star review on
Amazon. It doesn't have to be long.

CONNECT WITH ME:

Facebook: https://www.facebook.com/jimejsimon/

Twitter: https://twitter.com/JimEJSimon

Instagram: https://www.instagram.com/e.j.simon/

Website: www.ejsimon.com

Email: ejsimon@simonzefpublishing.com

PREVIEW FROM
DEATH IN THE CLOUD

Now Alex had the freedom he had always longed for . . . yet he missed his old life. Although he could eavesdrop on his old friends, it was different now. He was no longer a part of their everyday lives. He often wished he could return, to Queens, to his business, to the friends, the women and the bars and hangouts that had defined his social life. But he knew that would never happen.

And just as he'd had a premonition of danger when he left his home for dinner at Grimaldi's on that night he was shot, he now had another one, of something much worse. This time it wasn't some punk with a gun in a Queens bar. No, it was from a world he'd only glimpsed in the movies or on the news. Powerful forces and rogue nations with technology and weapons threatening the lives of millions of people and, once again, his own life. But this time death would be forever.

CPSIA information can be obtained
at www.ICGtesting.com
Printed in the USA
BVHW031812050123
655517BV00005B/58

 9 780991 256457